Seven Lives Saved

SEVEN LIVES SAVED

LYDIA MACCLAREN

III

"In him we have redemption through his blood,
the forgiveness of our trespasses,
according to the riches of his grace,"

— Ephesians 1:7

Thank you to my family and friends
who supported me all the way.

Soli Deo gloria.

Chapter 1

Kathka was dead.

The silver edge had sliced his throat, and he had laid upon the desert as his blood soaked into the parched earth. Hatred boiled away what life was left in his veins. There he died, abandoned and defeated.

Kathka's murderer knelt beside his body and pressed two fingers to his jugular. He found no life. As the old man withdrew his hand, he spoke. The only words Kathka would hear him say.

Words that cursed. Words that damned. Words that stuck like thorns into Kathka's soul. They bound him to his killer. He strained to speak, to move, to act, but he had no corporeal body, that had been buried by his murderer in the dust of the desert. He was a soul and nothing more, an awareness that saw the world of the living but unable to interact with it.

A soul cursed to remain tethered to his murderer, the Wise Man, the last of the gods. The only one who had not forsaken the land.

The damning words were the last Kathka would hear for a very long time. But time was a difficult thing to comprehend. His senses had become warped, all he knew was his murderer.

The god kept to his caves, large carved-out rooms filled with ancient tomes and sheaves of paper, quills and inkwells, little trinkets of rock and feathers, and glass jars filled with dried plants. There were no visitors, there was nothing but the god.

It was a strange limbo that Kathka inhabited. Every passing moment could be a day or a thousand years. In that uncertain expanse of time the old man shuffled back and forth between his books, tugging Kathka's soul along with every step.

Kathka seethed.

Unable to speak, he still possessed the ability to think. In his convoluted thoughts, he replayed every moment leading to his death, and his hatred for his murderer grew. He had come with his army to conquer, but he had met the Wise Man alone. Alone before the god. Then his blood was spilled. That moment looped in his mind, and he tried to discern how he could have avoided that fate.

His death seemed inevitable. His murderer was a god.

Still, he dwelt on the memories. The blade slicing again, and again. Rage had driven him to the wilderness to kill the old man, and that rage grew.

It consumed him.

The old man straightened at his desk, joints protesting with weary age. Then, he turned and caught Kathka in his gaze. Calm as a still pool.

Kathka's wayward thoughts ceased. Anger and fear wound seamlessly together until it was impossible to find the start of one and the end of the other or where he lay amidst it all.

The god knew. He knew all that went on inside of what remained of the man named Kathka.

"I will make you a deal." His voice, rough from disuse, shattered the fragile space. As if the god expected a verbal response he paused. Even if Kathka could speak, he did not know what to say. Ages had passed, or what felt like ages, and these new words were as dangerous as the last the old man had uttered.

"If you save seven lives, I will give you a second life."

The rage welled within Kathka. The Wise Man knew of the wrath that yearned for physical expression. He also knew the fear that Kathka's fury could not smother.

Fear that the past would be repeated.

"If you agree, at the right time you will know who to save. You will be bound to them; you will not be free until they are saved," The Wise Man explained. Confusion swept through Kathka, but the man simply repeated, "You will know who to save. Do you accept?"

Kathka could not respond, but he accepted the deal. He barely understood the proposition, but he would accept the terms. He would save however many lives to find release from the endless torture he endured tethered to the immortal god. Then, with his new life, he would finish what he could not in his previous.

He would kill the Wise Man.

The old man knew his intentions. Nothing was hidden from him, the god of wisdom. But he sighed, nodded, and murmured, "Then Kathka, we have a deal."

Chapter 2

With a great clap, scorched air filled Kathka's lungs. His pupils constricted as his eyes opened upon the looming sun. He lay stretched on a sea of sand and stared up at the orange globe that filled the sapphire blue sky.

His fingers dug into the granules. He reveled in the feel of feeling, in the sensation of his body, of his chest rising and falling, of the laughter rattling his bones as the reality of his second life crashed upon him.

The sunlight burned.

A beautiful heat.

He splayed his hand to block the harsh rays. Thin fingers cast a shadow across his face. They were not his hands. They were slim and smooth, and his rich brown skin had sunken to a dusty pallor. Kathka sat and splayed both hands.

The elation of life plummeted.

The old man had given him a different body. He could sense it within himself, the gaps left from a soul that did not fully inhabit the mortal shell.

Worse, the body was not from the desert.

The god had dressed it in a thick wool tunic, with an equally heavy woolen cloak, both too hot for the arid climate. A decorative brooch clasped the blue cape around his shoulders, and it revolted him. It was so delicately crafted, with silver curves etching out the wings, fangs, and claws of a dragon.

The symbol of the Islands.

The old man certainly thought himself clever, casting the desert soul into the body of an Islander. Kathka despised him for this new blow. No foul oaths could convey the rage that surged within him.

He shouted a few into the vast space anyway.

His fingers clawed into the sand until the red of rage eased to a simmer and his mind cleared. The god had given him two curses; seven lives, and the body he could not change. But it was useless to dwell on the insults of his murderer.

Time moved onward, and Kathka was plunged back into its flow.

The shimmering plane of heat rolled around him in the gentle slope of dunes. Kathka stood and turned in a circle. The same landscape flowed around him in mighty waves.

Blue above, red below. This was not where he had died.

According to the sun, there were four hours until sundown when night would rule and the sudden cold would render the desert more cooperative. Always travel at night, Acrius was fond of saying whenever they packed up camp. Always.

Kathka pulled up the hood of the cloak. It was too thick, and the brooch too dangerous, but he needed the protection from the fiery heat.

"Sorry, Acrius," Kathka muttered and took his first step into the shifting sand. He could not wait for the moon. Not when he had no provisions and a mission to fulfill.

He set his back to the sun, to shade his face and allow clear vision and hoped he was pointed toward something more than sand. The burning orb dipped lower, but not quickly enough.

Slow steps. Don't break a sweat. Mouth closed. Scarf pulled over the nose.

All he had learned in his past life was there for him to access in this new one. Kathka let those memories wash over him, but he banished any more thoughts of Acrius, or any of the Wayfinders. Dwelling on the dead would not save him.

Upon a ridge of sand, a figure shimmered into view. Kathka narrowed his eyes, uncertain if he saw a mirage or something tangible. It wavered, flickered, then reappeared. The swaying form of a camel. Kathka halted as the beast lumbered down the slope of the dune and into its shade. The details of the beast solidified as it approached and crossed back into the sunlight. Sacks were lashed to its back, and between them sat a rider with the hilt of a sword jutting over his shoulder.

Kathka was trapped, alone and on foot. He tugged the cloak tight around him and folded it over the brooch. The dragon would damn him.

"Hello there, traveler!" The greeting lacked any welcome.

"Hello."

The rider reined the beast to a stop a few feet from Kathka and tugged down his bandana to reveal a cruel, toothy grin.

"Not often you see a lone traveler."

"I was thinking the same."

The grin grew, and Kathka silently cursed. The man was not alone.

"So traveler, what brought you here?" the man asked.

There was no honest answer to the question, and there was no explanation for the brooch. He should have discarded the cloak.

"Got in a little trouble back in the last town." Kathka jerked his chin in a vague direction behind him. He regretted the action, it pulled up the cloak and exposed the white metallic edge of the pin. "Didn't have a choice to stay."

"I see." The rider dug his heel into the camel's side. The beast tilted forward, down to its knees, back legs soon following. Through the jerky motions the man kept his eyes trained upon Kathka. "You came a long way to cool your head."

"Not too far." Kathka knew he was discovered but remained committed to the lie. The truth was not something he could give.

"Oh, I'd say the Islands are quite far."

The man swung down to the sand. Instinct prodded

Kathka to run, but logic rooted him. The man was massive, with a sword and men nearby. Kathka was a scrawny lone foreigner.

A dry chuckle scraped from the man's throat then his hands were upon Kathka. He wrestled the foreigner to the ground and tugged back the cloak to reveal the dragon brooch.

"Should've stayed in that town, Islander."

With precious water Kathka spit. The man grabbed Kathka's tunic and hauled him back to his feet.

"Spirit is good, but don't get carried away." He dragged Kathka to the camel and lifted a length of cord from a saddlebag. "We have a long way to the city."

He laughed as he wrapped Kathka's wrists together. The fibrous cord cut hard grooves into his skin. The man tied it too tightly and tugged it even tighter to ensure his quarry was trapped. Satisfied with the knots, the man mounted the camel and nudged the sluggish creature to action.

"Don't worry, the others aren't far."

Yellowed teeth flashed in devilish mirth. Kathka could not stand the smile.

The camel lumbered to its feet then strode along the base of the dune, captive pulled behind, glaring all the way. They crested a low swell and followed its slope down, toward a valley between the dunes. Along the basin snaked a caravan of camels loaded with boxes and sacks. A merchant caravan, outfitted with riches and swords.

"Calster!" The call rose as the lone camel drew closer, "What did you find?"

"Miles of sand," The man replied to the other who detached himself from the flow of men and animals.

"And that?"

"A precious gem sitting amongst it all." Calster grabbed the rope and jerked Kathka forward. The pin glinted in the sunlight and the man's eyes widened.

"An Islander?" The man leaned forward in his saddle. "What are we supposed to do with him?"

"Staca," Calster crooned, "we can't pass up such a prize for our band. Bring him to a lord and there will be a reward for us. He'll be worth the trouble!"

"Sounds like a hassle," Kathka muttered. He used the opportunity of a still camel and slack rope to tug the hood back up over his head. The sun burned.

A booted heel made heavy contact with the crown of his head and sent him reeling until the cord snapped taut and swung him back. Kathka's head pounded as laughter swirled around him.

"Calster." Greed hollowed a smile upon Staca's face. "Keep our new friend in the middle, we won't want to lose sight of such a feisty foreigner."

"Wise decision." Calster chuckled.

Calster guided his camel into the middle of the procession where eyes rested eternally on the prisoner. Watching and waiting for him to make a move. But he knew how to behave. Kathka kept his head tilted down and focused on planting one foot before the other. Acrius would find his predicament comical. But he had forbidden thoughts of that man, so he cast aside the echoes of his mocking laughter.

Kathka was good at surviving.

If he were to be held prisoner, so be it. He had endured it before, and before it had not hindered him. He would not let his second chance be stolen away. He would not let the past be repeated. He would do what was necessary to end the curse upon his soul. He would suffer what was necessary, he would overcome what was necessary, he would end however many lives necessary to save seven.

Chapter 3

Two sacks of grain weighed Kathka's steps.

They liked to laugh at him, at the foreign brat. Their amusement through the sun-scorched days was always at his expense. Now they tested his strength and placed bets on how much weight he could carry.

They got to three.

At midday, the merchants let the camels sink to their knees and distributed water and salt. Even Kathka was allowed some, though most of his rations hysterically ended across the sand instead of in his mouth. As the merchants sat around him, Kathka remained standing. Dehydration parched his skin. He needed no more heat against his body, the Island garments trapped in too much of the sun's warmth.

A call rose from the front of the caravan and traveled lethargically down the ranks. The rest ended. Kathka preferred it that way.

"You've been silent," Calster commented as he mounted his camel. "Already broken?"

"Plotting your deaths."

A swift kick to the head and a sharp tug forward, and their laughter buzzed in his ear, like the crow of vultures.

He did plot their deaths. During the long march, he seared each face into his memory and swore to one day repay each one.

After he had saved seven lives.

Just as the sun met the crest of the dunes, a cheer rippled through the caravan. On the horizon, a sprawling city shimmered into existence. An oasis rimmed by dunes of sand. Adobe houses clustered at the fringes of the city, behind them speared dark towers and white palaces, and governing over it all was a square black building. There was no wall to hem in the city, an arrogant display of power.

Though the city dominated the skyline, Kathka did not recognize it.

His rage crumbled into unease as the caravan entered the shadow of the buildings. Into the streets the caravan advanced and Kathka was engulfed. Slow progress was made as sand was exchanged for brick and wide-open spaces for narrow streets.

Greedy eyes assessed the merchant's goods. Calster tugged the sword lashed to his back an inch from its scabbard. Steel grinned a dire warning, and the city dwellers kept a wide berth around the camels.

The noise, the smoke, the crowds, the city pressed Kathka's lungs closed. His breath scraped through his throat as his eyes caught on everything erupting before him. He did not recognize the city nor the contraptions that filled it.

In the unfamiliar city, he was a stranger in flesh and time, displaced in a foreign era.

Iron poles lined the roads, square boxes perched on top. Trapped within the glass was a steady, unearthly glow. Kathka squinted at the light, not understanding the fire. He was no closer to understanding when a grating scream tore his eyes from the fixture.

A wooden box burst into view. It trundled down a line of metal and hissed sparks of blue in its wake. Through the glass along its body, Kathka could see people. They pressed against the panes, trapped in the monstrosity, faces blank and unconcerned. The box passed from his view but was replaced by other unknown objects.

Everything looked different.

"Never been in a real city before?" Calster asked. Kathka seized the distraction. He focused on what he knew. The merchant, the camel, the sand crusting his clothes, the bandana masking the malicious grin crinkling the corners of Calster's eyes. He let that center his rage and smother the unease.

"Never one so filthy."

A jerk on the rope, a stumble forward, more laughter.

"This is Kanrin, capital of the Eastern Province. Lord Pashka governs here, he'll be interested in you."

"You flatter me."

"You won't feel so flattered soon."

In Kathka's past life, he would have killed any Islander he found. Calster's words held warnings, but he could not determine what kind. The world was filled with new rules, ones he would have to learn to survive.

He would survive.

Kathka memorized every peculiarity of the city for later consideration. The exercise continued as the caravan worked its way through the narrow streets toward the black box dominating the skyline.

The merchants called it the Square. It was a simple building, with no ornamentation, just thin slits of windows and a closed gate.

Within its shadow, the caravan halted. A single guard broke from the sentries. Staca dismounted and met the soldier. They discussed something, but Kathka was not close enough to overhear. The other merchants dismounted and unstrapped the goods from the camels. Between their bustling bodies, Kathka kept a watchful eye on the merchant and the guard.

Staca produced papers from an inner pocket of his cloak, credentials for the soldier. There was more talk. Kathka caught fragmented glimpses of the two discussing, perhaps arguing. The guard kept looking toward him.

There was an agreement. The guard took a small bag from Staca in exchange for a slip of paper. He shouted up to the watchtower and the gate creaked open. The caravan was allowed entry. Entry with their prisoner.

Staca grinned as he walked back to his band, waving the paper. Calster snatched it from his hand.

"Exotic predators?" Calster read. "What does that have

to do with him?"

"Where there was free space." Staca shrugged. "Lord Pashka returns tomorrow. With a little persuasion the guard was willing to let him be held here. Just keep an eye on him until Lord Pashka returns."

It was an unnecessary command. Their eyes never left him.

Calster untied the rope from the camel's saddle and passed the reins of the beast to another band member. With paper and prisoner, he entered the Square.

Strange bulbs strung along the tunnel and illuminated the corridor in a sickly glow. A fake light, the same as the light trapped upon the metal poles along the road. The tunnel ended at a forked hallway. While the rest of the band moved their goods to the right, Calster took Kathka to the left.

In the hall, they passed other merchants, some with empty shackles, some with muzzled animals. The merchants eyed their competitor's quarry. Appraising. When their eyes caught on Kathka they halted to watch and whisper. When they noticed the dragon brooch, their hissed words filled the narrow hall.

Islander. They spoke it like a slur.

Calster remained close at Kathka's shoulder. Not to shield, but to claim.

The hall ended in a room with a high ceiling where a great sphere hung suspended. Its weak illumination was nearly swallowed by the black slate of the building.

In the room, hitching posts and watering troughs were laid out in a square. Merchants milled about the center of the room. They grasped empty halters and discussed the whims of their buyers and the fluctuation of prices.

Calster led Kathka into the room, and the gazes shifted to him. Narrowed eyes considered the trader, and their contempt was tangible. Their conversations lowered, but Kathka could still hear their hissed anger.

Staca's band had found an Islander. Jealousy tinged the gossip hateful. Their greedy eyes lay hot upon Kathka's skin. They would have whatever prize he could garner for themselves.

Calster ignored the other merchants and approached the nearest soldier. While Calster presented the paper to a guard, Kathka edged as close to the rippling black surface of a trough as the extra rope would allow and stared down at the reflection he found there.

The rumors circulated through the room and he wondered what they saw.

He did not see himself.

The face in the murky water was too young, too lean. His square jaw replaced with a slim one, his brown eyes with slate gray, his broad shoulders with narrow. But more than the physical traits, he missed his age, the earring from his mother's village, the scar he received during the Wayfinder initiation.

In the water he saw a stranger.

The rope passed from Calster to the guard.

"Give me the pin," Calster commanded before the guard led the prisoner away. "I don't want it to get misplaced."

"What about his hair?" The guard slipped a knife from his belt and touched the razor edge against the short coils. Kathka jerked away.

"Cut it," Calster ordered.

The metal scraped cold against his scalp. The hair fell to

the ground in hacked off clumps. Kathka reminded himself that the hair was not his, but the humiliation still stung. The guard swiped a hand over Kathka's scalp to brush off the stray strands.

"Abay," he called to another guard. "Bring water, the man is parched."

Another soldier dutifully filled a bucket in the trough and offered it to the prisoner. Kathka drank only a few mouthfuls of the acrid water before the soldier upended the bucket over his head.

They laughed as the pail clattered onto the ground. Kathka glowered at the men and wiped brown water from his face.

"Get on with it," Calster said gruffly, but mirth crinkled his eyes.

The guard with the knife slipped it back into his belt and unpinned the brooch. The cloak slipped from Kathka's shoulders.

"What's this?" the guard asked.

Calster tugged the water-laden tunic down to reveal more of the marks crisscrossing Kathka's chest. He looked up to Kathka but found no answer in the prisoner's cold gaze. He was equally ignorant.

"It's a cultural thing," Calster said.

"What does it mean?" the guard asked.

"How should I know!" Calster snapped. "Just get on with it!"

The guard dropped the pin into Calster's palm then grabbed Kathka's forearm. While Calster inspected the brooch, the man leaned closer to Kathka.

"What does it mean?" he asked again.

"How should I know," Kathka spat back and earned a harsh shove forward. The guard led him to the back of the room and down a sloped walkway. Calster trailed close behind.

The room reeked of dung. Rows of cages filled the long, low chamber. Housed within were a variety of predators from hyenas to lions to leopards. Their tormented cries rose in the air and suffocated the space.

The guard halted Kathka before an empty cage. He unsheathed his knife again and cut the rope from Kathka's wrists.

Three punches. Kathka calculated that he could land three punches before Calster could call other guards for reinforcement. Not as an attempt to escape, but merely for revenge for the rough handling.

Three punches, but he determined that the closer watch was not worth the satisfaction.

The guard shoved him into the cell.

"Don't worry," Calster said after the bars had clanged shut. He twirled the brooch between his fingers. "I'll keep good care of this for you."

With a final chuckle, Calster left with the guard.

Kathka stood in the center of the cell. Blood oozed from the sores encircling his wrists and droplets of water ran in rivulets down the depression of his spine. He stretched his hands open, then curled them into tight fists. Open, then closed, and he regretted not punching the guard.

High above, barred windows filtered in diluted light. It was just enough to illuminate the haunches of animals, their glowing eyes, their slinking bodies. Cornered, caged, crazed.

Kathka closed his eyes to block out the sight of them.

He opened his hands, curled them into fists.

He could not block out the noise.

The roar of a lion, paws shuffling, an animal throwing itself against the bars. A cacophony that chipped at his concentration. He tried to focus on formulating his escape, but then he heard the staccato cry of the hyena. They laughed and he felt the chill of a desert night, smelled burning wood, and heard Acrius' energetic voice as he told a story.

The Islanders may look like the desert dwellers, but do not be fooled. Their skin wrapped not around a frame of bones, but around the empty carcass of a demon. They were evil. That was what Acrius had said, the tale he told all the Wayfinder initiates around the campfire.

Kathka clenched his hands into fists and let his fingernails cut into his palms.

Save seven lives, kill the Wise One.

That was his plan, and he repeated it through the night.

Chapter 4

"Hey, Islander." The iron bars fragmented Calster's brawny body and cut his smile in half. "It's time."

Kathka glared up at him and refused to budge from his cross-legged position. His rebellion endured as long as it took the guard to unlock the cell and drag him to his feet. Iron cuffs clamped over his raw wrists.

The grin grew across Calster's lips. It was a twisted humor he possessed.

"Let's go."

Calster led the way out of the holding stall. The guard

forced Kathka to follow with a firm grip on his forearm.

"Know your place," Calster spoke as they walked down a narrow hallway. His pace quickened as he spoke. "You're a prisoner. Don't speak, do as you're told."

The commanding words slid past Kathka unheeded. The merchant's fervid steps halted. Calster rounded, nose inches from Kathka's.

"This man," he hissed, "is a lord. It is good to be in his graces. You ruin this, I will kill you."

The threat was the last he spoke. Down the hall they continued, to where Staca stood before two large doors. He watched them approach with a severe frown.

"Ready?" Calster asked as he stopped beside the other merchant. He received no reply. They considered Kathka with wary gazes and hoped their gamble on the Islander would pay off.

Kathka glared at them.

The doors pulled inward.

"Remember," Calster muttered. He adjusted his collar, and as he stepped forward, he whispered, "I will kill you."

The guard and the prisoner followed the two merchants into a room so white it made Kathka's eyes ache.

The floor, the pillars, the domed roof, all carved from white stone. Cool palm branches waved in a gentle breeze that stole through the latticed windows and Kathka focused on their deep color. It was a safe color. A color of life.

"Lord Pashka," a servant called from the doorway. "Merchants Staca and Calster."

"Your Lordship," Staca crooned.

"Well," a voice boomed. It demanded attention, but Kathka was more interested in the veins of the leaves. "What is this you have brought to me?"

The guard stepped away from Kathka's side to leave him alone in the middle of the room. Prying eyes circled the perimeter, abstract shapes in the corner of his vision.

"An Islander, lost in the desert," Calster said from somewhere in front of Kathka.

"We thought first to bring him to you," Staca added. Their cloying words wove a tantalizing tale to garner a greater reward.

Ring-adorned fingers curled around Kathka's chin and snapped his head upward to meet the eyes of the lord. It was a young face, unmarred by the wrinkles or cares of age. It was a handsome face, with high cheekbones, broad nose, and brown skin flushed with a cool hue of purple. It was a dangerous face, with the braid of a warrior woven down his back, and poison swirling in red-rimmed pupils.

"Fascinating." Pashka's fingers slipped from Kathka's cheeks.

"An Islander?" a man scoffed and edged closer to the prisoner. He wore simple gray robes and squinted behind thick wire-rimmed glasses.

"He wore this." Staca extended the brooch which the lord took and inspected with raised eyebrows.

"Fascinating, indeed." Pashka passed the brooch to the gray-robed man who held it right in front of his face. He frowned deeply.

"And where did you say you found him?" The gray-robed man lowered the brooch just enough to eye Kathka again.

"In the desert, a four day ride to the east of here," Calster answered.

"In the desert?" the man repeated with obvious disbelief.

"An exile," Staca assured. He faked confidence well. "Obviously a move of desperation."

"But—"

"Malici." The young lord laughed easily. "Does it matter? He's a special circumstance, they will understand. Besides, they have proof."

The gray-robed man puckered his lips, but he said nothing more. The brooch sat in his palm; he could not deny its implications.

"Why does he look so haggard?" the lord asked to smooth aside Malici's concern.

"We had a long trek," Calster answered the question posed to him.

"They were not observant enough to properly care for their prisoner," Kathka answered the question not posed to him.

"You're a feisty one." There was laughter in the lord's voice as he backhanded the prisoner. Hard. Kathka stumbled, cheek stinging. The man adjusted his rings. "Well? Are you?"

"Sure am."

Staca jerked his chin down. A sign. Calster set heavy hands upon Kathka's shoulders and forced him to his knees. Kathka glared up at the men who appraised him.

"They are proud," Staca said in an attempt to assuage the outburst. The lord gave a slight nod, but he did not appear perturbed. His index finger touched the edge of the stiff cotton tunic and pulled it forward. His eyes traced the lines of the tattoo.

"A strange cultural habit of theirs," Calster supplied.

"They tattoo only their nobles."

Pashka's gaze finished its course and snapped back to Kathka's face. His smile was sharp. He knew Calster lied.

"I will take him into my personal oversight. You have done well to bring him to me."

"My Lord Pashka, it is an honor—"

"Yes, yes," the man interrupted Staca. "Malici will see to it that you receive compensation for your troubles."

He waved vaguely towards the other man. Riches supplied him the luxury of casual arrogance. Staca's attention remained on the lord. He needed to impress.

"It has been an honor, Lord Pashka. I hope our band can continue to please you."

"As do I," the lord smirked. "If it means you will continue to bring me such intriguing things."

Intriguing, he said. The word meant a closer eye, a tighter chain, a harder escape.

Pashka was a dangerous man.

Chapter 5

While Malici and Staca discussed, Calster removed his crushing weight from Kathka's slim shoulders. He clapped one hand down hard on his left shoulder twice before he ceded control of the prisoner to the guards. One fitted shackles around Kathka's bruised wrists.

"We'll miss you," Calster whispered, but the jeer was hollow. They had relinquished any power they had over him to Lord Pashka. The merchant band was no longer his concern, not until the deal was met and he came for their blood.

Kathka only had Pashka to concern him now.

As the guards led him from the room, the lord watched with a twisted smile.

The brilliance of the white room cast the rest of the Square's halls a shade darker. Everything as black as a starless midnight. It was impossible to see doorways and intersecting hallways until they crossed them. Kathka's eyes refused to adjust to the illusion, but the guards were unbothered. They navigated the twisting halls easily until they led him out a door and into the open air.

Hot light replaced the black. Kathka blinked multiple times before his vision cleared. Even then, he did not understand what the guards had led him to.

The strange contraption before him resembled the screeching box full of people he had seen upon his arrival to the city. Only much smaller. It was bright red. An extravagant color for an extravagant person.

One of the guards grabbed a handle in the side and swung open a section of the metal. The other drew Kathka toward the gaping maw. The guard bent down and slid into the beast, the metal cuff around Kathka's wrist forced him to follow. The guard left outside swung the door closed with a metallic click.

Inside, the space was suffocating. Uncomfortable and cramped. The interior was divided into two sections, a front and a back, both outfitted with a bench and nothing more. Another door opened in the front section, and the second guard slipped inside the contraption. The space became even more stifling.

Kathka breathed in evenly through his nose.

The thing lurched forward.

Kathka sat poised at the edge of the seat, fingers curled into the leather. Beneath the seat cushions the edges of the metal frame bit against his bones. The vibrations shivered up his spine and trembled inside of him. Each jolt over the brick road brought bile to the back of his throat.

The guard beside him quirked an eyebrow.

"No cars on the Islands?"

The short word had an awkward sound. The guard chuckled and shook his head. Ignorant Islander, deserving all the hatred that the desert dwellers heaped upon him.

Panels of glass allowed Kathka to watch the city pass. He tried to focus on the crowds outside and not on how the car seemed ready to fall apart with every bump in the road. The shaky box was an absurd method of transportation.

The world had leaped forward without him. The cities were different, the words were new, the technology was foreign. Even the color had changed, from brown and beige to black and silver.

Kathka watched the chaos of the city until a white wall blocked the view and it was replaced by a jungle of greens and the colorful blooms of exotic flowers. His nose pressed against the glass, breath blooming upon the panel. He caught a flash of something blue. A pool, hidden behind the foliage. He tried to mask his astonishment. But failed.

Even as king he had never possessed such splendor.

He loathed the brat who held him captive.

The jungle was trimmed tidy at the edges as the unruly garden was exchanged for an expansive paved yard. The road merged into the sandstone and the car continued on in a curved trajectory to meet the elegant staircase fanning from a great white building. A palace in the midst of the oasis.

The car rolled to a stop before the stairs with a shiver and a sputter. The metal frame groaned as the guard in the front opened his door and stepped out.

In the short interval of time it took for the guard to open the back door of the contraption, Kathka assessed the palace. He noted every staircase, door, balcony, any way of escape. Then the door opened, and the guard pulled him out onto the stone. The rattling of the road still vibrated in his bones and the ground was unstable beneath his feet.

A single guard pulled the prisoner up the stairs while the other returned to the car. It roared back to life behind them. Kathka filed the car away with the rest of the new contraptions for later consideration.

He had a palace, and his escape, now to consider.

The entrance hall was a wide expanse of tiled white with a great chandelier that filled the room with fake illumination. Before he had time to survey all the hall, the guard shoved him through a door and into a smaller side room.

This room was deep chocolate brown with accents of red warmed by the afternoon sun. The guard sat Kathka into a plush chair and fastened his cuffed hands to the armrest with another manacle.

"Lord Pashka will be here soon." The guard inspected the bound and simmering foreigner. "Any sign of resistance and he will use force."

Satisfied with the restraints and the threat, the guard left.

The warming sunlight soon became oppressive. Kathka hated the light, hated watching it inch along the wall. His eyes roved the room. There were three exits: the door behind him, a small door in the right corner, and a multitude of narrow windows occupying the west wall. A complex latticework of full blossoms overlaid each window. He squinted at the flowers and tilted his head. The lattice was made of metal.

Two exits, and a dizzying pattern of sunlight.

Inside the room were chairs, only chairs. The one Kathka sat in was part of a circle in the middle, all placed at just the right angles to host an intimate party of friends. Kathka imagined bodies occupying the silk cushions, eyeing him with loathsome gazes.

The sunlight receded with time. Lengthening shadows obscured the corners of the room. The heat began to abate, but it was little comfort. The longer he sat motionless the more the specters in the chairs resembled people he knew. People from his past.

People he had killed.

Kathka strained against the binds and forced himself to focus on the tangible pain and not imaginary figures. Pashka was toying with him, letting his mind play the tricks. It was working. But Kathka refused to let him win, this imprisonment was a momentary arrangement.

The doors banged open and the metal pressed deeper than Kathka intended. He hissed in pain and glared at Pashka as he walked past, a smoking pipe clenched between curled lips.

The fumes were intoxicating.

"Well, well." Pashka flopped upon a chair across from Kathka and crossed his ankles. Late afternoon sunlight flashed like fire off the golden beads threaded in his hair and the rings adorning his fingers. The tight hairstyle accented his angular features, but his hands were soft. The fingers around the pipe were long and delicate. Kathka wondered how great a warrior he could be with uncalloused hands.

"Hope you didn't mind the wait." A leisurely smile graced Pashka's face, aloof to Kathka's scrutiny.

Silence.

"I've never seen an Islander before. Rare down here you know." The pipe clinked against his teeth.

Retorts bit inside Kathka's mouth, demanded to be released. But he swallowed them back, though the words cut his throat. He would not bend to Pashka's whims.

"I'd ask you for your story." A lazy shrug rolled through Pashka's shoulders. He relinquished the pipe from his lips and pointed it at Kathka. "But I doubt you would give it to me."

"I won't."

A languid chuckle, a long draft of the pipe.

"Doesn't matter, I didn't bring you here for your lies. I brought you for something a bit more tangible." He set the pipe on the arm of the chair and stood. His steps were silent, like a desert cat as it stalked its prey. "Those merchants are ignorant, but we both know you are worth more than they could imagine. So many don't even recognize the marks anymore, the curses of the gods."

He brushed aside the loose tunic to reveal the lines tracing over Kathka's chest.

"Imagine, even the blessed Islands have been cursed. Whatever your past, the Bu Chak will be in my debt for bringing you to them. They are quite enamored by those tattoos."

Kathka was lost in his blather. Pashka withdrew his cool touch to retrieve his pipe and puff it back to life.

"We'll make up some story for you. Say you're a high

noble or some such. It'll be fun, creating you. Until then," he declared, "you will entertain me."

Kathka's eyebrows twitched together. He had never entertained. Imprisonment was filled with chains, cells, and cruelty. Not entertainment.

Behind the screen of smoke, Pashka smiled.

"Mell!"

The small corner door inched open and a boy entered. Thick black curls overwhelmed his slender, knobby body. The boy opened his mouth to reply, but his eyes landed on Kathka, and his words turned into a sharp inhalation of breath.

"Oh, be quiet." Pashka massaged his temple. With a twitch of his fingers, he motioned for the boy to approach. Mell's eyes skipped between the two men, but he obeyed. Pashka smacked him upside the head. "What's wrong with you?"

"It … he …"

"Stop stalling." Another smack.

"I didn't think the Islanders actually existed," the boy whispered as he cupped his cheek.

"Didn't exist!" Pashka's boisterous laughter echoed in the small room. Kathka found nothing comical in the situation. "You idiot! Go, look at him, touch him."

The boy's eyes grew incredibly wide.

"Go."

The boy hesitated between his master and the man with the murderous glare. He determined the greater of two fears.

He stepped closer to Kathka.

Calloused pads grazed Kathka's shoulder then retreated. His head remained tipped down to avoid meeting the foreigner's gaze. Pashka laughed.

"Get used to him, Mell. You'll be looking after him."

Mell swung to his master, chest heaving with a silent plea of desperate protest. Pashka paid no attention to the boy but instead considered the glaring prisoner.

"You've been silent, Islander. You've heard my plans for you. Nothing to say?"

It was a dangerous offer Kathka knew he should leave untouched. But he had already let so many opportunities for vengeance pass.

"I didn't pay much attention."

Pashka's fingers encircled Kathka's throat and smacked him back against the chair with a crack. The room swirled and his stomach rolled.

"I enjoy this, I do. But watch yourself, prisoner." His grip tightened, Kathka gagged. "Remember, I decide your fate."

Pashka's face floated before Kathka's shaky vision. There was malice and pleasure in the creases of his smile.

Pashka released his hold.

"Hope that doesn't bruise. I have to make you look like a proper Island noble." Pashka dragged in a deep draft of his pipe and blew the smoke into Kathka's face. It smelled sickly sweet, like over-ripened berries. "Start thinking of a story for yourself, next time I call you I expect quite a tale."

He turned to the boy who stood with head bowed and hands folded. "Take him to the Green Quarter, make sure he is well situated, understood?"

The boy's fingers twisted tight about each other, and the distress played in the corners of his downturned lips. He did not respond, which was a bad decision.

"Well?"

Mell nodded.

"And try not to kill him," Pashka said to Kathka as he walked past the chair and out of his sight. "I promised his father I'd look after him."

It was spoken with the light tone of a joke. But it was not one at all. It was one last jab at them both. Mell was pathetic, lanky framed, watery-eyed, and desperate to hide beneath his coils of hair. Even if Kathka wanted to kill the boy, he could not.

He would know, the Wise Man had promised. And he did. It was a constriction in his chest, a pull he could not deny, a solid assurance that this boy was it.

The first of seven lives.

Chapter 6

The Green Quarter was well named.

The floor was tiled lime, walls washed emerald, and drapes of light mint swung in the breeze wafting through the latticed windows. It was an ugly room.

As Kathka considered the quarters, Mell and the guard considered him. There was a hesitation, a shuffle of the boy's feet, and the apprehension stoked the frustration the green room had kindled.

"What?" Kathka wheeled upon the boy. Mell shrank small against the doorway away from the foreigner, away from the guard.

"The bath's through there." He pointed to a horseshoe archway on the opposite side of the room. The guard removed the cuffs from Kathka's hands, and the boy continued. "After you bathe, you will be chained."

"Not very hospitable." Kathka rubbed the tender skin around his raw wrists.

"There will be guards outside." Mell's words were practiced. He repeated the script he had been given. "I will remain in the room to attend to you, and to watch you. Pashka's compound is heavily guarded, escape will not be possible."

"We will see," Kathka growled at the unintended challenge. He had expected a reaction of some form, a flinch, or a retort, even a simple twist of his lips into a frown. But Mell remained impassive, hunched within the doorway. His lines finished, role complete. Kathka reached for the boy. His fingertips rested briefly upon his shoulder before Mell tore from the touch.

Kathka splayed his empty hands, but the action did not calm the boy. Eyes wide, he pressed against the stone, head tucked between hunched shoulders.

"I won't touch you, okay?"

The boy looked around a decade old, though he acted older. The hollows of his gaunt face pooled with fear and fatigue.

"Look." Kathka attempted to soften his voice, but he was not a gentle person. "I just want more information. I'm trying to understand."

Mell's lips twisted upward into what might have been described as a smile. But it was cold and lifeless. A grimace was a better description.

"You're Lord Pashka's prisoner," he said. "Do as he says."

"I've never been good at following orders."

"Then you won't survive long." Mell's words were clipped, stating a fact he had learned long before. Kathka laughed.

"We'll see," he said. To escape from the boy's empty gaze, he retreated to the washroom. The boy unnerved him. He was so young, yet so wearied by the world.

Kathka did not know how to save him.

He did not even know what it meant to save anyone. He hissed out a curse at his own folly, he should have asked the god for specifics. Eagerness to obtain a second life had clouded his judgment.

He repeated the curse.

In the washroom, a low stone bench stretched along one wall, a white towel and new clothes folded at the edge. A deep pool filled half the room, crystal waters distorting the swirling pattern of palm green tiles.

Kathka undressed and stepped onto the shallow ledge that ran along the edge of the pool. In the ripples, he watched the reflection of his new body undulate before him. He lifted his arms and inspected what he had been cursed with.

Stripped of the clothes and the brooch, it would be impossible to mark the body out as an Islander. If not for the brooch and the merchant's story, Kathka would have easily slipped back into the general desert populace.

If not for the brooch.

And if not for the black tattoo.

The dark lines were striking even in the weak reflection.

The clear marks of one cursed by a god. Fragments of myths flitted through his mind, and he retold himself what he could recall of the tales.

The gods cursed those who crossed them, a warning to any other who would dare do the same. Scala was the last to be cursed. Then the gods left.

But there in the water were the crisscrossed marks. A constant reminder that this body was not his to keep. He inhabited the shell for as long as he had seven lives to save.

If he failed, it was not his to keep.

Kathka stepped off the shelf and plunged into the pool to smother the building rage. In the recesses of his mind, he reminded himself that he could not swim. The water filled his ears and whispered to him, drowning out the reasonable concern. It pounded the rhythm of seven lives. Seven lives. But he did not know how to save even one.

His lungs begged for air. Kathka straightened his legs and was relieved to touch the bottom. With a gasp he broke the surface.

A dark shadow cast over the water. Kathka turned to the guard standing at the edge of the pool, arms crossed and eyes narrowed.

"Bedtime?" Kathka asked. The guard did not respond. The man was identical to the rest of Pashka's guards, with hair so close-cropped he could be mistaken as a vanquished warrior. Kathka swung his arms and skimmed his fingers over the water, splashing it over the edge of the pool and onto the guard's boots. The guard hastily stepped backward and Kathka smirked. It was childish, but it was satisfying. A retaliation that would not result in a chokehold.

"Get out," the guard snarled.

Kathka left the whispering pool. He dried himself with the towel and dressed in the garments Pashka provided.

It was an odd wardrobe. Kathka had not paid much mind to the clothes the desert dwellers wore, it had not mattered. But as he donned the attire Pashka had left for him, he noted the oddity of the material. The tunic was loose about his chest, with wide sleeves cut off above his elbow. Undesirable for travel in the desert, but at least it covered the lines marring his flesh. The material was silky and light upon his body, uncomfortably smooth and it matched the outrageous greens of the room. Green like grass, the collar of the tunic embroidered with wildflowers.

The pants were equally uncomfortable, made of a canvas material. It all reminded him that time had advanced without him. Even the simplest elements of life had not remained untouched. Everywhere he looked something was different.

Kathka buried the frustration. The emotion was not worth spending on clothing.

Garbed in Pashka's peculiar clothing, Kathka returned to the bed and offered his raw wrists to the guard who followed him out of the bath. The guard instead clamped an iron manacle around his ankle. He cast Kathka one last glower and left.

A heavy bolt slid into place and confined the boy and the prisoner amidst the green.

"Well." Kathka rattled the chain anchoring him to the bed. Pashka was thorough, which made everything more difficult. Dragging the chain behind him, Kathka settled in the middle of the mattress. It was a comfortable bed, which bothered him. Pashka continued to toy. "Might as well relax."

Bright hollow light flooded the room. A sharp ring

pierced the air as the illumination settled awkwardly over every corner. Kathka craned his head upward to the round spheres glowed.

"What is that?" He snapped his gaze to the boy whose finger was still poised over a square box in the wall.

"The light?"

"No. The sun is light, fire is light. This—" He jabbed a finger to the bulbs. "Is not light."

"Electricity." The boy spoke the new word more as a question, as if prepared to have Kathka strike down his second attempt to name the false light. The syllables were sharp upon Kathka's lips as he formed them.

"And the posts along the streets, they have this electricity?"

"The lamp posts?" Mell asked. Kathka quickly memorized the two new words and pressed on to the other items he had stored away.

"Those long boxes, like cars but bigger."

"Trains?"

"Trains." With Mell's vocabulary, he pieced together the fragments of the city. They were meaningless utterances to him, but together they formed the reality he now inhabited. Each question deepened Mell's frown.

The boy was suspicious. There was no way to avoid it, Kathka did not belong, and the boy rightly distrusted him. Trust was not necessary to save someone, so Kathka pressed forward with a new set of questions.

"How long have you served Pashka?"

Mell's brow crinkled.

"No answer?"

None was forthcoming. The flow of information severed

at the personal.

Kathka picked up one of the plush pillows littering the bed and ran his hand across the surface. He did not care to know, Mell's past did not interest him. But Kathka needed to know how to save him, and that included what and who he needed saving from. He gave the boy another moment to speak, then he ripped the pillow along the seams. Delicate white feathers spilled into his lap.

"What are you doing!" Mell rushed forward but halted at the bedside. Kathka dropped the empty pillowcase and reached for another.

"I'm playing his game," Kathka answered as he tore the next pillow.

"Stop!" Mell lunged to grab the pillow, but Kathka jerked it out of his reach. "Lord Pashka will not be pleased!"

"Good!"

More feathers cascaded onto the bed. A few slipped from the mattress and floated to the ground where they sat, almost looking like glass. Like her jewelry box. Fragile, easily shattered.

"Please stop."

Kathka's destructive hands stilled and he repeated, "How long have you served Pashka?"

Mell's eyes followed a feather as it floated down to the mattress. Once it alighted on the sheet, his gaze flicked upward to meet Kathka's gaze. It was the first time Kathka had looked into his empty eyes. But then Mell's gaze cast back to the feathers.

"If you stop, I'll give you this." Mell moved away from the bed and busied himself with a cabinet. He returned with a stone jar in his hands. The lid was studded with emeralds.

"Salve, for your wounds."

Stray feathers drifted across the sheets as Kathka moved to the edge of the bed. He stretched out his hand, and Mell set the jar in his palm. With the exchange made, Mell retreated to a corner of the room.

Kathka settled the jar on the bedspread and opened it. Thick salve filled the jar. Such an expensive container for something so common. Kathka shook his head in bewilderment and scooped up some of the ointment. He dabbed it on the open sores encircling his wrists. It was cool and soothing.

There was silence, except for the ringing of the electricity in the lights. Kathka looked up to the boy, but he was closed in upon himself and did not look at the prisoner.

Mell would not answer his questions, Kathka knew that. Though perhaps he did not need the answers. Perhaps the most obvious answer was the correct one.

"Here." Kathka clinked the lid onto the jar and extended it toward the boy.

Mell ventured back across the room to take the container. When his fingers curled around it, Kathka abandoned his veiled attempts to save Mell and asked, "Do you want to escape?"

It was the most apparent way to save the boy. Save him from the monster calling itself his master. Kill the monster, save the boy. Kathka was willing to fulfill the task.

"That's impossible." Mell took the jar and returned it to the cabinet. Without a glance toward Kathka, he walked back to the wall and flicked the switch in the box. The electricity snapped off. Dusk settled into the space the false light had fled. In the deepening shadows, Mell laid upon a sedan opposite of the bed. Back turned against the prisoner.

Kathka could barely distinguish his frame. He was far away, out of reach. With a sigh, Kathka picked up another pillow and emptied more feathers across the bed. Then he grabbed another. When no pillow remained intact, Kathka laid in the downy white. Upon the blank canvas of the ceiling, Kathka plotted the destruction of Pashka and the salvation of Mell.

Plotted until sleep overtook him.

In the dreamless darkness came the fear. The fear of a detached soul drowning in the void. He knew it was foolish to fear sleep. But in the darkness, he became too aware of how loosely his soul was secured to the new body. Connected by a flimsy cord. It could be so easily snapped, and it would be if he failed.

In his previous death, he had been tethered to the world of the living by the Wise Man. But the Wise One was not the god of death, that god had abandoned their world.

In sleep, he wondered what happened to the dead when there was no god of death.

Chapter 7

There was a connection. Bony knuckles against soft flesh. Kathka focused on the pain, it roused him from the depths and drew him back. Grounded him. When he opened his eyes, he saw Mell at the bedside, hand cupped against his cheek, eyes watery with shocked tears.

"What?" Kathka fell back upon the soft mattress in a puff of downy white. Sunlight filtered through the lattices and cast octagons of light across the mattress. Around him, the feathers floated back to their resting place.

"You have to get up," Mell said.

"Why?"

"Lord Pashka ordered it."

"Don't care." Kathka rolled to his side and closed his eyes. The world darkened. He shifted his fingers over the sheets to remind himself that he could still touch. That he was still alive.

"You have to," Mell repeated the first part of the command.

"I haven't been ordered around for so long." Kathka balled his hand into a fist around the silk and rounded on Mell's small form. "I forgot how to obey."

Mell's arms tightened around the cloth he held, head tilted away. The boy was frightened. Kathka did not care. It was easier to be angry than to admit. Admit the pressure in his chest, the tightness in his throat, how the darkness still crowded at the corner of his vision, that he did not know how to save Mell.

"What's this?" He snagged the edge of the fabric the boy held. It was light, delicate, ugly.

"It's for you to wear." Mell let the slick fabric glide from his grip and stream across the bed, the corner trailing upon the tiled floor. "You are to look nice."

The long sash was deep purple, but the color looked fake. Extracted by force from whatever substance caused such a horrendous hue.

"I would do anything for Pashka." He balled the silk and threw it across the bed. It unfurled and fluttered onto the edge, then slipped down and disappeared. "Except wear that."

"You'll get me in trouble."

"I don't care." He only needed to save him.

"At least wear the slippers," Mell mumbled, abandoning the scarf. He set the blue slippers at the bedside, then with slumped shoulders, he padded to the door of the Green Quarter. He rapped his knuckles against the wood and moved backward as it creaked open.

In the doorway stood two guards, dressed in full regalia. Their metal breastplates buffed so thoroughly they gleamed like mirrors, and from the tips of their spears dangled blood-red tassels matching the tunics beneath the armor.

They looked like Kathka's own soldiers. There was some solace in seeing something unchanged, though they were only there to control him. But with guards attired so finely, it was clear Pashka meant to impress. He crafted a grand display, but the show was not for Kathka. The prisoner was only one element arranged amidst it all. One element that would not be wearing the purple scarf.

Though the shoes at least had the potential to be useful.

Kathka slipped his feet into the flexible slippers as the guards approached. One unchained his ankle while the other clasped his wrists into shackles. There were no words, only actions.

From the Green Quarter, they led him down a hall. Kathka craned his head backward and was satisfied to see Mell trailing behind. Satisfied that he would not yet lose his first life, Kathka swung his head back and focused on memorizing all the details of the desert lord's palace.

The narrow passage opened into a courtyard overflowing with vibrant red, purple, and blue flowers. Balconies surrounded the open space, and from the safety of their shadows, guards and servants snuck glimpses of the rare specimen paraded through the garden. Every prying eye found him.

Red rage burned in his stomach.

The rumors would increase. Escape would become more complicated.

He was glad when the palace walls returned to surround him and cut off their view. They were persistent though, and as the guards led him past intersecting passages and stairways, a few servants stole a look at their lord's newest prisoner.

The guards led him through a doorway and into a long hall. There was nowhere for servants to hide in the room. Pillars stretched high above to support a triangular ceiling, and between the stone flashed the deep rich green from the garden surrounding the palace. Past the garden, past the high white wall, the dirty city stole a glimpse into paradise. Even further past the roof peaks, the desert swells marked faint shapes on the horizon.

True paradise, where Kathka would one day return.

But the Square was a smudge in his peripheral vision, an eternal reminder of Pashka's dominion.

At the end of the hall, the lord sat before a splay of food. He picked at the feast of fruits, bread, meats, and cheese, that cost a fortune.

"My prisoner!" Pashka stretched an arm over the table. "Come, join me!"

The guards unchained Kathka and forced him to his knees on a cushion opposite of Pashka. They retreated to the shadows of the pillars. Out of sight, but spears at the ready. Kathka noted their positions and glanced back down the hall to find Mell.

He remained at the doorway with head bowed so his

curls obscured his face.

Overlooked and ignored.

"You didn't wear the sash?" Pashka commented and Kathka turned back to meet the keen stare of the lord. He was dressed in multiple layers of silken sashes, his braids twisted together in a bun on the top of his head like a crown. "I suppose you're handsome enough without it. What is your name?"

Pashka mistook the silence as insolence.

"Your name." His voice dropped in warning.

"Kath," Kathka said before the second pause stretched too long. It was a lie, but the truth held weight. It was the name of a dead conqueror, not a prisoner.

"Well, Kath." Pashka tore off a chunk of bread and popped it into his mouth. He spoke as he chewed, "I heard what you did to my pillows. I'm not pleased."

Humor restored with the relinquished name, Pashka smiled when Kathka offered no response.

"No apology?"

"No."

Pashka laughed and pushed the platter of rolls toward Kathka. "Eat, you're nothing but bone."

Kathka reached past the bread and took a slab of pork.

"Tell me." Pashka propped his chin against his knuckles and watched as his prisoner tore at the meat. "Was it murder?"

"What?"

"Your exile," the lord clarified. "I assume the merchants were right, you did not come to the desert willingly."

"I'm not exiled."

"Is it the curse then?" Pashka continued his queries. His

smile was easy, but his eyes were sharp. He merely wanted a convincing story, something he could twist to fit whatever plans he had. But he was too close to the truth for Kathka to let him pry.

"It was murder."

Pashka nodded, but he did not believe it. "But not an exile. A fugitive? Who did you murder?"

"No one you would know," Kathka muttered and drowned a goblet of weak wine. Its color was too pale and it tasted too sweet. Pashka chuckled.

"I do like how this story is progressing, we will have to continue developing it later for the Bu Chak. But now we must focus on today's business." Pashka straightened at the table and called down the hall, "Malici!"

From behind, Kathka heard the delicate tread of the gray-robed man. He narrowed his eyes at Pashka, uncertain what he plotted. The lord looked content with himself.

Malici stood at the end of the table, hands tucked into the large sleeves of his robe.

"Lord Pashka," he said. "It is not yet time."

"No, but I would like you to explain to Kath what we are doing today."

Malici looked at the prisoner over the glasses perched at the end of his nose. Kathka had met men like him before. Pompous men who trusted too much in their titles.

"The Bu Chak have laws," he began. "I do not know about your Islands, but here we hold our laws in high regard. I am appointed to ensure they are obeyed. A lower lord has brought Lord Pashka a prisoner, I ensure that the prisoner is lawfully kept."

"An overseer? It doesn't sound like you have much

power then." Kathka sipped at the wine, though it disgusted him. He wanted the air of nonchalance to dig beneath the skin of the gray-robed man. It worked. He scowled at Kathka.

"Malici and I," Pashka stood and adjusted his scarves to fall properly about his lean frame, "we have an agreement. He keeps me mostly honest, and I ensure a few extra coins fall into his purse."

"How benevolent."

Malici bristled, but Pashka smiled. He resembled the jackal, the forager of the desert that survived on what could not.

His focus centered upon Kathka.

"You know," his voice was airy, dreamlike. His head tilted to one side as he considered the prisoner still sitting at the table. "There was something missing, and I just realized what it is."

From beneath the layers of scarves, Pashka produced the Island brooch from a hidden pocket. He crouched beside Kathka and pinned the dragon just below his collar bone.

"You would've looked better with the scarf," he sighed, then straightened. "You will accompany me to see this prisoner. It's an honor you can't turn down."

Kathka grabbed another slab of pork and followed as Pashka led the way down the hall, Malici at his side. The lord was barely taller than Kathka, but power swelled his stature. Young and overconfident, a dangerous status to possess. One that Kathka could topple if he made the right connections with Pashka's enemies.

But first, he had to save seven lives.

Kathka looked back at Mell. The boy remained at the

entrance of the hall, head still bowed. Silent, invisible.

At the end of the hall, a flight of stairs led down to a balcony. Palm and date trees provided a leafy protection from both the sun above and the peaks of the city behind.

A portly man stood a few feet in front of the balcony rail, just outside the reach of the shade, lips drawn into a wide grin. Too eager to please. As Pashka and Malici descended the stairs, he stretched his arms out wide in greeting.

"Lord Pashka!" The man's voice dripped honey. "Greetings from the Kasheen Plains!"

"Yes, yes." Pashka waved aside the pleasantries. The Kasheen lower lord had already exasperated the young lord. "What do you bring me?"

"Something of great interest." He winked, but the presentation faltered when Kathka stepped onto the stairs and into the sunlight. The light glinted off the dragon pin, impossible to ignore.

This distraction Pashka allowed. When Kathka stood glaring at his side, the young lord finally prompted the Kasheen lower lord to continue. "Great interest?"

"Yes, of course." His voice had lost its previous cheer. He snapped his fingers. From the shadows of the palms, his men forced a prisoner forward. "Of great interest."

The prisoner did not appear of any interest. Only the black tattoo that wound across his bare chest set him apart.

It was identical to the one marring Kathka's chest.

"Well, yet another." Pashka's eyes roved the man. "This meeting may not be a complete waste of time."

"As soon as I saw him I knew you would wish to see him." The man managed to find some way to spin the events in his favor, but he stumbled over the words. "He was found —"

Pashka raised his hand and the words died in the lower lord's mouth.

"Pardon, Lord Pashka," the man appealed. "I simply wish to assist."

"Pardon, indeed." Pashka stepped past the lower lord and inspected the prisoner. "I don't care to know how you found him, Malici will occupy himself with that. The markings are the only thing of interest to me."

"The Bu Chak will be interested in more than that," Malici commented. "This man is not like your Islander."

"Fine," Pashka sighed. "We will discuss trivialities."

He turned from the prisoner to join Malici beside the lower lord of Kasheen. The lower lord said something more in further attempts to sweet-talk Pashka. Kathka did not listen, the duty Pashka had set before him was complete. Impress the lower lord.

Kathka stood before the prisoner who shared his tattoo.

"How?" Kathka demanded. The prisoner startled at the forceful question. Slowly his bowed head lifted. His eyes passed over Kathka's torso and found the edges of the tattoo peaking from the sharp dip in the neckline of the green tunic.

"You." The prisoner snapped his eyes to Kathka's. There was strength in his voice, though hoarse from dehydration. A fervor lay just beneath the fragile exterior of desert chapped lips and shaven head. "When will the Bu Chak come?"

"How were you cursed?" Kathka ignored the prisoner's question and pressed his own. The man's eyes shifted across a multitude of things, but Kathka did not bother to follow his gaze. The prisoner plotted, planned, then shook his head and returned his focus back to Kathka. Resolution made.

"I'll save you both," the prisoner declared.

"No thanks."

Kathka's fist made heavy contact with the prisoner's ribs. Pain wound up his arm as the prisoner doubled over. His next blow would be for the softer parts of the man's lower back. He raised his elbow to strike but was wrapped in the mighty grip of Pashka's guard who pinned his arms against his sides.

Pashka approached, head tilted as he looked first at the doubled over prisoner then to the Islander.

"I believe punishment is in order." The habitual smile curled back onto his lips. He was enjoying himself. "For my pillows, and for the prisoner."

He nodded to the guard who shoved Kathka toward the stairs.

"Also." Pashka held up a hand and the guard halted. Malici, the Kasheen lower lord, and all the guards waited with bated anticipation for the next words that would fall from his mouth. All spectators of his show. He took slow, measured steps to stand in front of Kathka then plucked the brooch from where he had pinned it. "In the future, be sure to stand respectfully behind me. It is only proper."

The guard removed Kathka from the balcony. He seethed, but it was not Pashka's threats that had angered him. He had grown used to those, they were no different from the taunts of the Wayfinders in his previous life.

It was the prisoner's words that were new and dangerous. They were heavy, weighted by a plot he was ignorant of. A plot that could ruin his own inadequate planning.

Chapter 8

The wires scorched him to the core. Lightning whipped through his veins, sizzled in his blood, and tore screams from his lungs.

He had never experienced such pain.

No stab, slash, or broken bone had ever reached the same intensity. It left him numb.

Mell pressed into the corner of the Green Quarter as the guards laid Kathka upon the bed. New pillows perched around him. He wanted to tear them to shreds, but every muscle ached. The cuff snapped around his ankle, and the guards exchanged a harsh word, a laugh at his expense, then the door banged shut.

Kathka was left with the servant boy. He could feel his stare, but he had no energy to deal with the brat. His shattered mind slowly pieced itself together, stitching a jagged patchwork of rage.

"What was that?" It hurt to speak.

"Electricity."

The round spheres hanging from the ceiling seared his vision.

"Turn it off," Kathka ordered. It was intimidation, not authority, that made Mell shut off the lights. The bulbs went dark but round spots of red burned angrily where the light had inhabited the spheres. The red haunted him. He closed his eyes and still the spots hung behind his lids. He curled his tingling fingers around the sheets, solace in the pain. The physical world still existed.

"What do you know about King Kathka?" he asked for the distraction. He needed to piece together his own life. His own death in relation to this new world.

"You know our kings?" Mell's question was soft, coaxed by curiosity that overcame the fear.

"You do know of Kathka?"

"Of course, everyone does. The Blood King."

"Blood King?"

"Because of the massacres," Mell explained. It was the most confidence Kathka had heard in his voice. The most life. Though Mell spoke of things he did not understand. "He conquered the whole world by force, killed anyone who stood in his way. He was a ruthless king."

The title seemed displaced. The Blood King. The deaths had never seemed like massacres, only necessary sacrifices.

To conquer the world such actions were necessary. But that was the title the world chose to remember him by.

The Blood King.

"And since him?" Kathka asked.

Mell inched closer to the edge of the bed. The boy was barely there, a great craftsman of a careful life. A being that existed only when needed, and then only enough to fulfill his purpose. He teetered on the edge of existence to survive in the hostile world.

Yet curiosity drew him closer to the strange Islander.

"There hasn't been a king since."

Kathka snapped his eyes open, and Mell flinched. But he remained a foot from the bed, a question already formed on his lips. When Kathka made no further movements he asked, "Do you have kings on the Islands?"

"No idea."

Mell's eyes flitted to the ground. Kathka sat with a groan and the boy shifted away. Kathka's head pulsed, and his vision flickered. The boy seemed less physical and more spectral.

"If you don't have a king," Kathka asked, "what do you have?"

"The Bu Chak and the lords." Mell's responses remained curt, but Kathka needed more information.

"Who are the Bu Chak?" Kathka pressed. The title plagued him since Pashka had first uttered it in the chocolate room. It was used too often, directed too many of the lord's actions.

"They are what took the place of the Blood King," Mell explained. "They promised to restore our land, to free us from the curse. They haven't done much of either."

"What have they done?"

"Set up the lords." The boy scuffed his foot against the floor. A spark of frustration. A glimpse at a spirit not as completely broken as Kathka had believed. "They oversee the lords who oversee the lower lords, and the lower lords oversee the rest."

"And how do you become a lord?" Kathka asked.

"The Bu Chak appoint you," Mell explained. "They are in control, but the lords are the ones in charge. They oversee order. Some of the lords truly wish to govern well, though others, like Lord Pashka, don't."

He paused and gave a slight shrug. Kathka did not dare prompt him to continue, afraid the boy would become aware of his words. They did not fit into his script.

"Lord Pashka only cares about riches," Mell added, voice weak, barely above a whisper. "He is a despot."

"Despot?" Kathka chuckled, though it pained him. Mell's shoulders hunched against his neck, and he checked himself back into silence. "That's a large word for a little boy. Did Pashka teach you that?"

"No."

"Who did?"

"My father."

Kathka clipped the trail of questions. He was not interested in the boy's parents. Mell was adaptable, knowledgeable, and had survived this long in the hostile palace. Mell did not need his past. He needed a future. Kathka would give it to him. He would save Mell from what oppressed him, Pashka. Then the boy would be the cultural guide to this new world that Kathka desperately needed. Eventually, the boy would be compensated.

Once Kathka had saved seven lives.

"I'm going to help you escape."

Either shock or fear widened his eyes and drew his gaze up to Kathka's. Shock or fear, perhaps both, it was difficult to discern. The two were so closely related.

"Well?" Kathka pressed.

Mell looked away. The fear had won.

"I won't be his prisoner," Kathka said. "I will free myself, and I'm taking you with me."

After the declaration, Kathka lay back on the bed and let his eyes sink closed. Perhaps the electricity still jumped in his veins, he felt on fire. Save the first life, then conquer the land. He had done it once, he could do it again. Then kill the Wise Man.

"You can't free me," Mell said into the darkness. "I'm not a prisoner like you."

"Does it matter?" Kathka opened his eyes and tilted his head to look at the boy. "I can just as easily take you from his service."

"He won't let you escape."

"He can try." Kathka flashed a sardonic grin, all teeth and spite. Mell shrunk back from the sight. "Perhaps I'll even train you, you can help overthrow him. You should braid your hair, all warriors do."

Mell tugged at the end of a curl, then shook his head. "I'm not allowed to."

"Why?"

"Only Lord Pashka can."

Kathka smirked. "As if he's seen battle."

Mell bit his lip and averted his eyes. "Neither have I."

"But you are strong," Kathka countered. Mell clasped his

hands together and did not look up. The words did not reach him. "Who are you to him?"

"I am his servant, in exchange for lodging and food." He was quick to respond to questions with facts. The unease arose when the conversation veered toward the personal.

"Why would you accept that?"

"I didn't."

"Then who did?"

His gaze lowered to his toes, and he clutched his fingers tighter. "My father."

They had circled back to that man. It frustrated Kathka. That was the past, the present was saving Mell.

"Forget the man," Kathka grumbled with a dismissive wave. "If he would sell you out it's better you aren't tied to him."

"You're wrong."

The snap of Mell's voice startled Kathka.

"He brought me here because he cares for me," Mell continued, though the words were not careful, though they were unpracticed, though they revealed his own heart. "I will have a life here that he could never have provided for me."

The moment of shock stretched until Kathka chuckled. The boy had chastened him, and it stoked both hope and anger. Hope that the boy still fought. Anger that he had dared talk down to him.

"He gave you servitude," Kathka snapped back. "That's not much of a father."

"It was not a perfect choice—" Mell began but was interrupted by a sharp bark of laughter.

"A weak choice!"

"It was not a perfect choice," Mell repeated firmly. "But

he loved me, and I trust him."

"You're naive," Kathka snarled. "But it doesn't matter. I'll free you from his choice."

His words were firm and final. He did not need to be chided by a child who had not yet learned that no one could be trusted.

Chapter 9

"Finally, my entertainment." Pashka straightened at the desk and flipped back his loose braid. Sheets of paper littered the wood. Though he smiled now, Kathka could still see the knit in his brow that had begun to prematurely wrinkle his face. "How was your punishment?"

Kathka stood in the center of the study with the guards stationed behind him and Mell at the door. The pain gnawed at his stiff muscles. He gritted his teeth and refused to let Pashka find twisted satisfaction in his aching body.

"Wonderful."

Pashka pressed his hands on top of the papers and leaned across the desk. "Only the powerful can afford the price of sarcasm."

"I'm willing to pay."

"I should have you punished for that," he sighed and moved from the desk to collapse onto a sedan piled with pillows. Pashka possessed a great many pillows. "But, there are more pressing matters to address. I have a story for you."

With a single snap a female servant brought him a decanter of wine. He did not touch the accompanying goblet but drank straight from the container.

"I was a servant once, in a small village under the governance of Lord Naithal. Not that it matters, you wouldn't know where that was anyway. It was my mother who gave me to the lord as a servant." He shrugged and took another sip of the wine. "She had no money to provide for me, I hold no grudge. After all, how could I when servitude has led to this!"

He swept his arm up to the giant crystal chandelier, over to the rows of books, then toward the arched doorway leading to a balcony overlooking an inner garden.

"I was astute in business, which made me a valuable servant. I eventually served under Lord Naithal himself. He promised to make me his heir if I killed his lazy son. So I did, and I inherited all of his governance. Of course, that's my vacation home now."

He sipped the wine. Kathka considered each piece of information Pashka had given him, uncertain how the lord expected him to respond. The pause extended. Pashka settled the decanter in his lap and turned his eyes upon Kathka. A smirk curved the edges of his lips.

"That was all a lie you know." He propped his elbow on the armrest and cupped his jaw against his palm. The gemstones inlaid in his rings glinted in the electric light. "That's the kind of story you need to create for me. You're the one who is supposed to be entertaining me after all."

Kathka frowned. He did not know whether to trust Pashka's words. The story could be a lie, or it could be the truth. Pashka's twisted smile revealed no more clues about the veracity of his tale.

"You will have to come up with one soon," the lord continued. "They will be here and their favor is a positive advantage. I won't have you be the cause of their retribution."

"You're afraid of them," Kathka challenged. He did not believe it to be true, and Pashka's smirk confirmed his suspicion. The declaration was bait, to lure the lord into more talk of the mysterious group.

"Not fear, respect." Pashka took one last sip from the decanter then set it upon the tray and waved the servant away. Another came, a smoldering pipe in her hand. He took it and dragged in a slow inhalation. "I don't believe their rhetoric, but their cult allows the lords governance, and I desire to expand mine, so I must appease them."

With each word the purple smoke escaped from his mouth and twined in the air.

"The best way to obtain their favor—" He released the pipe from his lips and jabbed it at Kathka. "Is through you, the cursed. They are obsessed. I don't see why."

After a few languid draws of his pipe, Pashka asked, "How were you cursed?"

"Do you care?" Kathka asked and was answered with a

shrug. "Then what does it matter?"

"You're supposed to entertain me!" Pashka laughed as the toxic fumes swirled. Kathka's stomach rolled as the fumes layered around him and clouded his vision. "I've never heard of a cursed Islander. Was the curse inherited? But to think that the gods would curse one of you. Was it the Wise One then? But that doesn't make sense, the Bu Chak say he lives in the desert, not on your Islands. Did you see him?"

Fragments of ornate lies came to him in a dazzling composition that would satiate the man. With the fragments of information he had gleaned, Kathka believed he could produce a tale at least as plausible as Pashka's.

If his had been a lie.

Lies were easier than the truth, but harder to keep in line. The more he considered his lies the more glaring the holes in his knowledge. It was exhausting work. Pashka would believe he was lying either way. So he told the truth.

"I saw him."

"What's he like?"

"Old."

"Not very powerful then," Pashka chuckled. "A god who lets himself be old."

"The gods are old," Kathka rebutted.

"So they say."

"They say?" Kathka repeated. "You don't believe in the gods?"

"Why would it matter?" Pashka replied. "They abandoned us. But whatever the past, we're here now. That's all I care about. Do you believe in them?"

It could have been a question Pashka wanted an answer

to, Kathka did not know. But the lord did not press, his attention diverted as the desk began to rattle. A sheaf of paper slipped over the edge and floated gently to the ground.

The earth moved beneath their feet.

A guard grabbed Kathka's arm. As the man fought for balance, he shoved Kathka hard against the desk. Pashka's hands dropped to grip the sedan. The pipe slipped from his lips and broke upon the floor, scattering the half-burned contents. Embers died upon the cool stone.

Pashka's eyes were wide and wild. The earth was a great beast and Pashka a boy desperately attempting to slay the furious thing.

"Return the prisoner!" he ordered. "Make sure none escape!"

The guard attempted to obey his master, but the ground still shook. With unsteady steps, he hauled Kathka from the desk and heaved him to the door where Mell crouched.

They were all afraid.

Kathka did not resist as the guard shoved him through the trembling palace. Twice they stumbled against the walls before finally the shaking eased. The guard doubled his pace then, nearly pushing Kathka into a jog as he hauled him to the prison. Kathka glanced backward periodically to assure himself that the boy was still there, that the ground hadn't opened to swallow him.

The boy was always there.

They reached the Green Quarter and the guard rushed to open the door, to chain Kathka to the bed, to flee the room. He scowled at the guard's back as the door closed.

"What's wrong with him?"

The question snapped in the tense still, and Mell recoiled

at the sound. Or the question. He sat in the corner with his legs pressed against his chest and his arms wrapped around his knees, curled around himself as if that would provide protection.

"One tremor means more," he said, "and worse."

"Are there often earthquakes?"

"Always."

Kathka chuckled. It was not a comforting sound. It was not meant to be.

"Horrid place to live then."

"It wasn't always like this."

Kathka had experienced earthquakes, but not many. He wondered if that had been before, or if that was from ancient times. He did not know how much time had passed since his death.

He felt old.

But his hands looked so young.

"Have you spent time in the desert?" Kathka asked. Over his kneecaps, Mell looked at him. His stare incredibly direct for the timid boy. "Were you learning a trade before Pashka?"

"Why do you do this?"

"What?"

"Why?" Mell repeated. They both knew what he referred to. No one asked a servant questions, they did not matter. That much at least had not changed since Kathka's day.

Kathka had no explanation that would make sense. He did not have an explanation even for himself. He did not know how to save a soul; he did not understand the rules of the game he played. He hoped freeing Mell from Pashka would count as saving him, but he could not be sure.

So he shrugged.

The room swayed. The electric light above swung and sent warped shadows stretching across the room before it flickered out. Mell craned his neck upward as if he expected the ceiling to cave in upon them. The tremble returned the boy into his protective shell.

When the room had steadied, Kathka crawled onto the bed and sat in the muted light cross-legged. The world was oddly suspended, still and silent except for the shouts echoing down the corridor. Faint, but discernible. In the untouched Green Quarter, the prisoner and the servant were displaced from the harsh reality of upheaval.

Another tremble. When the tremors eased, then ceased, Kathka asked, "Do you play Crowns?"

Mell's brow furrowed, he gave no response.

"Do you?" Kathka pressed.

Curls bounced around his face as he nodded.

"Let's play."

Chapter 10

The wooden tiles scattered, a clinking melody of upset. The guard shoved Kathka face down upon them. His cheek pulsed, ears rang, and the voices warped. There were shouts, orders, and Mell scrambled away from the overturned table.

The tile game had been a horrid one anyway. Too complicated. Crowns was simple, transported only in the mind. Acrius had played it with him on many long night watches. But Mell preferred the tiles, and when dawn came they switched to that one.

Now they littered the floor.

The guard wrenched Kathka's arms behind his back and clamped manacles on his wrists. He hauled Kathka to his feet and pushed him toward the door. The anger was displaced, the prisoner an easy conduit for the unease the earthquake had roused in the palace. In the Green Quarter, the tiles had kept the two sane. Outside of it, the rest of Pashka's household anxiously waited for the next shiver in the ground that would bring the palace down upon them.

The guards forced him out of the retreat, Mell trailing after them.

In the hall, damage littered the palace. Cracks spread like spiderwebs up the columns and crevices splintered across the floor. Closer inspection revealed signs of past repair, attempts to cover the damage that had already been deeply felt. It had been a futile attempt. The new quake broke everything open.

Kathka noted every bit of damage he could find as the guards led him down the hall. Such damage meant greater chances of a new and unprotected breach in the stronghold. Their path diverged from the halls he had walked before. His eyes swept over the doors, windows, and stairs, but the guard's steps were hurried, and before he could account for each new escape route, they led him into a golden room.

The elegant room glittered in the sunlight. It was more magnificent than the white room of the Square, everything gilded gold. On a raised platform, upon a golden sedan with golden pillows and a golden blanket sat the lord. Fingers still adorned with all his gems, golden clothing still as crisply ordered, hair once again in a new style with two large braids cresting his head.

He grinned.

Mell resumed his demure stance at the doorway as the gray-robed Malici instructed the guard to lead the prisoner to the center of the room. He positioned Kathka beside the other cursed prisoner, the one he had punched two days prior.

The guard removed the cuffs, and as had become custom, stepped back to the pillars to stand at the ready in case of a threat.

Kathka was uncertain who to threaten.

At Pashka's side stood his antithesis. Dressed completely in gray, the man wore no ornamentation and unlike Pashka's elaborate hairstyles, his hair was drawn in a single simple braid. He was a miserable-looking man, lips curved into a scowl and heavy brow drawn low over eyes smoldering with disgust directed fully upon Kathka.

"Kath, meet Rain." Pashka rose from his reclined position. His head came to the man's shoulder. "Sent from the Bu Chak."

The group enamored by the curse. Pashka had promised they would come. Mell had warned of them.

"He is cursed?" Rain asked. His gaze remained intently on Kathka. It was a bad place to be, in his sight.

Pashka tilted his head and Malici shifted at Kathka's side. His hands brushed against Kathka's silk tunic. Before his shirt could be torn from his body, Kathka wrenched it upward to reveal for himself the black lines crisscrossing his chest. Malici stepped back to allow an unobstructed view of the cursed lines.

With measured pace, Rain descended from the dais.

"Careful," Pashka said, "he's quite wild." The usual mirth lacked confidence. Even the lord was wary. Kathka lowered the shirt as the man drew closer.

Rain dwarfed Kathka's slight frame.

"He doesn't seem like Islander nobility," Rain commented.

"The desert changes people," Pashka offered lazily. It was a poor excuse, but no one could refute it, not when the dragon brooch protruded from Rain's clenched fist. Pashka snapped and Malici grabbed Kathka's chin and forced his face upward to meet the amber eyes boring into him. Malici's fingers tightened as if by sheer force he could extract information from the prisoner.

Rain's eyes twitched narrow and he lifted a hand, palm open, and said, "No need."

Another snap and Malici released his hold. Kathka massaged his jawline, brushing his fingers over the indents of nails. Rain lowered his hand back to his side.

"Who are you?" he asked.

"Islander nobility." Kathka smirked. The man in gray's frown was harsh and did not waver before Kathka's dark jest.

"Why are you cursed?"

"Because I tried to kill the Wise Man."

"Lies," Rain hissed. "But I see you will not give the truth. That is irrelevant, I don't need it. You will be of use to the Bu Chak."

"Not if I can help it."

"You are haughty as a nobleman." Rain shook his head. The previous irritation had already left his voice. Now his words were hardened, possessed with a resolute assurance. "But your sacrifice is assured."

With the threatening words, he returned to the raised

platform.

"There is a third?" Rain asked. He stood at the base of the platform a few feet in front of Kathka. Still much too close. Behind Kathka stood guards with swords strapped to their sides. Behind them stood Mell.

"There is," Pashka confirmed. Kathka swept his eyes to the cursed prisoner who stood mutely at his side, then to the platform, then back to Malici at his right. He would soon be handed over to the Bu Chak. It was the only conclusion of events he could foresee. They would take custody and he would be taken far from his first life and closer to his second death.

He could not allow that.

"I have another cursed," Pashka said to Rain, voice curling in a tantalizing tale he would use to gently negotiate a higher reward. "Even more desirable than the Isla—"

Kathka dropped into a low crouch and swept out Malici's legs. The man thudded to the floor. There should have been a response, but in the moment after Kathka's first move, the room began to shake.

The tremor swept up Kathka's legs and shook him to his knees. On the dais, Pashka gripped the sedan for balance and shouted orders no one heeded. Rain pushed off the pillar he had been thrown against, ignoring the crack forming beneath his feet. His eyes were set upon the Islander.

Kathka ran.

He jumped over a kneeling guard and ran straight to Mell. He grabbed the boy's arm and hauled him from against the wall.

"We're leaving." He shoved Mell ahead of him. Mell stumbled, nearly fell, and the heaving earth slammed them both into the door.

"Capture him!" Pashka's cry tore through the fear. Kathka pushed Mell aside and hauled the door open. A guard stood in their path. Kathka landed a punch to his nose and followed it with an elbow upward to the temple. The guard crumbled. Kathka shoved Mell around the fallen man and out of the golden room.

A hand grabbed Kathka's wrist as he followed Mell. He twisted with fist raised to his new opponent.

He faced a thin slip of a woman with a shaved head, hands still cuffed together, and fingers clutched against his skin. Her eyes were darkness, and she saw through him. To his soul. She riveted him to the spot and simply looked at him. Her grip softened.

"Don't leave me."

There was movement at the edge of his vision. Rain. Pashka and Mell were shouting. One desperate, one afraid.

Kathka tore away from the woman.

He grabbed Mell's forearm and yanked him forward. Rain was close. The tremors lessened and eased to a finish.

"Wait!" Mell jerked from his grip and pointed to the left. "This way!"

Kathka veered into the side corridor. The round bulbs above flickered and died. The palace shivered dust down upon them.

"Take this hall!"

Kathka did not question the boy's directions and obediently took the hall he indicated. Mell knew the layout of the compound, the ways to escape. The earth lunged, the two crashed upon it. Kathka scrambled to rise and dragged Mell up with him.

"Halt!" Rain stood at the end of the hall and lifted something that glinted in the dim light of the arched windows. "Do not move. I do not wish to fight you."

Mell tugged at Kathka's sleeve. "Run straight. That lattice is wood, we could make it."

Guards arrived, filing in behind Rain. Pashka turned the corner and shoved through his men to stand beside Rain.

"Mell!"

At the sound of the name in Pashka's mouth, Kathka grabbed the boy and hefted him onto his back and ran. Ran straight, as Mell had instructed.

"Shoot!" Pashka ordered.

A great sound erupted in the hall. As loud as thunder and so close Kathka's breath caught in his lungs. Mell grunted, a small release of breath. The window was ahead. Mell claimed they could make it, Kathka was not so sure. There was another roll of thunder behind them. He took the chance.

The wooden lattice snapped and clattered down upon the sandstone. Kathka hit hard and lost his grip on Mell. He rolled until he managed to claw at the stone and stop. Kathka forced his lungs to fill, to deflate, to fill again. With a groan he sat, head spinning, but too aware of the figure that appeared in the broken window. He spurred his body to move, to grab Mell, to run.

Into the jungle he ran, smacking aside branches and vines, and desperately hoping he was headed toward the wall of Pashka's compound. Breaths became difficult. His legs trembled, he tripped, and ducked behind a thick tree trunk. With Mell's body gathered close against his own, Kathka listened for the sound of approaching footsteps. He only heard distant shouts. Distant cries. His chest heaved with exertion. He felt far from that warrior of old, that legendary Blood King.

"I think—" He sucked in another gulp of air. "We're safe. We'll find a way out."

Mell did not reply. It was then Kathka saw the red.

So much red.

Blood stained Mell's back. Kathka pried back the cloth and found a hole in his skin. He pressed his palm against the wound, but the bleeding did not stop. There had been no visible weapon, no visible blow, but whatever the thunder had done punctured Mell's very lifeline. Bleeding him to his soul. Mell was dying and Kathka had no idea how to stop it.

"Kath ..." Mell's voice was a whisper in the dry air. Kathka ignored him. He tore Mell's shirt and bundled the cloth against the wound, trying to fill the hole. "Stop."

"If I can stop it—"

"Stop."

"Then we can find someone—"

"Kath, stop."

"I have to save you!" The words were louder than he had intended. More desperate. There was a constriction in the back of his throat, but he refused to acknowledge it. Instead, he planned.

He would take the boy with him. To the desert. Far away, to a place where Pashka would never find him. To a school of some sort, if there was anything like that anymore.

But in the jungle, Mell died.

He deserved a proper burial, somewhere calm with a grave marker. Something like what the Wise One had done with his own body. At the time he had thought it a cruel act of spite to force his soul to watch his own burial. Now he understood it as a mercy.

His lungs burned, legs shook, arms ached, but he gathered sticks. He could not dig a proper grave, not with his bare hands, but he could at least construct something around the body. Though it was unnecessary, though it was a waste of time.

Kath tried to wipe the sticky blood against his pants, but the crimson clung to his skin.

Chapter 11

The desert accepted him back into its fold. It was where he belonged, where both his birth and final resting place could be found. Perhaps this life would be no different.

He had escaped through a crack in the white stone wall and slipped into the anonymity of fear. It had been easy to steal. In the bustle of people fleeing the buildings, Kathka let the grip of panic disguise him. He snatched a coat, bread, and a metal flask of water.

Then he left.

The admonishing gaze of the Square reminded him that

he was not a free man. Even his body was not his to keep. With the death of the boy, he may have failed already.

He ignored it.

He did not stop until he reached a craggy outcropping of red rock that tore from the desert floor. It would be a temporary hiding place. Neither Pashka nor Rain were men willing to let their quarry so easily escape.

"I'm nobody's prisoner," Kathka growled to hear the words aloud as he sank to the sandy ground. Far from the city, it was calm. Devoid of the contraptions that reminded him he was out of time.

The sun sank.

In a few hours it would be dark, and then Kathka's trek would begin. He needed sleep. The adrenaline that had coursed hot in his veins emptied and washed away his energy. But sleep did not come. He was too vulnerable, and when his eyelids did slip closed all he saw was blood pooling in the dirt.

There was a hot pressure in the back of his throat.

He bit his lip hard and buried the pain beneath his anger.

The bread was stale, but it filled his stomach and helped him pass the time. The sun was slow. He took a swig from the flask, it tasted metallic.

Behind him there was a noise, the ricochet of falling rock. He lowered the flask and listened. Before him the barren desert stretched to infinity. Behind the city was a dark stain on the landscape.

Again, there was a noise. Closer. Someone was near.

He slid forward in the sand and whirled about in a low crouch to face the coming fight. Water sloshed from the flask and disappeared in the loose earth, but he could not focus on the loss. Someone was there.

Perched upon the brittle peak of the rock like some strange bird was a woman, thin lips perked in a taunting smile.

"If it isn't my near savior."

He stared at the prisoner. The one he had left behind. Then her smile widened to display her crooked teeth and he refused to tolerate her derision.

"How did you find me?" Kathka demanded as he stood.

"The boy's dead."

"How did you find me?" he repeated.

She jumped and fell heavily on the sand on her hands and feet.

"That is sad," she continued her one-sided dialogue. She stood and patted her hands free of the gritty granules. Her smile had diminished to a mere perk of her lips. She matched his height and when her eyes lifted they met his with a snap.

She was all bones and sharp personality wrapped beneath tawny brown skin. But it was her eyes that brought the hate to edge his words. They were a void. An endless depth. She saw too much.

"Answer me," he growled.

"He saved me," she answered. "He's much nicer."

"Who?" His teeth gritted harshly against each other.

Her wide smile returned, and he nearly threw the water bottle straight against her teeth.

"Red."

"Who?"

"The other cursed one," she explained. The crazy prisoner, the one who claimed he would save Kathka. "He has an … agenda."

At her pause Kathka groaned. She knew as little as he.

"How did you find me?" In her circular responses, he returned to his original query. He needed to know. If she had found him the others would be close.

"I followed you."

"How?" He gripped the bottle hard.

"I'm cursed," she said, which was no explanation. She touched her fingers against the protruding marks along her exposed collar bone. "We're both cursed."

"Great." He collapsed back against the rock and focused on the desert. Though its solace did not calm him. She remained a haunting specter in the corner of his vision, a piece of the city dislodged in the upheaval. He clenched his hand into a fist until he felt the release of grounding pain.

"Pashka and Rain will be here soon," she said.

"I know." He spoke curtly. He wanted her to leave.

"You're not a very nice person."

"Did you think I would be?" he scoffed.

"After you left me behind?" She sat and mirrored his position, with legs splayed into the sand. Her feet were bare, gauzy blue dress loose over twiggy legs. "No."

Curses danced in his mind. He should have used them all, instead he took another sip of his precious water. He needed to conserve his energy.

"How did you die?"

He choked, coughed, and doubled over as he dragged in a burning breath and coughed again. She watched as the fit raked his lungs. When he could inhale enough oxygen, he glared at her.

"I'm cursed," she repeated as if it explained any more

than it had the first time she had said it. She reached out, fingertips searching for the marks on his chest. "Like you."

He knocked aside her arm.

"Go away."

"No." She crossed her arms over her chest, smile still curling her lips. "You have a strong soul."

Nothing she said made sense and there was no arguing with insane people.

"So, how did you die?"

"I'm not answering that."

"I just thought ..." She shrugged. Her shoulder brushed against his. He shifted further from her. "It'd be nice to talk. As we waited."

"Waited?"

"For Pashka and Rain."

"We're not waiting for them."

"Then why are we sitting here?"

Kathka breathed evenly through his nose and capped the flask. He focused on the workings of his jaw as he clenched and unclenched his teeth. She watched him. Waited for him. He pointed to the horizon.

"The sun needs to set. It's best to travel the desert by night."

"The desert?" Her voice pitched upward on the last syllable. "Isn't that dangerous?"

"For you, yes."

"Not for you?"

"I'm a Wayfinder."

"A Wayfinder?" She whistled one long low note. He ground his teeth. "You must have died a long time ago."

"I will silence you."

"What about water? Food?" She continued and ignored the threat. "A desert can be very barren."

"I know."

"And won't we be out in the open? You can see for miles."

"If you're so concerned, you can take your chances back there." He thrust his thumb backward. She glanced at the rock behind them, and her lips contorted in a funny twisted line.

"They are there," she whispered. Her gaze was on him again. He wished she would not look at him. Her eyes were too perceptive. "Who killed him?"

"Rain," he said. Though he had not seen it, he was sure the thunderous noise and fatal blow had come from the contraption he had held.

Her gaze softened though he was not sure who for. Either way, it was a weakness she expressed. Better to bury the pain with the rage.

"He did something," Kathka continued, though he did not intend to. The deepness of her eyes enticed the words from his mouth. He knew it was irrational, so he told himself that he only searched for more information to avoid the same fate. Still, it was easier to turn away from her gaze. "There was a noise, but no blow. No blow, but still a wound and blood."

"He was shot," she supplied for his lack of terms.

"There was no arrow," he countered. He regretted it when she chuckled.

"Not with a bow, with a gun and a bullet. Do you know what a gun is?"

"I do," he defended, though he did not.

"I'm sure you do." She smirked at him. She knew it was a lie. His fingers curled around the metal bottle. "So, as we wait—"

"We?"

"The city is no safer than the desert."

"Listen." He strained to keep his voice even. He was losing the battle with patience. "If you insist on following me, you listen and obey. No questions."

"That doesn't sound fair."

"Doesn't matter. I'm deciding to keep you alive," Kathka snapped. "You obey. And no more talking, I need to think."

"I don't like silence."

"Not my concern."

She pressed her legs up against her chest and curled into a ball around herself. Like Mell had done.

He felt it then. It had not been immediate like it had been with Mell. But the Wise Man had said at the right time, and this must have been the right time because it was unmistakable. The constriction, the pull. The reorientation of his world around the singular existence.

Kathka groaned. He propped his head against the rock and trained his eyes upward. In the frustration mixed relief. There may still be a chance, another life to save.

Night gradually stained the sky dark. Soon the stars would reveal their light, and then he would chart, he would move, he would escape.

"My name is Nana," she supplied after he had not bothered to ask. "What's yours?"

"Kath," he conceded in an attempt to silence further questions.

"Kath," she repeated. A star appeared, a fleck of light

high overhead. "Nice to meet you."

More stars joined the first. Together Kathka and his second life watched them appear.

Chapter 12

They walked barefoot on the cold sand. Kathka held the palace slippers crumbled in his fist. They invited too much sand but discarding them would leave a trail. The rough granules rubbed the soft flesh of his soles raw. Beside him the woman trotted lightly, dress whipping in the wind and tangling between her legs.

She smiled.

He frowned.

The stars pinned above directed toward places Kathka was not certain still existed. There was no time to plan all scenarios, so they followed the guidance of the stars in hope that it still led true.

"Red is strong." Nana persisted to speak despite a few threats. She did not seem to understand silence. He had given up at some point, he could not remember when. "I think he was trained, the guards were nothing."

There was a pause. She always gave them to him, he never took them.

"And his tattoos were fake."

He consulted the stars and asked why he had been cursed to this. They told him nothing, so he doubled his pace. She kept by his side.

"Well, the tattoos were real, but …" She made vague gestures over her chest above the tattoo hidden by the coat hanging from her frame. She had complained she was cold until he had grown tired of her voice and had given her the stolen garment. "They were wrong."

"Hmm," he offered when she would not stop watching him, expecting something.

"Why would he fake a curse?"

Kathka shrugged. He did not care, it mattered little. Red, or Pashka, or any of the others. Mell mattered, Nana mattered, and the five others as well. But a sliver of doubt wedged into his certainty.

She had mattered, but she had been hidden. The connection that had been so instantaneous with Mell had not been with Nana. At the right time, the Wise Man's voice echoed in his mind. Kathka hated the wording.

"Aren't you even a little curious?" She was so close. "At all?"

"Not one bit," Kathka said, though his confidence had faltered.

She fell away from his side, but he could feel her gaze. Penetrating past the fake skin his soul wore. She could see everything.

A great scar cut across the desert. It appeared suddenly before him, and he halted at the edge. Sand displaced from his steps spilled into the crevasse where a breeze caught it up and transformed it into a tool to sculpt rock into twisted formations.

"Sarian," Nana said as she returned to his side. She saw it, the narrowing of his eyes, the furrow in his brow. "Did you know it by another name?"

"Knife Canyon." Her lips quirked into a smile, and he busied himself with surveying the great chasm. The system had been given a simple name during his time. Everything seemed to have become more complicated as time passed, from tiled games to names.

The cold desert night slipped around his still body. Without movement, his feet began to ache with the cold. He walked along the edge of the gorge to stop himself from shivering.

As he walked, he scanned the rocks for access down. The night obscured the structures and hid the valley bottom from view. More granules of sand slipped down and were swept into the abyss.

"They'll come here, it's the most obvious escape."

"It provides water and shelter." Kathka eyed an outcropping that sloped down into the gorge. It was close enough to reach. "We'll lose them."

"You're so confident."

"Be silent and watch."

He tightened the strap of the bottle over one shoulder

and tucked the slippers in the band of his pants, then jumped. The jagged rock bit against his palms as he caught himself. After he stabilized his footing, he released his hold and stood on the formation. He brushed his stinging hands against his already bloodstained pants.

Nana clapped. "Very nice."

"Jump," he ordered.

She did. She landed, scrambled against the rock, and rebounded at his side, smile maintained through it all. "Now what?"

Her cheer infuriated him. Kathka pushed past her to stand at the edge of the formation. The floor of the canyon was still far below, past arches, tunnels, and channels of rock.

"There." Kathka pointed to a flat rock face below that sloped upward to a black opening. "That cave, we'll rest there. We'll get to the bottom tomorrow."

Kathka dropped down to the surface below and ran up the slope of the rock to catch the lip of the cave and haul himself into the bowled floor. He did not bother to see if Nana followed. As his eyes adjusted to darkness without stars, he slid his hands across the rock and hoped no animal had made the space its home. The cave would be large enough for two, and if they kept to the curved right side, they would be protected against piercing light or prying eyes. But it was small enough that their combined body heat would fill the space and stave off the desert chill until the sun rose.

"This is pleasant." Nana slipped into place beside him. He could barely make out the outline of her form. Her exploring fingers bumped against his knees before she veered away and ventured further back than he had bothered to search. He let her adventure and finished the last of the water before she returned. It did little to sate his thirst.

He laid down upon the uneven ground. The new body was weak, pathetic, and needed rest. He could only run from the consuming blackness for so long.

A curious hand found his shoulder and rested there.

"What are you planning?"

He heaved a sigh that filled the space with frustration. He had a plan, one when Mell was alive and he was sure what the boy needed to be saved from. But now Mell was dead, and a new life sat at his side, and he had no plan because he once again did not know what to save her from.

Nana's hand remained on his shoulder. A small connection. One he did not appreciate.

"No idea."

He rolled to put his back to her. Her touch fell away. Connection severed. He listened as she settled in the cave.

"This is fun," she whispered. "I've never spent much time outside a city."

She gave him the pause again. He did not reply.

"What was it like, being a Wayfinder? Was it fun? It sounds fun, living in the desert, always an adventure!"

"Not nearly."

Her silence was heavy with a multitude of churning questions, and he regretted giving her even a little response to encourage any new inquiries.

"Is that how you died?" She finally chose her most pressing interest. "When they were destroyed?"

"Be quiet and go to sleep."

"I like history, it's important to remember."

"Be quiet"

"I'll tell you a story if you tell me how you died."

"Why are you so curious how I died?" Exasperation broke his will. He was exhausted of her questions, of the frigid desert night, of the rough surface his tired body laid upon.

"I want to know. How did you die? Why were you cursed? You're the only other cursed I've met."

"How about you then, you tell me how you died."

"Died?" There was laughter in her voice. "I didn't die."

He clenched his jaw and attempted to soothe the mounting exasperation with the pain. "Then how did he curse you?"

"He?" she whispered. "Did he curse you? He didn't curse me. You're the exception, you're the one cursed by him."

"Then who cursed you?" He sat, head inches from the roof of their cave. They were close. She sat with knees pulled against her chest, arms wrapped about her legs.

"Well, he did. But not just him, all the gods did. I'm Scala's descendant, I've inherited his curse."

"Scala?" Kathka scoffed. "The rebel? He's your ancestor?"

"Yes," she said with complete assurance.

Pashka had asked Kathka if he believed in the gods. In his previous life, he had never considered the gods or the myths of Scala. The gods were insignificant, when he was in the lowest ranks of the Wayfinders and when he was a king. Insignificant, until he was killed by one. But he had never considered if Scala had ever truly lived. He was simply part of an unimportant creation myth.

The first tendrils of yellow sun tinged the dark with muted light. In the cave, Kath could just discern the frown pulling Nana's lips down.

"Did you see him?" she asked. She did not need to clarify who. He knew. The Wise One. The only god still left.

"Does it matter?"

"If you won't tell me how you died, will you tell me about him?" she pleaded.

"No."

The single word was harsh and cutting. He expected more words from her, but she was silent. He settled back on the ground with his back to her and tried to ignore the sensation of her so close beside him.

She felt far away.

Silent and far away.

Chapter 13

———

Kathka awoke when the sun still reigned. He rolled to his back and threw an arm across his eyes to block the probing rays of light. The sun was a warm reminder that he still lived. His lips cracked in the heat, his throat scraped like sandpaper when he swallowed, and a pulsing pain settled behind his eyes, but he was alive.

Sleep pulled his eyelids down and lured him back into the wasteland of slumber. He tilted his head to the side and found his unwanted companion before he succumbed to the weakness of his body.

Nana sat with her forehead resting against her kneecaps.

When he woke again, the sun was sinking and her position had not changed. Kathka sat, arm tingling with loss of blood. At his movements, she lifted her head. The waning sunlight highlighted the edges of her face golden brown. A smile still graced her lips. He had entertained the thought that after a night in the desert her perpetual cheer would have faded. He had been wrong.

"Morning!" she greeted. "Or night, I suppose."

"Did you sleep?"

Her smile faltered. "Sometimes it's hard."

He flexed his numb fingers and ignored the calculations his mind automatically ran through. The Wayfinders did not accept liabilities, he had to learn how to avoid being one.

He did not need the assessment to know she was his biggest weakness.

"You better keep up." He crawled to the entrance and swung his legs over the edge. He did not care if she followed, he would just as willingly leave her, his burden.

But he needed to save her.

In the failing light, he examined the landscape and found nothing but rock and sand. He lowered himself down onto the sloping formation and stretched his sore muscles.

"So, where exactly are we going?" Nana hopped down beside him.

"If there's still a city at the western end of this," Kathka swung to the west and swept his gaze along the flow of the valley, "then there."

"There's still a city."

"Then there."

Kathka took the lead. It made him feel more in control. He eased down the rock, conscious of the steep drop on either side. Though the night encroached, there was enough light to illuminate the winding pathway that trailed along the bottom of the canyon. It looked dangerously far away. The night had a way of making things more ominous than they were in the daylight.

At the precipice of the rock, he jumped to the ledge a few feet below, then to another ridge further down. In a slow snaking path, Kathka worked his way down until his feet landed on the sandy bottom.

Nana perched on the first ledge, watching him.

"Come on." He stepped back to allow her space to follow. "Unless you want Pashka to find you."

"I'm more concerned about Rain."

The coat billowed around her as she followed his descent. She almost appeared to be flying. Weightless. But she was tethered to the ground like everyone and landed with a heaviness beside him. She bounced back up with a smile full upon her lips.

"Rain's an excellent tracker," she added to explain her previous comment.

"You've been tracked by him before?"

"Many times."

He swore. The word floated between them awkwardly. Her brow crinkled, as if she did not understand the word, but she did not ask for clarification. She did not say anything. That silence he could not stand so he continued down the sandy track toward the city that had withstood time.

"Why is he so obsessed with the cursed?" he asked. The silence had followed him, and he wanted to be rid of it.

"It's not him specifically, it's the Bu Chak."

"Why do they even care?" Kathka tired of hearing their

name.

"They take Scala seriously." It was a slight. He stopped and turned back to her. She remained where he had sworn.

"What does that mean?"

"Do you know of Scala's Revenge?" she asked.

His breath was shallow. He tried to inhale, but a dread clamped around his lungs and refused to let them fill. He bit the inside of his lip and focused on the pinch of pain.

Nana kept her even gaze upon him. Dark and deep. Haunting, searching. But she could not possibly know. She could not know that he knew of Scala's Revenge, that he had sought it, that he had failed. She could not know, and he would keep it that way.

"What does that have to do with anything?"

"So you do know?" she pressed. He tried to look away, but her steady gaze held him captive.

"Doesn't everyone?" He tried to sound nonchalant and added a jerky shrug. "It's just a myth. To be the rightful ruler, you have to avenge Scala, accomplish what he could not and kill the gods. Myths, that's all."

"No, that's everything." Nana stepped closer, and he could not move. The words tumbled from her mouth and he wished they did not hold truth. But they did. "Scala killed Caizin and tried to overthrow the gods. But they cursed him, then left our world. Many have tried to accomplish what Scala could not and kill the Wise One, but they have all failed. But the Bu Chak, they see things differently."

She stopped within arm's reach.

"They are seeking Scala's Revenge. They believe Scala was right, that the gods were evil and needed to be overthrown. But the Bu Chak, they think they know the key to why all the others have failed. They think that to destroy the Wise One, they first need to destroy all the cursed."

She pointed to her chest, though the coat hid the marks.

"Destroy the curse, destroy the Wise One, then our people will be freed. The Bu Chak will become the gods." Her finger swung to him, outstretched to touch him. Instead, she pointed. "And your people will not be protected by the gods any longer."

"The Islanders?"

Her hand dropped back to her side. There was a line between them, a sharp one drawn by her words.

"Yes."

"I'm not one of them," he said, and she knew. She knew he was a Wayfinder, but she shrugged, and her dismissiveness hurt.

"It doesn't matter to the Bu Chak. By appearances, one of the blessed is cursed. Not that it matters, they don't need to understand, they simply need to destroy all the cursed."

"So, they want to kill us both?"

"Exactly!" Her affirmation was exuberant, and the intensity of her words evaporated.

"If they want you so much, and Rain is such an excellent tracker, why hasn't he caught you yet?"

"I'm an excellent escape artist!" She laughed as if it were a joke. As if any of the situation was comical.

He could take no more of her smile. He tore himself from her eyes and continued walking to escape her pull.

"Maybe not in the desert, Wayfinder." She pouted and trotted back to his side. "But I know my way around a city."

"I'll take my chances in the desert."

"I don't think these paths are as secluded as you seem to

think."

He laughed then and let himself join her dissociated comedy. "You let me worry about keeping us alive."

She touched him, a light pressure against his forearm.

"Thank you."

He stepped away.

"Let's just widen our distance from the Square."

"Yes, let's!" she agreed. "Kanrin is not a pleasant city. I miss Lyria, we should go there."

He groaned as she launched into a commentary about the beauties of a city Kathka did not know. The further her discussion drifted from Scala, the more the tightness around his lungs loosened. Her words were inane, but they distracted. If he let himself, they would sweep him away and make him forget that they were not going to Lyria, the city of flowers.

High above them, the sky was a curled ribbon of black velvet set with diamonds. A faint glimmer of starlight reached the canyon floor, and in that light, they made slow progress to the main gorge and the path to the western city.

While Nana discussed the monkeys in Lyria, the information she had provided looped in Kathka's mind. Her words became a drone as he thought of Scala's Revenge.

Fulfill what Scala could not, it had always been a noble quest for those wanting to prove their power. Now the quest had been fashioned into a cult.

He was cursed to protect the very one they craved to kill.

Chapter 14

Blood filled his dreams.

He woke with a start and smacked his forehead against the low ceiling of the cave. He grumbled a string of profanities and lay back upon the ground.

The blood was gone. It had never been there, though he could smell the faint scent. It had never been there, he reminded himself firmly. It was just a memory. A memory dragged from the depths of his subconscious. Memories of his past life so utterly stained with blood.

The Blood King, Mell had said. He could hear the whisper of the boy's timid voice as he spoke the words. They had sounded foreign and strange, but perhaps now he understood them more. The title was warranted when he thought of Scala's Revenge. Zalna had been obsessed with the quest. He had not cared, not when there was so much of their own realm to conquer.

Kathka slid his hand over his forehead and squeezed his eyes shut. Hard. Acrius and Zalna, Scala's Revenge and the Wise One, Mell and the fatal blow. He took each memory and buried it deep, beneath the blood and the broken glass and the cracked bones. The tang of iron filled his mouth as his teeth bit too hard into his cheek.

His eyes snapped back open, and he sat with care to avoid the outcropping. Nana lay curled on the opposite side of the cave. Still asleep, and he was grateful she was and had not seen him struggle.

Kathka edged to the mouth of the cave and peered out. The sand was still hot after a day in the sun, though it would cool quickly as the moon rose. Still, it would remain warmer at the bottom of the canyon, warm enough that Kath could appreciate the sunset. The red hue of dusk cast the brown earth in a blush. It would look peaceful, if Kathka could forget they had so much ground to cover, and pursuers following behind.

They needed to move.

"Hey." Kathka nudged Nana's foot with his. She scrunched tighter around herself. "Time to go."

Nana uncurled and stretched as much as she could in the small space before she sat with a smile full upon her lips. He grit his teeth.

"Good night," she chirped. "How did you sleep?"

"Come on." He slipped out of the cave and onto the

ledge that ran along the edge of the cliff face. In fragmented protrusions, it swung down to the canyon floor.

"I slept well," Nana said, as if Kathka had returned the question. She followed behind him until she reached the sandy track then returned to his side. The coat brushed his arm. Always so close.

"At least you got sleep." He sighed.

"At least," she repeated. Her words held more cheer than his. "It is always a gift when it comes. Though, I never do dream. I wish I did."

She mentioned dreams and iron returned to his tongue. He reminded himself that he had bit his cheek. It was just his blood. That was all.

"Tell me about the city we're headed to." In the corner of his eye, he saw the tilt of her head toward him. Eternal smile wide. She mistakingly believed she had succeeded in crumbling his refusal to speak.

She had not. He had simply learned her. To veer the conversation away from dreams he had only to bring his own topic.

So, he let her think she had triumphed to bury the memories.

"Well," she began. "It's an old city, but I think you already know that."

"Yeah, I got that," he muttered.

"I've never actually been there," she continued, "but it's an important trade city between the provinces. Lots of supplies, lots of merchandise. I don't think it's the … cleanest of cities."

Kathka nodded along with her words, but he only partly listened to her commentary. Though it would be useful to learn about the city, his attention had to be trained on the chief of their concerns. Water.

As they walked, his eyes roved the hollows of the rock formations and searched. He knew there would be springs. There should have been one already, but the canyon seemed drier since he had last trekked through its snaking path.

A trickle of water dribbled from a crack in the wall. A spring muddied with sand and red rock, and though his mouth was dry and the bottle empty, he refrained from drinking. They would follow it until they found where it joined with other streams.

He would have to explain to Nana who would certainly ask. Should have already asked, but she was not at his side. Kathka turned and found her trudging along, chest heaving. She was silent at least, but she was falling behind.

"You're slow," he said and regretted it. Words invited more.

"I'm dehydrated."

"This isn't good enough for you, Scala's Daughter?"

"I should ask you, aren't you supposed to be an Island noble?" She smirked despite his reproachful scowl. "After you, Wayfinder."

The bite in her words quirked his lips. He followed the trickling water. Dusk had passed to night, but the moon was nearly full, and he was glad for it. It made the water sparkle.

Another muddied stream joined the first and doubled its size. The stream followed the flow of the canyon, splashed around fallen columns of earth, and spilled down a precipice and into another gorge of the canyon system.

"There." He picked his way over the craggy rocks and surveyed their new obstacles. The stream was narrower than he remembered. Everything drier. Less hospitable. "Just need to get down."

"Kath."

Fear rose in the edges of her voice. He turned back to her.

"Don't move."

The dagger against Nana's skin forced him to heed the command. Moonlight winked off the razor-sharp edge. The wielder was shaking. The hilt of the dagger was too large, the decorative pommel clearly visible even in the moonlight.

A dragon.

Chapter 15

"Who are you?"

"And you?" Kath retorted and earned Nana's glare.

"Don't toy with me!" The woman tried to sound forceful, but the blade quivered in her hand. Nana winced. The silver edge darkened. The woman did not notice.

"Kath," he supplied. "My name is Kath."

"I don't care about your name!" The woman inhaled an unsteady breath. Her fingers curled tighter around Nana's wrist. Her hold was awkward, loose, easy to break even with the threatening blade. As she gathered her thoughts, Kathka noted every pressure point Nana could hit to escape from the woman, the ones he could before she slit Nana's throat. If she was even capable of the act.

"Who sent you?" The woman began again with her reworded question. "The Ja Nrai? Jayla?"

"Neither," Kath answered because it was true. But it was not the response she wanted.

"You have to be from one! Did he send you?"

"No one sent me."

"Then how did you know I was here?" she demanded.

"I wasn't looking for you!"

"Liar!"

"Just let her go."

For the first time, the woman considered her captive and noticed the blood. The shaking worsened.

"Not until you answer me."

"I did!"

"You lied!" Her voice rose. "How did you find me? Where are the others?"

"Let Nana go!" he shouted back and took a step closer.

"Stay away!"

"You're not going to kill her." He took another step. He was so close he could reach out and touch Nana. "Let her go."

The knife dropped from Nana's throat and the woman shoved her forward. Nana stumbled, grabbed Kath for balance, and slipped behind his back. Her hands bunched in his shirt, and she peered at the woman over his shoulder. With both hands, the woman held the knife stretched before her.

"If you come a step closer, I will kill you."

"Doubtful," Kathka muttered. "Now it's my turn. Who are you?"

She was still shaking, and it revealed what she tried to hide. She was afraid, not crazed. Or at least, she had not been. She was clothed in an elegant purple dress, though its hem was now sullied by sand and the sleeves ripped by the rock she had hidden behind. Her thick dark hair was twisted into an intricate braid down her neck, though now large pieces of it curled around her face.

"Leave me."

"Who did you think I was?" Kathka continued posing his questions.

"She said you are an Islander, I thought that ..." The woman's voice wobbled and tumbled to a halt. The ferocity of her previous demands wavered as she questioned the words she had overheard.

He wondered just how much she had overheard.

"You are being followed?" he asked.

Dark shadows obscured her features and silenced any reaction. But she could not stop the shaking.

"We're like you." Nana propped her chin against Kath's shoulder. "We're being followed too."

"Leave me alone," she hissed, blade still raised. "I want nothing to do with you."

Kathka pushed Nana against the canyon wall and pointed to where the stream disappeared over the edge of the rock shelf.

"Follow the stream, you'll find clearer water," he said. The woman did not move. "But better water means more chance of being found, and you're out of your element."

The woman glanced at the water, then back to Kath.

"You'll die down here," he told her, with a dreadful measure of certainty.

"I'll survive." She kept the knife poised between herself and the two strangers as she edged closer to the rock lip. With her toes she felt for the rim. When she found it, she stood with her heel hovering over the edge. She inhaled and exhaled slowly, prepared for the betrayal she believed would come. But when she turned her back and slipped down the edge, Kathka and Nana remained still. She disappeared from their view.

"Come on," Kath said after a few moments passed. Long enough that the Island woman would no longer be braced at the bottom, frightened enough to use the knife. Not too long to lose the woman whose soul pulled at his own. "Let's follow."

"You care what happens to her?"

"Not one bit."

But he was supposed to save her, the Islander, his third life.

Chapter 16

He filled the stolen bottle with murky water and considered the women on either side. Nana knelt at his right by the stream, pooling handfuls of water into her parched mouth. The edges of her eyes crinkled as she smiled. The dehydration and sleep deprivation affected her more than he had expected.

On his left, further up the stream, knelt the Island woman. His third life. The water pooled in her cupped hands, and she frowned at what she saw. Most of the water had dripped from her palms before she took her first tentative sip.

She did her best to ignore her two followers. She had set the unsheathed dragon knife at her side, and on her other side, out of sight, she had tucked a bag.

"Any provisions in that sack of yours?" Kathka stood and slung the bottle around his chest. The woman separated her hands and let the water splash back into the stream.

"Why are you following me?"

"You need me." He faced her; thumb hooked on the leather strap. "That is, if you want to get out of this place alive."

"What do you know?" She rested one wet hand on her thigh and placed the other on the dagger's handle.

"Rather a lot," Kathka responded, words as sharp as hers.

"Just not about current affairs!" Nana chuckled before taking another gulp of water.

"Enough," Kathka hissed.

The foreigner's frown deepened.

"Are you truly an Islander?" she asked.

"That's what most have decided about me, yes." At his response, her eyes twitched narrow.

"Don't follow me."

"You're stubborn," Kathka muttered.

Her spirit snapped and burst into a self-righteous flame.

"What do you know?" she repeated and stood, dagger in hand and pointed again at Kathka. "You expect me to follow you without question, to trust a complete stranger?"

"I said nothing about trust."

"Look at you, you're soaked in blood!" She tipped the blade to his stained pants. His hands balled into fists. The comment was unfair. "And how did an Islander come to be with a desert dweller?"

"How did an Islander come to be stranded down here?" he retorted. "You're the one who knows nothing, that much is obvious!"

"I'm warning you," she hissed. "If you dare get in my way, I will kill you."

"You can't kill anything, you're just rich and spoiled!"

Nana pressed her hand against Kathka's chest and pushed him back. He had not realized he had taken a step forward.

"If you two keep shouting, we will be caught." Her voice was soothing, low and musical. She kept her palm flat against Kathka's chest, right above his heart. The weight was constricting.

"We don't know why you are here," Nana continued. The woman lowered the blade. "You don't know why we are. But we're all running, and I think we could help each other."

"I don't trust you." The woman's tone remained sharp.

"I understand." Nana smiled. It was a powerful weapon on her, it disarmed the woman. "But Kath's right, you won't survive here long. You don't know this canyon, we do. We can help you."

"Why would you help me?"

"I never met a true Islander before, but now I have and we're both running." She chuckled. "I think we are more similar than you think."

The two women regarded each other silently, neither wavering. Then the lady sighed and caved to the smile.

"Fine." She sheathed the blade in the scabbard strapped to her hip, partly hidden in the pleats of her skirt. "I will travel with you, but don't you dare come near me."

Nana flashed her brilliant smile back to Kath as if she

had accomplished something. Kathka grabbed her wrist and lowered her hand from its constraining hold.

"Just don't fall behind," he said through clenched teeth.

"I'm not following you." She crossed her arms over her chest.

"You are, I'm the only one that can keep us three alive," he spoke as evenly as he could. They could not argue because he was right, and they all knew. Still, she did not acknowledge him. Her words prodded the fire of his anger and he moved past the two before he retaliated. His teeth worked harshly against each other, pain solace in the anger.

"We need to find a cave," he said as he marched down the bank of the stream. "The sun is rising."

"A cave?" The woman's voice twisted in shock and disgust.

"Sleep under the sun then." Kathka kept his stiff pace, it would be unwise to look back at the Islander. The rage warmed him.

"Princess," He muttered to himself, as if it were a curse word.

Behind him, he heard the footsteps follow. Then another set begrudgingly trailed the first.

"My name is Nana," Nana offered to the wall of stony silence beside her. She did not seem to understand that she was supposed to hate the woman like Kathka did. The Islanders, protected from all the hardships of the world. "He's Kath, and he's as horrible as he seems."

No response.

"He's an Islander but, not truly," Nana provided unneeded information. Both sets of eyes fell heavy upon him. Confused. Uncertain.

His fists curled and uncurled, straining his muscles, and focusing his mind away from the conversation behind him.

"Can I at least have your name?" Nana tried again to coax words from the woman.

There was a long stretch of silence, then, "Cyrah."

"Cyrah," Nana whispered as she considered the precious piece of information she held. "What a beautiful name."

A tremor shivered up Kath's legs and he halted. Far above them, the stars remained motionless. Around them the world trembled. Loose stones clattered across the rock outcroppings, slipped over the edges, and tumbled against stone formations all the way down to the valley floor. Kath eyed the closest rock pillars, waiting for them to slide like melting wax to the canyon floor.

"What is happening?" Cyrah's shrill voice broke his concentration.

"An earthquake," Nana explained. Somehow her voice retained its habitual calm.

The quaking shivered to an end, but it was an uneasy still. Kathka heard her approach, steps soft in the sand, then felt her presence at his shoulder.

"This is why they search for me," Nana whispered as he watched the stars and waited for the next tremble in the earth. "The earth yearns to be united, for the curses to be erased. The desert, the shaking, the drought, it's all getting worse."

Nana bore the marks of the curse etched across her chest. Though they marred her skin, they were not hers. They belonged to Scala.

But she suffered.

"We can't stay here." Kath turned away from her and did

not confirm what Nana knew to be true. The world was falling apart.

Chapter 17

"This is disgusting," Cyrah declared. Kathka was certain she would simply turn around and walk away from the cave. She did not leave, but she did turn to look back at the canyon. Light tinted the black sky and her focus landed where the inky depths were shaded gray. But then she sighed and consented to crawl tentatively into the cave.

Cyrah positioned herself on the opposite side of the cave, as far from Kathka as she could.

"I'm supposed to sleep here?" she muttered.

"Just sleep," Kathka growled.

"You could tell us dragon stories instead!" Nana beamed. She sat between the two, glancing back and forth in search of someone who shared her enthusiasm.

"No stories," Kathka snapped. Nana's shoulders fell and he looked away from her crushed expression. "You both need sleep."

Cyrah frowned, though she did not argue. She combed her fingers through her hair in an attempt to rebraid the tangles.

Kathka lay down with his back set against the two, forehead pressed against the cool curve of the rock. Eventually, he heard the shuffling as they settled into more comfortable positions.

He tried to rest, but his sleep was disturbed by their worries, by the known and unknown followers, by the lingering truth that he did not know how to save them. It all made rest impossible. The concerns at least occupied his dreams and kept the tangible blackness at the fringe of his consciousness. He still feared it.

A pressure on his shoulder roused him from his restless slumber. He rolled to his back, blinking to clear his vision. The sun was high, and even in the darkened confines of the cave, he could clearly see the frown etched across her face.

"Are you the Blood King?" Nana whispered. The question pressed against his ribs and he had no air to answer. "Are you?"

"Go to sleep." He tried to roll back against the wall but her hand upon his chest kept him pinned.

"You are. Is that why you were cursed, for what you did?"

"You're insane," he muttered, but it was a flimsy defense.

She hovered above him, eyes wide and urgent.

"You are the Blood King."

"You don't know that."

"I do."

"No, you don't."

"Zalna told me."

Her body crashed against the floor and a sharp cry of pain burst from her throat. Shattered in the air. Like broken glass. Their roles reversed and he was above her, chest heaving. The foreign woman slept, and he choked back the angry oaths boiling in his veins.

He was shaking.

"Don't ever say that name." He released his hold on her shoulder. "Ever."

She scrambled away from him. Eyes wide, afraid. She knew. She knew he was dead, she knew he was the Blood King, and she knew of Zalna. The metallic tang was in his mouth. The memories thrust from their grave and scattered about him in a mess of bloodied broken bones.

Demons never seemed to die.

"How?" Kathka demanded. Nana rubbed her shoulder blade, where her body had hit the ground, and did not look at him.

"I told you, you won't listen," she muttered, her words bitter barbs. "I'm Scala's Daughter."

"That means nothing to me!" he hissed, maybe too loudly. Cyrah stirred. They sat in silence as she settled.

"It means," Nana continued, "that I've inherited the curse the gods gave to him for killing Caizin. He was cursed to bear the weight of those who had died. I bear it now."

"Mell."

The name came unbidden to his lips, and it rested between them, a small connection. A pain in the back of his throat. Her hand slipped to rest on the ground and her eyes flicked up to meet his. So deep, he could not understand the emotions filling them.

"It doesn't work like that."

"You bear the weight of those who died, you just said that."

"You have seen him and yet you understand so little." She shook her head. "I bear the dead to be tormented."

"Then what happens to those who don't torment you?"

"I don't know," she whispered, and it was the most solemn words he had ever heard.

"Then you understand as much as me," he snarled, because the pain pricked at the back of his throat, and he needed the distraction of fury.

"She said you were fierce, but you're just rash."

He wanted to retort that Zalna was a liar, he was not rash, he had been justified. But her gaze was dark, and she could see his lies. The cracks in his tales. He had not meant to be the Blood King, but he would be again.

"Don't speak of her," he said instead. He lay down, back rigid against her. Her curse was irrelevant, what she dragged from his past was irrelevant, the pain and the fear were irrelevant. He only needed to save her. The dead were dead, they did not matter.

But the pain stung in his throat. He clenched his teeth until his jaw ached. He circled through the plan he had constructed for his new life until the pain eased.

He would save Nana and Cyrah. He would save the remaining four lives. Then he would be free. Then he would complete what Scala could not, what the Blood King could not.

He would kill the Wise Man and he would prove that he needed no one.

Chapter 18

Thunder rumbled. It was too loud, too close. Kathka opened his eyes to daylight. There were still a few hours before the sun would set and they could continue their march.

But the thunder.

"It's a car," Nana explained his silent confusion. He sat and she shifted backward.

The space between them was taut with unspoken words. But he did not know how to unravel all that should be said.

So he said nothing.

"A what?" Cyrah hissed.

"A car," Nana repeated. Her focus shifted to the foreigner. "A large metal thing, used for transportation."

In the desert, he had been able to forget that he was displaced in time. The strange contraptions with their strange names forgotten. But the thunder was a reminder that he did not belong. That everything had advanced and left him behind.

A reminder that he was lost.

"Pashka?" Kath asked. Her gaze momentarily passed to him, and she nodded.

"You brought them to me," Cyrah accused. She tightened her protective hold around her sack. Kathka crawled to the opening of the cave and peered over the edge.

Below their cave, on the canyon floor, a metal monstrosity had stopped. Men disembarked from the flat open bed of its frame, their movements sluggish in the heat. They knelt beside the stream to break for a cool rest. A guard dragged a prisoner from the back of the contraption and shoved him into the water, face down. They laughed as the prisoner floundered in the shallow stream until the guard had mercy and released his hold. The prisoner gasped on the bank. It was Red, the prisoner with a fake curse.

Beside the car, dressed all in gray, Rain observed the men. In his hand, he clutched a flimsy blue slipper.

Kath ducked back into the shadow of the cave. A curse hissed through his teeth. He felt the band of his pants and found only one slipper tucked against his side.

"He's going to find us," Nana whispered.

"We're hidden," Kath countered.

"Rain's an amazing tracker," Nana reminded. It aided little. There was heat in his blood. It was mounting. He gritted his teeth. She watched him.

"You brought him here, do something!" Cyrah's voice pitched high with irritation. But she was right, he had brought this danger upon her. Even in the diluted light, he could see it, the panic in her eyes.

"Sorry about that, princess."

"I'm not a princess!"

"What do we do?" Nana intervened and focused both back to the immediate threat. The question lodged in his brain, stuck in the convoluted thoughts. Rain was a problem he did not know how to solve.

"There are six of them." Before, he could have overtaken them easily. The knowledge was in his mind, but his body lacked the prowess of his previous. They could run, but they would be swiftly overtaken by the machine.

"We take the truck," Nana whispered as if she had followed the course of his thoughts.

"How do you even use it?" Kath muttered.

"I know how!" she assured. For a moment, her hand alighted on his forearm, but she withdrew it. "Kath, it's the only thing we can do!"

He pressed the back of his head against the rock, focused on the pain, and heaved a sigh.

"We steal the car," he conceded and threw the useless slipper upon the cave floor. Her smile was too satisfied.

"So," Cyrah said from the recesses of the cave, "we run toward them?"

"Cyrah, you run toward them, get on the thing. I'll worry about the men," Kath instructed. He held out his hand to her. "I need your dagger."

Her eyes narrowed immediately. Kath kept his empty

palm extended and she faltered. Despite her braid, she was no warrior. Her gaze dropped to her hands, filled with her sack. She slipped the blade from the scabbard and handed it to him.

"I can't wield it," she offered as an excuse.

His fingers curled around the hilt. The diamond eye of the dragon winked at him. The unfurled wings slipped into the handle, and the curves settled perfectly in his grip. It all felt familiar, the weight, the balance, the feel of an instrument of destruction.

"Let's get that car."

Chapter 19

The rock clattered against stone as it tumbled down the slope. The noise of its descent ricocheted through the canyon's twisted sculptures. Shouts rose, and from his vantage point, Kath watched four of the men rush toward the opposite canyon wall, away from the car. One guard remained beside Red at the river.

Rain stood beside the car, gray boots planted on red soil.

"We have to go now," Nana whispered.

"I'll distract Rain, you get the car." Kath repeated the plan to be sure she understood. He hoped she would listen. Armies had been at his command, but never two women with questionable battle skills.

There was a silent agreement. An exchange of glances. She slid past him and down the edge of the outcropping, hidden by a column of corroding earth. Cyrah grabbed Kath's shoulder before he could follow, nails biting into his arm.

"What if we're caught?"

"We won't be." He jerked from her grip and slid down the bank, loosening a shower of dirt. He winced and peeked around the column. Rain stared directly at them.

"Run."

He jumped down and rushed forward. The dagger whistled through the air, a tune that ignited his blood, kept his heart thudding as Rain unsheathed his short sword and called for his men. This felt right. This felt like himself.

In a clean sweep, Kath brought the blade crashing down.

Cyrah's dagger was thin and shuddered as Rain swept his sword up to deflect the blow. Kath twisted to the side and let his blade glide across the metal. Like a dancer twirling with a partner, he stepped into Rain's parry and let it spin him to the side until his dagger chimed off the blade and he slashed upward with the momentum. Aiming for the throat.

Rain lifted his arm to take the blow. Steel bit through cloth, sliced flesh, and found the inner river of red.

The butt of the shortsword dug into Kath's ribs. He stumbled backward and splashed into the stream. He regained his footing in the sandy bottom in time to dodge an arch of steel. Rain recoiled and stilled, blade poised in the air, prepared for another blow.

The knowledge of swordplay flitted through Kathka's mind. He knew how to toy with Rain, how to coax him to reveal his weaknesses and then use them against him. But Kath's body was too weak. Too slight. Too short. Too malnourished.

Rain was a perfectly crafted weapon. Every movement meticulously analyzed and executed. He noted the swift rise and fall of Kath's chest and attacked. Kath flipped the blade to lay against his forearm and lifted his arm to deflect the downward strike. Rain recoiled and lunged, and Kath dropped his arm to block the blow to the right.

The attacks were not aimed to kill. Each precise blow crumbled Kath's defenses through sheer exertion. Rain's intent was to bring him down through his own frailty. He would succeed.

Kath needed a distraction.

A scream ripped through his focus. Not Nana — Cyrah. Kath jumped backward to avoid a swing and, with precious time, glanced at the car. Nana scrambled into it. Cyrah lay on the flat back, fingers still extended to the bag wrestled from her grip.

Her screams stung.

Rain seized his opportunity. Kath caught the glint of steel, moved to parry the blow, but was unprepared. Beneath the weight of the strike, the dagger wrenched from his grip and winked in the sunlight before it splashed into the muddy water.

Rain remained poised and regarded him with cold calculation. His gaze darted to the right. He dropped his shoulder just as Red rammed into him. He grunted at the impact.

"Go!" Red shouted as he grappled with Rain.

Kath ran. Behind, Rain's men closed in upon him. But

they recognized the distraction too late.

Their feet splashed into the stream as Kath ran toward the machine. It roared to life. Nana turned in the seat and caught his eyes.

"Kath!" she called. The beast lurched forward.

"The bag!" Cyrah screamed as she kicked at the guard clutching her ankle. Kath grabbed the useless thing from the sand and slung it over his shoulder. He landed three quick jabs in all the uncovered spots of the man's torso. His grip loosened. Cyrah's heel made heavy contact with his nose, and he collapsed into the sand.

Kath threw the bag upon the machine and jumped. He found little purchase on the sleek metal and his feet dragged across the sand, pulling him back to the shouting guards.

Cyrah grabbed his forearms. With her as an anchor, he clambered onto the back. He sat with chest heaving and hands plastered against the metal to keep from being shaken off.

Nana was not good at controlling the beast.

"Kath, you okay?" Nana called over the noise of the thing.

"Yeah," he managed.

"Stay low!" she cautioned.

A peal of thunder rumbled and there was a spark to his right. He reeled to the left and slammed against the frame. Behind them the men shrank. Rain ran toward them, then halted and raised the metal weapon. The gun. He grew increasingly small. His arm fell back to his side.

They were too far away.

A smile tore across Kath's face.

"We did it," he said, relieved and amazed that the plan

had worked.

"Is Rain mad?" Nana asked.

"Furious!"

She laughed. The sound settled deep in his bones, wrapped into his blood. It was a pleasant sound. Chest still heaving from adrenaline and exertion, Kath turned to look at the two women. Nana in front, Cyrah at his side.

Tears painted her cheeks wet.

"What's wrong?"

Nana's laughter died at his question. Cyrah's shoulders shook and she clutched the sack tightly to her chest.

"Were you hurt?" Kath leaned closer to search for a red bloom. There was thunder, there could be a wound. A wound like Mell's. One he would not be able to stop.

Crimson stained the bag. Her grip loosened and the sack fell open. Two eggs sat nestled in the folds of cloth, shimmering white like crystal. The shards of a third were littered amongst its brethren. A small reptilian body lay still in the debris. Dead. Thick blood seeped from where fragments of shell had punctured its scaly flesh.

"Are those …" Nana passed her gaze between the road before and the sight behind. "Are those dragons?"

Cyrah cried.

Chapter 20

Only the noise of the metal beast accompanied their voyage. They drove the rest of the day and through the night, distancing themselves from Rain and his men. Kath sat beside Nana and watched her hands glide over the wheel as she navigated the rocky terrain. He needed the distraction.

Cyrah remained in the back, huddled over her sack. She cried for a long time. He did not look at her, but he could hear each ragged breath as it wracked her body. Eventually, her cries, then ceased, and she was silent.

No one discussed the eggs.

Gray edged into the sky and smothered the stars. One by one they winked out, not strong enough to withstand the light of dawn. Nana abruptly stopped the car, throwing Kath forward. He caught himself against the front panel. She called it the dashboard.

"What?"

"I think," she began, and he knew what she would suggest. It made him nervous. "We should trade the truck for provisions. It's better to be in the desert."

"Yeah."

"The city's not too far ahead."

He looked at his hands splayed across the dashboard to avoid Nana's direct gaze. If it were just the two of them they could have gone in together. But now Cyrah was with them, and she was still a crumpled heap. A crumpled heap with two dragon eggs.

"I'll exchange it," Nana said, knowing all that he considered.

"Nana—"

"We can't bring her to the city." She wrung her hands around the steering wheel. "She would stand out too much, and I don't know if it would be a good idea to bring … them. And you need to stay with her, she won't be safe alone."

"And you will be?" His gaze shifted slightly to look at her long oak-brown fingers curled around the wheel. She chuckled.

"I know my way around a city," she chuckled. "Remember, Wayfinder?"

He wanted to argue, but she was right. She was right and it frustrated him because the thought of parting from her constricted his chest.

"Don't worry, I'll come back." Nana clambered over the seat. He wanted to reach out, grab her arm, and insist they find an alternative plan.

But she was right.

Nana knelt beside Cyrah and spoke gentle words too low for Kathka's ears. They were not for him. He was an intruder.

Cyrah's hands were bloodied from removing the shards.

Nana asked a question, and Cyrah's chin dipped in a single nod. Another question, and Cyrah gingerly gathered her sack. With Nana's help, she descended to the sand.

"Find a cave," Nana instructed as she climbed back to the front seat. "Stay there until I come back."

He did not move.

She crossed her arms over the wheel and leaned against it in a careless calm. "I won't be long."

Her smile aggravated him. He slid to the sand, legs wobbling on the still earth after hours sitting in the rumbling machine. He pointed to a ridge in the cliff where a chain of caves dotted the rock face.

"We'll be in that one," he said. "Sell the beast and go there. We'll be waiting."

She laughed. He wished she wouldn't.

"It's a truck, Kath."

In a plume of sand, she left the two behind. He watched until the sand cleared from the air and settled back upon the earth and revealed only an empty canyon passage before him. The ruts of the truck were distinct. The wind did not reach down so deeply in the canyon to shift the tracks back to oblivion.

An easy trail for Rain to follow.

"Come on."

Cyrah followed as he led her up the steep slope, sack clutched in her arms. Kath grabbed the lip of the cave and climbed into the basin he had pointed out to Nana. It was large and shallow. Not good for hiding, but it would have to do.

"Here." He extended a hand down to Cyrah. "Give me the bag."

She gathered it tightly against her chest.

"Give me the bag," he growled. "Then you can climb up and get it."

She looked down at the bundle, frowned, but lifted it. "Be careful."

In his hand, it felt so light. There were two eggs in it, but he tried not to think about that. He set it beside him and reached down with both hands to grab Cyrah's wrists. He hauled her up, though the stress tore through his muscles. A burning had settled into his arms and shoulders from the short spar of the previous day. Yet another reminder of his weakness.

Once in the cave, Cyrah snatched the bag and pressed herself against the cave wall, balling protectively around the sack and its contents.

"You okay?" The question felt awkward to him, offered in a messy bundle of jagged edges. He was not surprised she did not answer. But she refused to even look at him and it made the rejection harsher. Kath heaved a sigh and laid down on the ground. He stared up at the cave ceiling.

He was tired. Tired of traveling, tired of running, tired of scrambling with what little leverage he had to keep the two women alive and fulfill the deal. But he did not want to sleep, not when the darkness was so suffocating and not when Nana was out there, somewhere in the desert.

"You don't know how to play Crowns, do you?" he asked.

"Crowns?" Cyrah repeated. "What is that?"

He chuckled. "Never mind, just sleep."

"How can I, after that?"

Her voice was a whisper. Scratchy and rough. Pain still laced her words.

"You need to," Kath muttered. There was a long silence. He was sure she wouldn't say anything more, when suddenly she did.

"I was sworn to protect them."

Cyrah's words were fragile. He did not care to hear, but it was he who had instigated the response. He did not care to hear of the eggs, but she continued, and he let her.

"I failed."

In her voice was the threat of tears. Soon they would wet her cheeks, a waste of water. She had already wasted too much. Such emotions were a weakness, one she should learn to stifle.

"You still have two." He sat, unslung the water bottle from around his torso, and slid it to her. She drew her palm across her cheeks and smeared the tears. She did not take the bottle, just stared at it. "Don't complain, you were the one who brought them here. Should've just kept them in your palace, princess."

"You make it sound so simple, but it's not."

They were at an impasse, and neither would yield. He did not want to understand. He simply had to save her. Only her.

Not the dragons.

Disheveled curls of hair slipped over her sagging shoulders as she reached for the water bottle. Her braid had long since been destroyed.

"So," he started as she drank some of his precious water. "These people after you, should we worry about them?"

"No." She screwed the lid back onto the bottle and placed it on the ground. "Worry about your man. He's familiar, they are not."

"They'll still be after you though?"

Cyrah pushed aside the cloth of her sack. The eggs glowed even in the dim light of the cave. His eyes gravitated toward the unearthly sight. Cyrah's fingers danced over the white surfaces.

"Yes, and they'll be mounted."

Mounted. Kath rubbed his hand over his tired eyes. Mounted on dragons. When he dropped his hand, he found her narrowed eyes inquisitively upon him.

"You've never heard of the Ja Nrai?"

"Ja Nrai?"

"You truly know nothing." She listed forward and rested her forehead against the smooth shells. Her regal countenance corroding in the sand.

Bu Chak. Ja Nrai. He did not care for the sound of either.

"Who are they?" he asked. She tilted her head to look at him, still doubled over the eggs. "If I may have to face them, I want to know who they are."

"They're the dragon riders. The Island guard."

"Why did you take them?" he asked. It was clear why the dragon riders pursued her; the white eggs were answer enough. Why the eggs were in the desert was something else entirely.

"Not your concern." She straightened and pulled the bag back over the eggs. "You're no more Islander than any of these people. Our business doesn't concern you."

"Alright," Kathka conceded. She was right, he was not one of her people. He may have been branded one, but his soul belonged to the desert. To the hot days and cold nights, with their campfires and dances that mirrored the wavering flames. "Keep your secrets. But you did bring them here, what are you planning on doing with them now?"

"I thought …" She stopped.

"What?"

After a moment of worrying with the sack, she continued, "The legends say the Wise One remained. If that is true, I am going to take them to him."

Kathka could not help his laughter. It was dangerous, it would attract attention. But her shock was worth the threat.

"Oh really? And how will you do that?"

"I …" The single syllable remained as she searched for more to defend herself with.

"Listen," Kathka interrupted her attempted reply. "I will take you to the Wise Man, alright?"

"You know where he is?"

"I do." He nodded. She still looked at him with narrowed eyes, but he did not care to give any further explanation. There was no need for her to know more. No need for her to know that his location was general desert knowledge passed down in myth. Certainly no need for her to know that Kath had visited him once before and for all his threats he had been killed so quickly.

"I'll take you to him," he said instead. "And then I'll leave you alone, okay?"

"Why are you doing this?" she asked.

"I'll get you to the Wise One." He lay back on the ground, hands clasped behind his head and foot propped on his knee. "That's all you need to know."

She did not question further, and he pretended he was asleep until he heard her settle around the eggs. Soon her breathing evened, and emotional exhaustion drew her into a deep sleep.

Kath opened his eyes, resolve to remain vigilantly awake unbroken.

In the silence, Kath listened intently for any sign of Nana's return. He traced the cracks and grooves of the cave ceiling with his eyes and plotted through the new trajectory of their flight.

Kathka would bring Cyrah to the Wise Man.

He hated the twisted humor that would bring him back to the god's desolate wasteland. He would have killed them all, dragons, and Islanders, and Wise One.

Now he aided them all.

Chapter 21

Cyrah shifted constantly in her sleep, though she remained curled around the eggs. At least she slept. He listened to her movements as he watched the shadows shift across the entrance of the cave.

Though resolved to remain alert, exhaustion occasionally forced his eyes to close. Each time his heart would beat a rapid rhythm and the black would crowd close around him. Sleep reminded him that he should not be alive, that he too should be a dead specter haunting Nana's consciousness.

His eyes would snap back open and each time he expected to see her with lips curled into her eternal smile.

She was never there.

Every faint sound was either Nana returning or Rain descending upon their fresh, wide tracks. As the sun completed its race across the sky, the two in the cave remained undisturbed. With each passing moment, Kath regretted letting Nana go.

Night pressed upon the earth. As the cave darkened, Cyrah sat. With sluggish movements, she sipped from his flask. She laid it aside with the cap off. Empty. The last of their water. Her hands wandered over her sack and pressed over the firm shapes of the remaining eggs.

"She hasn't returned?" she mumbled. More frustrated statement than question. She sighed and slipped her hand through her tangled hair. "We would have time for you to teach me Crowns."

He smirked.

She rebraided her hair, though he did not know why. It would just get tangled again and fall apart. But she focused on the task with great care. With a thin slip of purple cloth, she tied the end of the braid tightly and ran her hands over her handiwork. With such staunch resolve to keep the braid, perhaps she was more of a warrior than he had credited her to be.

Task completed, she was left to be consumed in the waiting.

He could teach her Crowns.

"Kath!"

He jerked upright and found her before him, all sun-kissed skin, laughter lines, and a shimmering smile gracing her lips.

"Nana."

She disappeared and heaved a bag into the cave, then two more, before sliding in after them.

"Miss me?"

"What took so long?" he growled.

"Well, I'm sorry." She sounded unapologetic. She opened one of the bags. It was filled with metal squares that smelled of pungent spices. "Just making sure we didn't starve."

Nana snatched one of the boxes and flipped open the lid. She took out strips of dried meat and tossed one to Cyrah who managed to grab it while keeping a hand protectively against the sack. The Islander turned it around in her hand with a frown. Nana passed another to Kath.

"There's also dried apples, some salt, and water. I got each of us a traveling tent and a backpack for each. Trucks go for quite a bit. I even managed to save some money too." She stuffed the the meat into her mouth. "I bought coats for you both. I should've gotten you a new shirt though, Kath. That green is a terrible color."

Kath ignored her last comment. He took the metal box from her hand and considered the contents. The scraps of meat were tantalizing, but he did not touch it.

"What're you thinking?" Nana crouched at his side. So close. She chewed at the jerky and looked down at the food in his palm as if she could find his trail of thoughts there.

"How many packs of meat are there?" he asked.

"Ten tins."

"Don't eat more than four pieces." He flipped the cloth back over the meat. "We need to ration it if we're going to survive the desert."

"Where are we going?" she asked.

The question teetered near the edge. It was fragile and he

was not very good with fragile things. Zalna had a jewelry box. He could remember it clearly. It had glass panels all held together with gold. He did not know how she had obtained it. All he knew was that he had not given it to her. It shattered easily on the floor, and she was hurt.

Hurt easily turned to hate.

He had not seen Nana's hate yet, only her hurt. He had deserved it. Trust shattered on rock. He feared seeing her hate, though he deserved it.

His pause lengthened and her smile faded. He could not leave her question unanswered forever.

"To the Wise One," he said, and as he spoke, he heard shattered glass chiming on stone floor.

"The Wise One," she repeated. Her smile gone. He busied himself with the bags she had brought. He emptied their contents and began to distribute the food, water, and canvas tents evenly in three packs for each. She watched him, but he refused to meet her gaze.

"I've tried to find him." Her voice was flat, the cheer from her success so quickly extinguished. "It's impossible."

"I found him," Kath said shortly.

"How?"

"I think he let me," he admitted and lifted his eyes to meet hers. He could not ignore her. "And I think he'll let me again."

Her lips were a thin line. She said nothing. Her silence was worse than her incessant speech. There were questions, ones she did not ask. He feared them and the answers they would require.

He lifted the first sack of provisions toward her. She took it.

"Why do you think that?" Cyrah asked and Kathka gladly took the opportunity to tear his eyes from Nana's transfixing gaze.

"Because." Kath extended a sack to her which she took. "He let me once, why wouldn't he let me again?"

It was not a lie, but it was also not the truth. He did not explain further because he did not need either of them to know. The Wise Man promised to give him a second life if he saved seven lives. He was sure that to save Cyrah he needed to lead her to him.

It was possible it was also the way to save Nana. A way to save her from the curse she bore that was not her own.

"Cyrah, that coat is for you." He motioned with his chin toward the coat on the ground as he slipped into the second one.

Her brow furrowed and she picked up the coat with two fingers, as if it were dirty. Her robes were elegant, the more time he spent with her the more he noticed the intricate details stitched into the fabric. There were dragon motifs across the skirt, wings unfurled in delicate loops and regal snouts with bared teeth. Her clothes looked like something he knew, not like the clothes he and Nana now wore. Not like the coat Cyrah awkwardly slipped into.

"There's food, water, and shelter in each sack." Kath hefted up his backpack. "Let me know if they are too heavy. They shouldn't be."

Neither seemed confident in Kathka's words, but they had no choice but to accept them. If he could take them to the Wise Man, he could do something no one else could.

Kath hoped he had guessed the Wise Man's plan accurately.

"Let's go."

Chapter 22

Kath balanced on the ledge, body pressed against the wall of the canyon. With one hand, he cautiously reached up and was relieved to feel his fingers curl around the edge of rock. He turned his head to protect his eyes from unsettled sand as it drifted down.

Two packs slung across his back and weighed down his already weak body. Cyrah refused to carry both the provision pack and her bag on her back, so he bore the extra weight as they climbed.

His body was exhausted.

With a stabilizing breath, he grabbed what little purchase

he could find and hoisted himself up. He kicked against the canyon wall and scrambled over the edge and onto the desert floor. Chest heaving, he crawled forward and sat.

The sky unfurled around him. Without the constraints of the rock walls, the deep velvet expanded in all directions, and he stared up at the great dome of stars.

It was beautiful to be so free.

They had wasted most of the night on their vertical ascent. Though no sunlight yet dimmed the white pinpoints, the horizon stirred with the first considerations of day. They still needed to put distance between the canyon and themselves.

Kath slipped Cyrah's backpack off and stood, neck still craned upward, chest still heaving for breath.

Nana clambered over the edge, hands clawing at the shifting ground. She stilled, but the sand slipped beneath her and pulled her back toward the canyon.

"Get away from the edge." Kath grabbed her arm and pulled her past him. He caught a glimpse of her smirk before she slipped away into the desert. He knelt at the precipice and peered over. Cyrah stood on the ledge below. Her arms shook as she gripped the jagged edges of the rock face.

"Take my hand."

She tilted her head upward, cheek pressed against the rock and looked at Kath's extended hand. Just looked at it.

"Take it!"

Cyrah scuttled her hand upward toward him. She refused to separate herself from the stabilizing rock. Her hand rested right below his.

"Come on, Cyrah!" Nana cheered. Too loudly. Her voice echoed down the canyon.

Cyrah inhaled sharply and let go of the rock to grab Kath's hand.

"Give me the other!" Nana crouched beside Kath and reached down for her. Cyrah pressed her forehead against the rock and Kath wondered if she was even breathing at all. Then in a sudden burst, she reached out and grabbed Nana's hand.

"Pull!" Kath ordered. The two strained to drag Cyrah up, fighting against her weight, the shifting sand, and their own weakness. Cyrah kicked at the canyon wall until her knee caught on the edge and she crawled into the sand and collapsed in the desert.

All three lay with heaving chests. Kath and Nana stared up into the host of stars, Cyrah stared down into the host of sand.

"They won't expect that escape!" Nana laughed.

"If we don't keep going," Kath grunted and stood, "they will find us."

Cyrah propped herself up on her elbows and reached back to check the contents of her bag. Kath kicked her backpack and it toppled before her.

"You take that now."

Cyrah gave no protest. She sat and twisted her bag to settle against her chest. Protected. Then she slipped the pack onto her back where it belonged.

"So, we keep walking?" Nana bounded upward and stretched her arms high before doubling over to touch her toes.

"We need to get away from here."

Cyrah craned her head upward to the sky.

"And the Ja Nrai?" she asked. The sky was void of

winged beasts, but that was not promised to last.

"Just walk." He started forward knowing they would follow. They had to. They needed him to find the Wise One, they needed him to survive.

"Trust him." Nana's voice was soft behind him. It was a bad choice of words. Nana knew better. "He knows how to survive in the desert."

He trudged through the sand and focused solely upon the stars that pointed him onward. He tried to rid his mind of her voice, but then she was at his side and he could not ignore her.

"How did you become a Wayfinder?"

She asked of things long since passed. It felt like a lifetime ago that he had roamed the sands as a Wayfinder. It had been a lifetime ago. Now she looked at him and waited for his answer. A smile curved her lips, but he could only think of her body hitting the ground. Of glass shattering. Of the hurt in her eyes.

"I was captured by them."

"I thought Wayfinders were free men."

"They are. The ones that are caught are used as a diversion. If they are clever enough to survive, they're accepted as equal."

"What about your family? Didn't they try to get you back?"

Of all the memories he had, she asked him of ones he did not despise. Ones that were so faint he barely remembered them at all. The earring was a reminder they had even existed at all. Acrius taunted him, claiming that one day he would lose the ear because of the ornament. But he liked the feel of the smooth disk and the few memories it evoked. A smile, a warm dish, a thick blanket on a cold night.

Acrius never knew it had been his mother's. He would have called him weak.

"They were already dead," he said in a carefully monotone voice.

"That's horrible," she whispered.

"That was life."

"That's not how it should be," she murmured. He had not thought about what it should or should not have been. It simply was.

Nana glanced back to Cyrah then in a lower voice she said, "I can possibly talk to the other Wayfinders."

"Why would I want to speak to them?"

"I thought …" She waved her arms aimlessly as if that would clarify her thoughts. It did not. "Maybe they could offer some advice. To survive?"

"They won't be helpful."

"Not even Acrius?"

"Stop doing that!"

Her eyes widened as if surprised by his outburst. As if it had not happened before. As if she did not know who he was.

"Doing what?" Cyrah asked. She had halted at his shout. They all had. Kathka gritted his teeth and started forward.

"Nothing," Nana replied for Kathka as he marched on. She returned to his side, persistent. "Is it embarrassing to ask for his help?"

She was not very good at listening.

"The dead are dead, Nana. Their voices have been silenced."

"You're quite talkative for a dead man."

He halted once more, but Cyrah had not yet continued to follow, and he could feel her wary gaze. He kicked the sand and set a quicker pace.

Nana kept at his side.

"Why don't you want to talk to Acrius?" she pressed.

"Because," he hissed. "Because I killed him."

She fell away from his side. He did not know what else she expected, but it still stung.

"Didn't he tell you that?" he asked, though she may have stopped listening.

"He didn't say that," she responded after a moment's hesitation. He had hoped she wouldn't. He did not want to hear what the dead had to say. "He only said you had ended the Wayfinders."

"I killed them."

"Why?"

"They were in the way." He did not understand how her simple questions forced so many words from him. Even after he spoke, he found more gathering on his tongue. "They didn't agree with consolidating power."

"You killed Acrius, even though he was like a father to you?"

Kathka laughed. "Did Acrius tell you that?"

"Dead men don't speak, remember, Kathka?"

She dropped back to match Cyrah's pace. He did not look, but he felt her presence retreat, her parting words ghosts that remained to haunt him.

"Dead words," he said aloud though there was no one to hear. Acrius was dead and it made no difference what he or Zalna or anyone else from his past whispered to Nana. Dead words.

He thought instead about something breaking, snapping with pain. The fire that it would bring, and the rage that would smother the hurt and give ground to action. It covered the twisted wounds her words uncovered, grounded him with each step he took.

Save seven lives, kill the Wise One.

He thought of breaking and forced himself to forget that it was Acrius who had taught him the ritual.

They walked that way for a while, Kathka leading, Nana and Cyrah lagging.

Then came the words, like music. Soft and melodic, they floated in the air and broke his concentration. Nana's words, punctuated infrequently by Cyrah's clipped responses. But there were responses, and a conversation began. There was laughter. Her laughter. He could not fathom what the foreigner had said to elicit the response.

He could not. He only succeeded in bringing hurt.

He was better at killing than saving.

"We set up camp here," Kath said curtly and halted. Behind him the conversation ceased. It was what he had wanted.

The backpack thumped to the sand, and he rolled his stiff shoulders. He still felt the residual sting of the duel with Rain. The hard leather straps of the backpack were not helping.

"Eat your rations," he continued and knelt beside his pack. He worked with precision, unpacking his dried meat and fruit, and the small canvas tent. "Set up the tent, you'll want to try and get to sleep before the sun has fully risen."

"Yes, sir!" Nana mirrored his actions, even with the same

brisk movements.

Cyrah glanced between the two of them, then looked at the sack in her hands.

"Are you going to get to work?" Kathka speared the main tent stake into the sand. He glanced up at Cyrah as he shoved more sand around the metal with his foot. She still looked down at her hands. "Well?"

"I ..." She chewed her lip and looked out over the flat desert. The dunes began miles off. Kath hoped they would reach them the next night. But currently, Cyrah was his worry. "I don't know how to."

"Of course you don't."

She glared at him.

"I can help!" Nana bounded up, leaving behind her own unfinished tent. "I'm sure I don't have as much experience as our Wayfinder here, but I've done it enough times to remember how!"

Cyrah relinquished her backpack to Nana. As Nana unpacked the supplies, Cyrah mouthed, "Wayfinder?"

"Setting up a tent is below you, princess?" Kathka asked to keep her from voicing the question he saw on her lips. He feared the response she would have received. He had no confidence that Nana would keep his past a secret.

He succeeded in his distraction. Cyrah's eyes snapped to him, eyebrows drawn low, mouth opened to retort. She faltered. Her attention flicked to Nana who had already buried the second stake into the sand.

"Why do you keep calling me that?" she mumbled instead. Cyrah knelt and delicately set her sack in the sand. Her fingers slipped one by one from the fabric, and she stood. For a moment longer, she looked down at it before she turned to Nana. "Let me help."

"Because of what Kath said?" Nana smiled at her. "Don't worry about him."

"No." Cyrah shook her head. "I want to learn."

"You would make a good princess." Nana's eyes crinkled as her smile widened further. Before the smile Cyrah's defenses lowered, and she returned the smile with her own timid one.

Kath watched the two women. Just watched. There had been moments like this with the Wayfinders. Moments between the thievery when they set up their camps, swapped stories, and ate. There had been a camaraderie, built between the men and women who had nothing else.

For a moment, the two women looked happy. He tried to remember if he ever felt happy with Acrius. With the Wayfinders. He had not allowed himself to think of them after he had killed them.

He wondered what it would be like, to save anything.

Chapter 23

In his exhausted sleep, Kath did not immediately realize that the high-pitched sound was a scream. And even after that, he waded blindly through the darkness, unable to connect the noise to anything real.

He was lost in the void. Nothing more than a lifeless soul.

Scorched air rushed into his lungs, and he jerked upright. The red sun filled his vision. It was too much, but not enough. He tried to ground himself, but the sand slipped so easily through his fingers.

The scream continued.

He blinked. Around him objects cleared. The canvas of his shelter sloped on either side of him, across from him Cyrah sat under her lopsided shelter. She grasped her bag, eyes wide and begging him to move.

Between them, Nana screamed. She writhed on the desert floor, tangled in the canvas meant to shade her.

Kath crawled to her side. His hands hovered above her. Her face contorted in a grimace, veins raised across her skin, ligaments of her neck straining.

"Nana," he spoke too softly, call drowned in the pitch of her cries. "Nana!"

He grabbed her shoulders. Her skin was hot. She burned him. The heat traveled through his veins, to his core. Her eyes snapped open and the screams caught in her throat. Her dark gaze filled with toxic danger and tears pooled in her eyes.

"Scala."

The heat was in his head. He blinked to bring her face to focus, but the blackness that was still so near to his memory edged his vision. The heat seared him.

"Is she okay?" Cyrah's voice was murky and distant.

"Yeah," he heard himself respond. Nana shook between his hands, tears slid down her cheeks. "Go back to sleep."

Kath did not know if Cyrah listened. His focus was on Nana. Her hands were against his arms.

She burned him.

His hands shifted over her shoulder blades, an awkward attempt at comfort. But her eyes were upon him and he froze in his efforts.

"You have a strong soul." Her voice was raw from her screams. "You keep the dead away. Even Scala can't withstand you."

She was close, arms resting on top of his, sending shivers of heat down his spine.

"I use you. To keep the others away."

"Then use me."

"I'm afraid you're just as horrid as Scala." She withdrew her hold and the heat sapped from him. He was left hollow, emptied as her eyes turned away and left him only with the blackness in the back of his mind. The past and the present were tangled inside of him. She knew. She understood the contradictions of his very being. But even she could not begin to unravel it all.

They were both cursed. The living to the dead, the dead to the living.

Nana wrapped the coat around herself and curled into a ball, back against Kath. He tried to say something more, but even speaking felt as if it would hurt him. Everything had been seared. He shifted backward, and she did not look at him. He righted the tent over her, and still she did not look at him.

When he turned, he found Cyrah watching them both.

"Is she okay?" the woman whispered. Her grip around the bag had loosened, and there was a softness in the question. A concern.

"She's fine." He knew it was a lie. As did she. Her eyes flicked to Nana's curled body.

"She is…" she began, then hesitated and looked away from Nana as if embarrassed by the words she almost said. "She is Scala's Daughter, isn't she?"

She had heard. Kath grit his teeth and silently berated his careless words. Cyrah's gaze flicked finally up to him, an unease pooling in their depth.

"Does it matter?"

"No." She lowered her gaze. "It doesn't anymore."

"Just go back to sleep."

He did not say it to Nana, he knew she would not sleep. Neither would he. The dark and the heat were too near to them both.

Chapter 24

The incident of the day was not mentioned upon waking for the night. In silence, the three repacked their shelters and ate their rations. The night was ahead, with its stars and darkened sand and safety.

"We follow the Center Star." Kath pointed to the bright pinpoint above them. The two women stood on either side, their presence a heavy weight upon his soul. Two lives to save. "It'll lead us to the Coran, we'll find shelter there, and towns to refill our supplies."

"What is the Coran?"

"Mountains," Nana replied. "They'll be expecting that."

"Doesn't matter, it's the way to the Wise Man." He walked away because he was tired of their questions. He was tired by everything. Sleep had eluded him, the fear and the heat coursed in his veins. He had spent the day aware that Nana was also not asleep.

He was exhausted.

"Will there be an opportunity to bathe?" Cyrah asked. Kath sighed.

"Tired of how much you reek, princess?" He forced the response, though he just wanted to ignore her inane question.

"I'm not the only one in need of washing," she huffed.

Nana laughed. It was a good sound to hear. She had seemed distant, drawn inward from the events of the previous night. When Scala had haunted her. He wondered what he had said to her, his descendant. Whatever he had said, it had made her scream.

The sound was still fresh in his ears.

"When we do get to the mountains," Nana said, voice returning to its usual rapid clip, "I will have to get some spice cookies for you, Cyrah. You must try them! They are made with cinnamon and are delicious. I have only ever had them there."

"Cookies?" Cyrah did not sound at all enthused at the prospect.

"Do you not like sweets?"

"No, it's not that," she corrected. "I do. It's just, I don't have them much. No one does. It's not the wisest use of the Island resources and I assumed our Wayfinder would think the same."

Kath grimaced at her use of the term. He was glad he

walked ahead of them so he wouldn't have to see the smile that accompanied Nana's chuckle.

"She's right," he said shortly.

"No sweets?" Nana sighed. "That's too bad, the cookies are so good. They are called snow drops because they are powdered and look like snow. Or at least, that's what they are supposed to look like."

"You haven't seen snow?" Cyrah asked.

"You have!" Nana gasped.

"Only a few times."

"What's it like?" Nana's voice was so exuberant even Kath smirked at the excitement. It was just snow.

"It's cold, and white," Cyrah said. Nana must have been visibly upset because a moment later she added, "It's fragile, and it melts so quickly. It sparkles when the light hits it just right."

He had never seen snow either but could not imagine what Cyrah described. Not when the dunes finally began to swell around them. But behind him Nana sighed.

"That's marvelous!"

"It's just cold," Cyrah dismissed. "At night I half expect to find it here in the desert."

"I have read about snow," Nana said wistfully. "But it sounded more like a myth."

"You read?" Kath snorted. He could not picture Nana sitting idle with a book. Not with her energy, and not with her curse.

"I used to read all the time," Nana replied. "When my parents were still alive."

"Oh," Cyrah murmured.

Kath grit his teeth. She was Scala's descendant, but her

lineage had never crossed his mind. She asked him about his death, about his past, about him. She tried to know him.

He had never tried to know her.

"But, Cyrah, your parents must also be dead since you are now the Dragon Priestess, right?"

Kath halted. The question had been innocent, but it was more than Nana should have known.

"How do you know that?" Cyrah asked, and her voice was dangerous.

Kath turned, and in the glow of the moonlight, he could see Cyrah's glare.

"You do know," she accused Kath.

"He knows nothing." Nana twirled about to face Cyrah. "We're just more alike than you think. We all die."

"Ignore her." Kath grabbed Nana's arm and pulled her forward. "She's insane."

"But—"

"No more talk," Kath interrupted Cyrah. "Don't get us caught."

Which they all knew was an excuse. She had said it did not matter. He did not want her to change her mind.

"Let me go," Nana demanded, and Kath released her arm. She placed distance between them, though she matched his pace. She did not trust him. Her words from the day before turned over and over in his mind. He may not be safe. He did not feel very safe.

"What are you doing?" he asked.

"She knows," Nana said. The cheer remained, but at his side he could hear the truth. It was a facade, and underneath was the result of multiple sleepless nights. She sounded exhausted. "She knows I am Scala's Daughter. Does it matter what I say?"

"Not everyone knows that Scala was cursed to commune with the dead."

"It's not communing," she retorted, but Kathka could care less. She looked behind at Cyrah. "What do you think he will do with the eggs?"

"I don't care."

"You must. The gift the gods gave, returned to the only one left, what does it mean?"

"Why would you care?" He turned the question back on her.

"If he takes the dragons back, maybe he will take back Scala's curse."

"You want that?"

"Who wants the dead in their head?" Nana easily laughed aside his question, but it haunted him. Dragons and curses, he could not discern what plan the Wise One had in motion.

"What if he doesn't?"

Her screams echoed in his mind. They would not leave him. She spoke of the future, but she lived in the past. She ran a hand over the downy hair of her scalp. Her hair was growing back.

"He's the only god left, if he doesn't take it back … then I am only left with what I had at the start." She offered the smallest smile. It was so different from the exuberant ones that usually filled her face. "I just want to understand."

Kath did not understand the old man or his dealings. He did not know if the Wise One would answer Nana's desire, or if that would save her.

There was so little he understood.

He hoped Nana would understand better than he could.

Chapter 25

Kath's feet ached, raw from sand and weary from the eternal march. The sun was his respite. As it rose, he stopped.

Nana and Cyrah assembled their shelters as best they could. They were lopsided things, barely able to be considered tents. Nana improved, but Cyrah's struggle continued. She groaned as her sheet fell once again into the sand. The desert was corroding her decorum. As Nana talked her through the tent-making steps, Kath scanned the horizon.

Searching for Rain, for Pashka, for dragons.

Finding nothing.

He turned back to the women. Cyrah had threaded her dress between her legs and tied it about her waist. She knelt on the sand and attempted to balance the poles and the canvas while Nana encouraged her with words too bright and cheery for what her efforts deserved. Cyrah's braid was untangling, and her precious bag sat to the side. For a moment, forgotten.

It moved.

"Cyrah." Kath nudged the thing with his foot. A series of chitters came from within. "Your bag."

The tent tumbled to the sand. Cyrah turned as a white reptilian head emerged. It was tiny, the thing staring up at Kath, far from the fearsome beasts of legend. Brilliant golden eyes latched upon him. Warmth seeped into his chest, as if the gold itself filled the cavity.

The beast lurched forward. Leathery wings flapped in awkward intervals as it stumbled from the bag. Kath stepped back as the reptilian creature approached.

"What have you done?" Cyrah screamed.

"Me?" Kath retorted. He dared not look from the beast to Cyrah. The creature's clawed feet churned the sand, and its tail snaked back and forth over the granules as it persisted toward him. "I didn't do anything!"

He kicked a spray of sand against the beast and it halted. It shook its head and blew sharply out its nostrils. Nana's hands closed about its little body and lifted it from the ground. It squirmed in her hands and squeaked profusely.

"Put it down!" Cyrah snapped.

"This is a dragon?" Nana held it at arm's length. With a great spread of its jaws, the dragon roared and revealed a line of sharp needle-like teeth. A bloom of fire rolled from its belly and dissipated in the air. Nana giggled. "It's cute."

"It's not cute." Cyrah marched to Nana. She extended a hand, but the thing nipped at her fingers, and she drew back. "It's a noble creature."

"It's an abomination," Kathka muttered.

She rounded on him, and he regretted drawing her attention. There was fire in her dark eyes. Fire and fury.

"You are terrible," she hissed. "I should have you killed."

"Killed?"

"You are unworthy, you have no blessing of mine!"

"Unworthy?"

Cyrah pressed her fingers against her temples and inhaled a shaky breath. "A dragon binds to the first person it sees."

"Me?"

"Yes, you!" Her hands flung outward, gestures wild as her voice pitched higher. "You fool! It's bound to you. Without my permission."

"I don't want it."

"I don't want you to have it!"

"Kath." Both gazes swung to Nana. She still held the dragon as it flailed dramatically. "What will you name it?"

"It's not mine."

"It should not be yours!" Cyrah shouted back. "You're no Islander."

"And I want nothing to do with your Islands."

"It needs a name," Nana persisted.

"Then call it b—" Nana's gaze was steady upon him. He faltered and altered the name from obscene to cruel. "Brat."

She looked just as disappointed.

"No." Cyrah's voice was strangled. Hatred grew. "No,

absolutely not."

"If it's mine, I name it Brat."

Her slap stung. His hands balled into fists, but Nana grabbed his wrist. She had released the dragon and it slinked swiftly through the sand, clawed up his pants, and spiraled its way to perch on his shoulder.

It chittered and nudged his cheek with its scaly head.

"You are a terrible person," Cyrah whispered. There were tears in her eyes.

"You shouldn't have brought them down here," Kath growled. The anger still coursed hot in his veins, and the gold filling his chest only provoked him more. He had enough attachments.

Her hands shook, but the dragon was in her way. Tears slipped down her cheeks.

"I had to protect them, I had no choice." She wiped angrily at her eyes. "You've ruined it."

She grabbed her sack, cradling the last egg against her chest, and tugged the canvas back onto the support. It was a badly done shelter, but she did not care. She simply needed to escape him.

Cyrah showed too much of her emotions. It was better for her to stifle it. But as he watched her, he did not feel frustration, just confusion. She sacrificed so much for the eggs, and he did not understand her passion.

The dragon nudged his cheek.

"You won't kill it right?" Nana whispered. She knew the legends, how Scala's Revenge ended with total conquest and the utter destruction of the beasts alongside the untouchable Islanders. She knew he had died seeking to achieve just that.

Kathka let the question remain unanswered.

Chapter 26

A weight pressed on Kath's chest. He blinked his eyes open to the fading light of evening and stared up at the canvas of his shelter. The darkness of fatigue cleared slowly, but the pressure remained. He lifted his head and locked eyes with large golden ones.

The white beast curled on his chest.

It chittered a greeting and lifted its head from its silver claws. There was a pause, then it tilted its head to the side and seemed to wait for something. Kath did not know what for.

Nana chuckled. She sat beneath her shelter across from

him with her knees against her chest and watched the baby dragon.

"It won't leave you," she whispered.

"It should." He sat. The thing tumbled from his chest and landed in a heap between his legs. It writhed in the sand, then, with a beat of its wings and a violent stretch of its legs, it rightened itself. It sat with its head pointed up toward him and continued to wait.

Kathka had no time to babysit the beast. He looked to Cyrah. She sat with her back resolutely against him. Her tent was packed, and she busied herself with discarding the shards of eggshell from her bag. The failing sunlight caught off their jagged edges and the white fragments glistened like glass.

"You're leaving a trail for them."

She flicked another piece onto the sand.

"Do you know what it wants?" he asked. The thing continued to stare.

"Food," she responded curtly. Kath knew it would be the answer, he had wished to avoid it.

He tore his shelter down and folded it into his backpack. Nana followed suit. The dragon slinked around his feet as he worked. He ignored it. With his tent packed, Kath took out his rations. Brat chirped and butted its head against Kath's shin. He grunted in pain. The smooth brow would leave a bruise.

"Go away." Kath jerked his leg up and the beast tumbled forward, head burying in the sand. It perked upright, sand sliding off slick scales. Its head snapped back to him, and it chirped a second time. With a sigh, he tossed a scrap of meat to the beast.

A waste.

Nana sat on the side of the dune and ate her dried apple as she watched the dragon tear at the tough strip. With both woman and dragon preoccupied, Kath took the moment of solitude to plot their survival.

They had camped beside the slope of a dune that rolled steeply up. All around them the sand swept in a great current. It was difficult to see far through the waves of sand, but it was a waste of energy to climb a taller dune for a clear vantage point. He relied on the stars to lead him forward to where the sand tumbled against mountains, solid ones that did not shift places.

There they would find the Wise One.

Cyrah remained cross-legged with her back to him, head tilted back to stare up at the blackening sky.

"Did you eat?"

Her back straightened, and in pointed, crisp words, she answered, "I ate the fruit."

"And the meat?"

"I gave it to the dragon."

"You need it."

"What I need is not your concern." She folded her hands on top of the bag in her lap. "I will worry about myself."

"You'll die," Kath said. "Then who will take care of the dragon?"

To that, she had no answer. She gathered her hair over one shoulder and began to braid.

Kath grabbed his rations from his pack and took a single strip of meat. The dragon chirped at the sight of it, but it had already eaten more than its share, and at the expense of the one he needed to save. The one who refused to look at him.

"Still want to have me killed?" he asked, offering her the meat. He was sure she would take his bait, and she did.

"I can't," Cyrah muttered. "The dragon would be rogue."

"Rogue?"

"Rogue," she repeated with a nasty snap. "A dragon only binds with one person. Without you, what would that leave your dragon? Uncontrolled, uncontrollable."

At his feet, the dragon sat with its tail curled about itself, and its muzzle pointed straight at the meat in his hand. It was so small now, but he had seen the outlines of dragons in the sky. He had seen the dark shadows they cast over the earth and felt the hollowness in his stomach.

Why the gods had given the dragons to the Islanders and left the desert so vulnerable, Kath could not fathom.

Cyrah had reason to fear.

"Eat." He dropped the strip of meat into her lap. "Then get up, we're leaving."

Her anger followed him as he tucked the rations into his pack then hefted it onto his back. Her bitterness wrapped around him, sharp like thorns. He tried to convince himself that it was her fault, not his.

Still, he felt the sting.

"Let's go."

He followed the pinpoint of the Central Star. The dragon struggled to keep pace beside him, each step down buried its claws deep into the sand. It fell behind.

"You should apologize," Nana said as she stepped into the place the dragon had occupied.

"What for?" he muttered. "I did nothing wrong."

It still stung.

"Sometimes saying sorry doesn't mean you did something wrong." Her hand skimmed against his. "It means you understand the pain."

Acrius would have disagreed. Rage and revenge were all — anything else, a weakness.

Kath halted. The dragon took the opportunity to plow through the sand and twine up his body to perch on his shoulder. He turned and stomped back to where Cyrah still sat, meat untouched on her lap.

"I'm sorry."

She looked up at him.

"I'm sorry the egg broke, and that this one hatched."

Cyrah kept a tight protective hold around the egg in her arms as she stood. She struggled to swing her pack onto her back as she juggled the egg and the strip of meat. It would have been easier to set it down, but she did not.

Kath stood still, not sure if he expected another glance, or words, or any acknowledgment at all. Cyrah offered the meat to the dragon on his shoulder who greedily accepted. She passed Kath without responding.

Kath released his bated breath, but the sting remained.

"That didn't do anything," Kath grumbled to Nana as he passed her to follow after Cyrah.

"Maybe not for her." She shrugged and kept at his side. "But perhaps for you."

He bit his tongue. Words pooled in his mouth, and he blamed the night. With the darkness and obscurity, with the gemstones in the heavens, and the infinite expanses. Their travels were disassociated with the reality of life. It was a dreamlike state where it felt natural to protect rather than destroy. He could almost believe they would always be there, in the desert, marching endlessly in the night.

Three wanderers, escaping a brutal reality.

"I'm sorry," he said. "For hurting you. In the cave."

He quickened his pace to pass Cyrah and reclaim the lead. But he had seen it. Her soft, sad smile.

Chapter 27

Their voices carried behind him. Snippets of conversation floated across the distance between them. He did not care that Cyrah did not like fruit, or that her favorite flowers were lilies. But she faced the brunt of Nana's endless questions, and he let the incessant noise continue as long as it protected him.

But he could not avoid her forever.

"Kath!" He cringed at the call, at the sound of her voice directed once more to him. The dragon on his shoulder twisted back to look at the woman. "The sun is rising."

Ahead of him, the light of dawn tinged the sky and the

brilliant glow of the Central Star faded to nothing.

Kath did not slow his pace.

If he slowed that would mean a reprieve from the monotony of walking. It would mean sleep, darkness, and silence. It would mean that the emotions barely submerged would have an opportunity to pierce his consciousness and demand release. He tried to think of snapping bones. Even the memory of a broken arm couldn't force the emotions back.

The dragon turned its gaze back to him, as if it too waited for his response.

"We'll keep walking," he called back. "Cyrah was kind enough to leave them a trail, I want to put more distance between us."

It was an excuse to keep walking. Cyrah scoffed.

"Your pursuers must be very adept if they can find us from that."

"Oh, Rain's very good!" Nana agreed enthusiastically. There was even a note of admiration.

"Certainly better than your pursuers." Kathka flicked the dragon's snout, it puffed out a breath and shook its head. Kath shook his hand, finger smarting. The scales were tough. "We haven't even seen signs of them."

"Maybe I'm just better at outwitting them," Cyrah retaliated. "Perhaps I am better without you, Wayfinder."

Kath stopped and turned. Behind the two women, a sliver of yellow peeked over the gray dunes. It continued to rise. Nana's lips were quirked in a smile, and a smaller one curled Cyrah's.

They both knew it was a ridiculous statement.

A slight smile perked Kath's lips. When Cyrah looked at

him, it was not with loathing. Though there was space between them, it was not sharp. The stinging had eased.

They had stopped in a valley between two hills of sand, it would offer protection from searching eyes, a good place to rest for the day. He heaved a sigh.

"Fine, we stop here."

Their sacks thudded to the ground as soon as the words left his lips. They did not even question his sudden change of mind. Nana rolled her shoulders and twisted her neck. Cyrah knelt to settle her sack carefully upon the soft ground and peered inside to ensure no harm had come to the singular egg.

"This is lovely!" Nana sighed as she raised her fingertips toward the few remaining constellations.

"Just get your shelter around." Kath grabbed Brat from his shoulder and set it on the sand. His shoulder was stiff after a day of carrying its weight. It chittered at him and curled its sleek tail about its body and watched him. Waiting, as always.

Nana sat on the sand and pulled out her tin of rations. Brat slunk to her side. Kath took advantage of the dragon's absence to eat and avoid sacrificing his own rations to its pathetic gaze.

Cyrah did not eat. Instead, she pulled the canvas tent from her sack.

"Have you eaten?"

"No," she said simply and shoved a stake into the sand.

"Why?" Kath asked. She stiffened at his low voice.

"I am not hungry."

"Doesn't matter," he said. "You have to stay alive."

Her silence unnerved him. He set aside his rations and

marched across the sand to where Cyrah propped up her tent. She made no objection when he snatched up her backpack and turned it upside down. The tins lodged into the sand. He grabbed one and flipped it open. Empty.

"The dragon." His voice was strangled, he spoke as evenly as he was able. "The dragon ate it. All."

"Dragons eat," Cyrah defended. She abandoned the tent and drew the last egg close to her. "A lot. She's a newborn, she needs nutrition to keep up with her rapid growth."

"She? Well, she just killed you."

Cyrah glared at him. The caustic words corroded the shaky trust that had begun to build between them. He regretted it but did not know how to undo it.

"You would rather her die?" Cyrah asked.

"I'm trying to save you!"

"I never asked you to," she snapped. The anger reignited, the apology of the previous day so easily crumbling to meaninglessness. Kathka's hand balled into a fist around the empty backpack.

"We can get more food," Nana assured as she slipped between the two. There was solace in her gaze, a calm in their depths, but he refused it.

"How?" he demanded.

"There are oases on the western edge of the canyon," she said as if it were simple to turn back. "We have extra money from the truck, I'll get us food."

"Even if we could, then what? We'll still have the beast, and we can't feed it."

"Then what do you suggest?" Cyrah scrambled to her feet behind Nana, egg clutched in her arms. Any answer sounded wrong. Any words would cut like shards of glass.

Their gazes were upon him. Questioning, hoping, fearing. Brat curled between his legs and stretched upward, claws catching on his pants, mouth opened as it awaited more food.

He just needed to save them.

"We kill it if necessary." It was the wrong response.

"Kath," Nana chided.

"The dragon or your life." He pointed at Cyrah. "You choose. Or did you bring them down here to die with you?"

"Kath!" Nana stepped back from him. "Why are you doing this?"

Their hatred justified his anger, which was easier than the desperation suffocating him. Their hatred was easier than their trust because he did not know how to save them, especially not now. But he could not admit that.

It was easier to crack a bone than to heal it.

"Didn't the dead tell you?" he asked even though Cyrah listened. He wanted to justify his anger, to see her hate. Nana's eyes danced over his face. His heartbeat pounded loud in his ears. Her lips parted, and he wished she would not speak, though he had forced the words from her.

"The dead," she repeated. "They always, always, always seethe about how you murdered them. So many, for nothing but rage. Zalna speaks often. Why don't you want me to mention her?"

The adrenaline of the fury vanished. Her eyes were dark and stormy, wet as if it had just rained. He knew then that he had underestimated her.

"Because she was your wife? Because she betrayed you?"

"Stop speaking."

"Or because you killed her?"

He grabbed her forearm. The heat seeped into his body. Blackness swirled around him and the words choked him. He thought of the cave and did not know what he had intended to do next. It felt foolish.

She looked sad and tired.

"Is that why you don't want to trust us?" Nana whispered. "Because you couldn't trust even her?"

Cyrah shouted something.

Thunder rolled and sand exploded near his feet and sprayed against his shins. He reeled backward, hand slipping from her skin. The heat disappeared and the desert snapped back to focus. Red sand and gray sky and an approaching rider.

"They found us." Fear strangled Cyrah's voice.

A horse careened down the dune. More riders crested the sand and descended in its wake. The lead rider neared. Sunlight glinted off the metal weapon in his hand.

Pashka.

Chapter 28

Cyrah ignored Brat's squeaks of protest as she wrenched her from Kath's leg and shoved her into the bag beside her unborn sibling.

"They can't take them." She thrust the bag into Kath's arms. He grabbed it, but she did not let go. "Don't let them."

The five riders circled like vultures. Black hooves thudded into the ground and sprayed sand. Their circle tightened around the three fugitives. A rider broke from the others and reined in his horse to a restless prancing. He grabbed Cyrah's braid and yanked her backward. She screamed. Pashka laughed.

"What's this?" He reined his mount to a halt in front of Kath and leaned forward in the saddle, a sneer smeared across his lips. His hair was twisted in yet another style, partly braided and partly loose and that was enough to set the anger burning in Kathka's stomach. "Runaway prisoners? What a find."

"I didn't expect to see you again, Lord." Kath dropped the bag between his feet. He willed the dragon to be still. He tried to focus on the golden warmth in his chest. If they had a bond like Cyrah said, he hoped she understood his plea.

Be still.

"I don't let my prisoners go so easily." Silver winked as Pashka leveled the gun at Kath. In its reflection his body contorted and he saw blood in the alley, Mell's lifeless form. "Especially ones so lucrative."

Thunder clapped and a burst of sharp pain struck his shoulder as metal grazed past and exploded into the sand behind him. His lungs caught in the flash of heat. He could not breathe.

Be still.

"Though," Pashka lowered the gun, "it seems I've received interest."

A rider dismounted and grabbed Cyrah's wrists as she clawed at the man clutching her hair. She struggled against his hold, but she was so small. Weak.

"Unhand me!" she cried, voice strengthened with the anger of her broken dignity. Her braid was utterly undone.

"Am I wrong in thinking this lady is an Islander?" Pashka asked, voice laced with twisted delight. He did not need an answer to know he was right. Her elegant dress, the dragons curling around the hem. "Take them both."

Cyrah resisted as Pashka's man forced her hands behind her back and tied them. Nana, however, complied. She had learned to save the struggle for escape.

"But you." Pashka dismounted and approached Kath. "I have something special for you."

The fourth rider forced Kath's hands behind his back and tied the rope tightly around his wrists. The movement inflamed his grazed shoulder with fresh pain. With a swift kick to the back of Kath's knee, the rider forced him to kneel and crossed his feet to tie them.

Pashka kept a constant gaze upon his prey and smiled with cruel pleasure. He stepped near and pressed his gloved thumb against the torn flesh. Stripes of blood grew thick down the coat.

"Does it hurt?"

"I've had worse."

Pashka lifted the pressure and stepped back. He laughed as he slipped the gun back into its place on his belt and unsheathed instead a dagger.

"That deserves punishment."

The blade sunk into Kath's thigh. Only when Pashka's fingers slipped away from the hilt did the pain come. Hot white pain. He bit his cheek hard, but it was insufficient to smother the hiss it forced from him.

"That will keep you here," Kath faintly heard Pashka's almost gentle words. The lord stood before him, but he seemed so far away. So unimportant. "Don't worry, Rain is close behind, he'll retrieve you."

Pashka shoved him backward. He hit the sand, and the breath left his lungs. Fiery pain swelled and black dots burst across his vision. He stared up at the sky and thought of fat droplets of red seeping into sand. A fine drink for a parched land.

A drink he had offered once before.

Pashka shouted orders to his men. Cyrah screamed again. The flurry of activity around him was dizzying. He focused intently upon the blue above to keep his consciousness from the black.

Be still.

Gradually, the pounding hooves grew distant and Pashka and his men stole two lives from him. Two lives he was supposed to save.

He had been no savior in his previous life, and he had died on the desert floor.

He would be no savior in this life.

Chapter 29

The heat intensified as the sun rose. Sweat slipped across his skin and soaked his clothes. The wind swept granules of sand and tumbled them against each other. The melodic sound whispered for him to sleep, to rest. But he could not. He feared the darkness, that this time he truly would not awaken. Kath was almost relieved when the roar of an approaching car broke the lull.

The sound grew louder, until, with a great groan and a sputtering pop, it ceased. His vision flickered and when it returned a figure hovered at his side, clothed completely in gray. Rain with his solemn scowl.

Amidst the pain, Kathka felt the tug on his soul. The undeniable confirmation.

"Still alive?"

Kathka grit his teeth and laughed. "Barely."

"The violence was unnecessary," Rain sighed and shook his head. He knelt beside Kath and lifted the fabric the knife had pierced. "But you'll live."

Rain grabbed Kath's shoulder and forced him to sit. Kath dug his heels into the earth as his stomach rolled. He forgot about the bag. It tipped, fell, and the egg rolled from within and lay like a gem upon the sand.

The strange object reflected in Rain's dark eyes. His fingers spread out to touch it.

Brat slithered from the bag and perched atop the egg. She hissed and bared her teeth. Rain snatched back his hand.

"What—" he began, but the words died upon his lips. There was a shout and a thud from behind, and in his distracted state, Rain reacted too slowly. A strategic blow was placed to the back of his head. In a heap, the man collapsed before Brat.

"Severely underestimated," Red muttered as he flexed his fingers.

The dragon puffed her chest heroically as if she had done anything.

"Idiot," Kath muttered.

"Hold on." Red circled Rain's unconscious body and tugged the key ring from his belt. Red deftly unlocked his chained hands while fixing a wary gaze upon the dragon.

Kath did not trust Red.

Red dropped the shackles to the sand then turned his attention from the beast to the knotted rope around Kath's wrists.

"What are you doing?" It seemed to Kath the most obvious question to ask. He could not offer much else in his state.

"Making good on that promise," Red replied as he knelt. Kath focused on making sense of his words. "For a second time."

"Didn't I tell you not to save me?"

"Good thing I didn't listen." Red unbound Kath's wrists then moved down to untie his feet. "You'd be dead twice now."

"What do you want from me?" Kath demanded.

"I want to get you some medical attention. You need it." Red finished with the knot and pulled free the rope. He stretched it taut then moved back to the unconscious body. With his foot, he flipped Rain to his stomach and knelt to tie him as Kath had been. Though his body was gaunt, his movements were precise and forceful. "I'm taking you to our leader."

"Leader?"

"Someone who will heal you."

Kath did not trust Red, and he did not trust this leader. But he could not argue when his body was damaged and death was his other option. When Red finished securing Rain, he returned to grab Kath's arm and pulled him to his feet.

The world dipped strangely as Kath stood. He clamped his left hand to his injured leg, but the pressure sparked more pain. Brat spiraled up his body to perch on his shoulder. She was heavy, but it was a comforting weight. She hissed at Red.

Red leaned back to widen his distance from the dragon, though his palm remained lightly against Kath's elbow. Kath wobbled without the support, but he stubbornly refused to sink back to the earth.

"Stop staring or she'll bite you."

Kath relinquished his hold on his injured leg. He waited a moment for the pulsing pain to subside, then, with jerky movements, scooped the egg from the sand. He cradled it carefully in his arm, like Cyrah had.

"Can you make it to the truck?" Red asked. Kath looked at the metal thing and the two guards slumped beside it, then down at the egg. It had felt cold to the touch at first, but the longer he held it the more he noticed the heat emanating from inside. "I don't want to remove the knife yet, can you walk?"

Kath nodded. He took slow, painful steps forward. Upon the undulating sand, each step landed heavily and uneasily. Red firmed his hold around Kath's forearm and offered the grounding Kath needed to lift himself onto the metal monstrosity.

Kath collapsed on the back of the truck, breaths heavy, frustration searing. Brat curled on top of the egg tucked in the crook of his arm, and her presence gave him some solace. Red left his side, and he was glad for it. The man's presence was intolerable. When he returned, dragging Rain's body, Kath had formed his words of resistance.

"I don't trust you."

It was the best his pain-addled brain could manage.

"You don't have another option," Red grunted as he pulled Rain up beside Kath. He left the other guards unconscious on the sand. Red's chest heaved from the exertion, and he sat for a moment to catch his breath. But only for a moment. With the metal cuff that had been around his own wrists, Red snapped one around Rain's wrist and the other around a bar on the side of the truck to ensure the man could not even consider escape whenever he came to.

Red would not underestimate Rain.

"Soon enough Pashka will wonder what happened to Rain. He will return and if I don't help you, when he returns you'll be turned over to the Bu Chak. Do you trust them?"

Red clambered to the front of the truck. The metal beast roared, and its frame shivered and sent vibrating pain through Kath's body.

"Rest," Red called back over the noise. "I'll protect you, trust me."

Kathka did not. The truck lurched forward, and they set off, toward the leader and whoever had tattooed a fake curse across Red's chest.

Chapter 30

The sky was an unchanging force of heat. It shimmered, and Kath was certain he could see the red and yellow waves of heat passing through the air. He followed the currents lazily with his eyes until his vision flickered, and he was lost in the black world, exhaustion and pain forcing him to succumb to slumber.

A detached soul.

A soul cursed for eternity for attempting to kill the last god.

He wondered if he would be one of the souls bound to haunt Nana. Then the truck beneath him would lurch and shards of pain brought him back to the hot earth. He was not dead. Not yet. But he was dying. Again. Or at least, he thought he must be.

Red said something. It might have been a response to a question, one he had posed. But Kath could not remember. He strained to hear but only caught mention of Nana.

Pashka had her. And Cyrah.

Two people he was supposed to save, lost.

The sun burned. He shut his eyes once again and saw her lips curl into a smile. His chest constricted, and it was hard to breathe. There was a pulsing in his leg. He ignored it as he studied her face and tried to anticipate what her next words would be.

But this was just a memory.

He already knew what Zalna would say. She would suggest disassembling the Wayfinders, creating something more. He would do it.

Another jolt over the sand. Kath's eyes snapped open, and he vomited on the bed of the truck. His stomach rolled a second time, but he had nothing more for it to empty. He lay back down and pressed his palm flat against the smooth egg. It felt cool against his hot body.

Then his eyes shut, and the black came again. The past and the present were fluid things. He saw Nana's smile, Zalna's tears, innocent blood on his hands, Mell's blood in the dirt, armies at his command, the Wise One's blade, all jumbled images of his life. Of his two lives.

A white muzzle explored his slack features. The touch roused him from the black and solidified the world around him. She was real, she was in the moment, the small baby dragon.

Brat growled, as hands caged her wings and lifted her from him. More hands grabbed him and forced him to sit. The world swirled. There was Red, then Rain, then a camel and men he did not recognize.

Brat writhed in the grip. She snapped her small jaws and spit a ball of flame. There was a shout and the hands released from around her body. She flapped unevenly in the air, she was too far away and too young to fly. She landed heavily on his leg, talons pressing below where the dagger was still lodged. Bile rose in his throat.

All eyes stared at him. At the dragon.

The pain brought darkness crashing down upon him.

Chapter 31

Sunlight illuminated the canvas in a warm yellow haze. Kath stared at the material as his vision flickered from light to the darkness that terrified him. With time, the world grew concrete, and he understood that he was alive.

A heat resided in his calf, a dull ache that flared whenever he shifted. His fingers found the bandage beneath the loose cotton pants. Pain sliced a clear temporal line in his consciousness. An excruciating reminder that they were gone. That he had failed.

He slid his eyes down from the peak of the tent to the floor. A woven rug of deep blue and orange stretched across the ground. Sand spilled in where the canvas met the rug. It had a way of getting everywhere. He found no entryway, so he twisted his head to the other side and found a heap of white scales.

The dragon.

He placed his palm on the cool white. Brat's head popped up. She curled her neck back to sniff his face with hot breath that smelled like burning wood. She chirped a greeting.

"Hey," he rasped through his parched throat. The pads of his fingers shifted over the grooves of her scales and wandered over the knit of her armor. She was larger than before, the size of a hunting dog. He was uncertain how much time had passed.

He slipped his hand from her flank to the cot to steady himself as he sat. Bile rose. He swallowed heavily to ignore it and swung his feet down to rest on the rug.

He was sure he would vomit.

Brat sat between him and the tent entrance. The flap was pinned shut, sunlight seeping around its edges. Inside the tent, the filtered light and encompassing warmth made time sluggish. But from outside, sound trickled in, the murmur of voices in conversation punctuated by a shout of instruction and the whinny of a horse.

Time had not stood still.

Ignoring the queasiness in the pit of his stomach, Kath stood. He stepped unsteadily toward the flap. Brat remained close at his heels. She pressed her snout against his palm, breath blooming against his bare skin.

They stood before the entrance. Still and silent. Kath listened to the voices, but he could not piece together who they were who had sheltered him, bandaged him, clothed him. The only way to find out was to confront them, so he slipped the wooden pins from the loops of the cloth and pushed the flap aside.

Sunlight flooded the tent. He reflexively lifted his hand to shield his eyes. Bright white faded to reds and tans. Blinking away the burning, Kath lowered his hand to survey the camp.

There were about fifteen canvas tents dotting the sand, all gathered in a circle around a fire pit where the embers from the previous night's fire still smoldered. Shade screens were assembled a few feet from the heat. Beneath the stretched canvas sheets sat the camp dwellers, cross-legged and lounging upon rugs beside low tables. Kath estimated around fifty in the camp center. Under the nearest shade screen, the residents crowded around a large black box set upon the table emitting garbled speech. The camp members passed occasional remarks and dried fruit as they listened to the box.

Red sat there. He sat angled away from Kath, elbows rested on the table, and chin cupped in his palm as he listened intently.

Brat growled.

A few eyes turned. Then more. Red's hand dropped, and he turned to see what had captured everyone's attention.

Kath felt exposed.

"What are you doing?" Red rose and strode swiftly across the sand. He grabbed Kath's arm. "Back inside."

Kath stumbled backward into the tent. Brat slipped between the two men and growled as Red entered.

"You should be resting." Red slipped the pins back into place then turned to Kath with his arms folded across his chest. "Lying down."

"I don't think so," Kathka laughed but sat down on the cot. The world swirled and his calf burned. "I don't take orders from you."

"So I see."

"Where's the egg?" Kath demanded.

"Patience." Red glanced at Brat who kept her golden gaze intently upon him. "Rest, get your strength back. I'll get you some water and food."

"I want answers."

"You'll get them," he assured.

"Now."

Red heaved a sigh. "I'll get Tai, he'll explain."

"Who?"

"The leader."

Kath wound his fingers around the metal frame of the cot tightly and tapped the foot of his injured leg. He needed the pain to focus him.

"Stay here." Red jabbed his finger at the cot and slipped out of the tent. The breath left Kath's lungs in a rush and his rigid back folded. He rested his elbow against the kneecap of his good leg, and he contemplated the intricate design of the rug to stay back the nausea. The pain had failed him. It only made his wounded body weaker. White scales slinked into the edge of his vision. Brat rumbled low in the back of her throat, like an overly large cat.

"Why am I stuck with you?" he sighed.

"Strange words for a dragon."

Kath straightened, though the pain still pulsed. An older man stood in the entry, braided hair gray with age but back ramrod straight with the persistence of a strong soul. He crossed his hands behind his back and stood in attentive silence as he waited for a response. The overwhelming knowledge that this man was the fourth life rolled over him.

But there was something unsettling in the keen gaze fixed upon him.

"Just a dragon," Kath muttered.

"Just a dragon, quite." The man shook his head, mirth upturning the corners of his lips. He chuckled as he slipped a hand from behind his back and rubbed his trimmed beard. "Dragons are often considered more than a simple 'just'."

Kath curled his hands into fists. The pain pricked, but it did not focus his mind. He thought of Nana. Of her pained eyes. Gently, he eased his hands flat against the cot and took a steadying breath.

"You're Tai?" Kath tried to keep his voice calm.

"That is what most people here call me, yes."

"Then you have answers."

"Everything will be explained in the proper time, do not worry about that." His hand returned to clasp the one still held behind his back. He spoke with a rhythmic cadence, smooth and easy. Too slow for the unease twisting in Kathka's chest. "First, let me check your wound."

"It's fine."

"Contrary. You were stabbed, you're fortunate the damage was minimal."

"Not fortunate," Kath muttered. "Pashka is calculated."

"An accurate observation. No lord would intentionally damage the Bu Chak's prize."

The observation felt like a barb and lodged deep, coloring Kathka's mind red.

"Answers," he hissed.

"You are not very patient." Tai moved along the edge of the tent to a chest. Kathka kept a cautious gaze upon the older man as he lifted the lid and rummaged through it. "For patients, patience is key."

The lid banged shut and, with items in hand, Tai turned to Kath. A wide smile spread across his face, amused at his wordplay. Kathka glared.

"Where's the egg?"

"It is safe." Tai moved back to the cot. His smile had fallen, but the wrinkles of frequent laughter remained prominent around the corners of his eyes and lips. His eyes were too soft, and Kath was uncomfortable with their regard. Tai tapped his hand on a chest at the end of the cot. "We placed it here. If you have any other requests, we would be pleased to oblige as best we can."

Kath had no request. He knew as little about dragon care as they did. Cyrah knew, but she was gone. In her absence, he felt an obligation to look after it. He was not charged to protect it, but he was charged to save her, and he knew how she had cried over the shattered egg.

"May I?" Tai asked, extending his hands to show the fresh bandages and two medicinal containers.

Kath nodded. Brat responded to the grudging acceptance within him and shifted backward, though she remained tall and imposing at Kath's side. Tai did not appear perturbed by her presence. He knelt beside the cot and set his supplies on the twisted sheet. Wrinkled hands passed gingerly over Kath's shoulder and unwound the bandages there. Kath had nearly forgotten that wound. A small taste of what Mell had suffered.

He looked away.

Tai changed the bandage quickly, then moved down to the second wound.

"May I?" Tai asked again. Kath gave a single nod. Tai pulled the loose pants up to reveal the tightly wound bandages. He unwound the bindings to reveal the carnage beneath. Sickly purple flesh encircled the red gouge. The wound was grotesque, but it was cleaned and stitched while he was unconscious. It was grotesque, but it would not kill him.

Tai discarded the old bandages on the rug then took one of the medicinal jars and opened it. Its scent was heavy and cleared the pain that flooded Kath. Tai waited as Kath caught his breath. Once he did, Tai dabbed his fingers into the paste and smeared it across the wound.

"I am the leader here," he explained as he worked. It forced Kath to concentrate on his words instead of the pain. "We call our camp Haven. We are not so much a resistance group as an assembly of refugees. We take in many harmed by the Bu Chak. Do you know much about them?"

Kath hissed out a no. It was simpler than explaining the scraps of information he had cobbled together.

"They are a religious cult. After the collapse of the kingdom of the Blood King, they convinced many people that what our land needed was to overturn the curses upon us."

The marks of the curse looped across Kath's chest, and Tai glanced briefly over to them. But he continued with his care, and continued with his tale.

"The Blood King had ruled through ignoring the old legends, but that failed. They claimed he failed because of the curses. They say that to thrive our people must remove the curses of the gods. They promised that they could undo those curses, and upon that promise they gained power. They rule this land, through fear and hope."

"Hope?"

"Hope." The lid clinked on top of the jar. Tai set it aside and picked up the clean bandages. "Lift your leg."

Kath obeyed. He trained his eyes to the peak of the tent and tried to swallow down the bile.

"They believe," Tai continued, "that if they destroy the last god, they will make themselves god. They believe that by destroying the curse they are eradicating the last stronghold of the gods' power in this land. Their singular aim is to kill the Wise One and those who bear the curses."

"Nana," Kath said.

"Their ultimate quarry, the bearer of Scala's curse. We have attempted to free her many times, but she's a flighty one." Tai chuckled. "Red was sent to—"

"Why'd he let her go?"

The old man pinned the end of the bandage in place and sat back on his heels. "If you let me speak, I would explain. Isn't that what you want?"

Kath lowered his leg and touched the clean linen. Brat sniffed the bandages. He flicked her muzzle. "Continue."

"They want Red, they believe he is cursed though you may know that he is not. We tattooed him, to get him to where Nana was. To free her. They wish to kill her, but such death is the very reason why the gods cursed our people."

Kath did not care to hear more about the ancient legends. They complicated simple matters. But he remained silent and waited for the next words and the information that would make sense of Tai's stories.

"When you intervened, unfortunately, a decision had to be made. Red chose to save you and the dragon."

"But there are two others, Cyrah and Nana. What about them?" His words were strained in a mix of pain, nausea, and anger. "If you know that Nana is Scala's descendant, if they know, why would you let them take her?"

"There is still time to save her." Tai gathered the old bandages and one of the medicine jars and stood. As he spoke, he moved back to the chest to replace the medical supplies. "They believe that she must be killed on the same day that Scala was cursed. The first day of our calendar."

He closed the chest and turned to face Kath.

"We simply intervene before then to save her."

Kath had no response. Tai knew so much, Kath so little. The curses, the gods, the legends of long ago, everything was jumbled together and everything groaned for peace. For solace. For rest.

Kath felt exhausted.

Tai pointed to the jar still on the sheet. "Use that for your skin, it will soothe the burns."

"Why?" Kath did not look at the jar but kept his gaze trained on Tai. "Why did he decide to save me?"

"We know how to save Nana," Tai replied. "We don't know what they would do to you or your dragon. A cursed Islander? It's never been heard of."

Kathka frowned. The logic was infuriatingly sound.

"I will save Nana," he said to make clear his intentions to the leader of the group he now found himself among.

Tai's eyes flickered to the beast at the bedside, then back to the angry man.

"We could use your dragon."

Chapter 32

Kath lay on the cot with one leg propped against the side and the other dangling off. He stared at the canvas ceiling and listened to the din outside.

They ignored him.

Tai had left him to rest in solitude with the dragon for company. Only Red visited. Kath preferred him over Tai.

The first time Red visited was just after Tai left, and he brought a loose shirt which Kath took, glad to be rid of Pashka's garish green tunic. It brought him at least a small measure of solace.

After that visit, Red brought only water and food. Soup,

flatbread, and dried fruit. He would stay long enough to ensure Kath ate it all.

Between his visits, Kath was left with his thoughts to plague him. He refused to think about Nana and Cyrah. He could not. It brought too much weakness, with thoughts of loss and failure and Mell. So instead, he occupied himself with the twisted legends.

He had been told the tales on long night watches around the fire after Acrius had tired of playing Crowns. The myths, embellished with fanciful details, were spoken in haunting words to scare the young recruits. He had not cared then to discern what was crafted and what was true. Then it made no difference. Knowing the truth would not have saved him from a swift death as a Wayfinder.

Now it obsessed him. Two of the lives he was bound to save faced death because of those tales. So he told himself the stories again, and again, and again. He stripped down the legends to their cores and compared all that he knew to all that Tai had told him.

The gods had charged Caizin to rule the mortal world, that was how all the lore started. But Scala murdered Caizin. The reason why changed depending on the teller. Some painted him as good and others evil. Kath had no opinion. All he knew was that Scala had committed the crime and the gods had cursed him. Caizin's faithful were raised, Scala and his zealots brought low. That was the fable, though no tale could account for why the gods abandoned them.

Kath had ignored the myths during his rule. It was Zalna who had listened attentively to Acrius. She had hung on each word that promised true conquest. True freedom.

At that time, the myth went that to release the curse, the

god had to be killed. Now the cursed were placed on the death list, and the prize was to become a god.

Kath did not know which myth was true. He doubted either one was. All he knew was they all knew nothing at all. That was what he learned after he had been killed by a god.

The god of wisdom was the only god their world had left, and he had a plan.

Kath just didn't know what it was.

Red entered the tent at his usual time, at noonday, just as the sun crested the peak of the tent to begin its descent. He pushed open the tent flap with his shoulder as he balanced a tray of food in his hands. He looked less like a prisoner each day and more like the warrior he was trained to be. The camp's food filled out Red's lean muscles, made him more dangerous.

"Here." Red set the tray atop Kath's chest. Brat's white muzzle appeared at the edge of Kath's vision. Her nostrils flared as she inhaled the rich scent of meat. "To perk your mood."

"Leaving here would be better."

"You need rest." Red moved back to the entrance of the tent, to widen the distance between man and beast. "How's your leg?"

"Fine," he grumbled. It was not wholly a lie. Compared to the first morning the pain had settled into a manageable throb and his blistered skin was healing with the help of the soothing salve. There were fewer instances of the bile rising in his throat.

"Give it time."

"It's been three days."

"And you're healing." Red's gaze slipped over Brat's sleek

body. "When we're ready to move, we will."

"If we know where they are, we should move now."

"It's best to be fully prepared for our strike. We have time, we know when the sacrifice will be held."

Kath lifted the tray with one hand and sat. He placed the tray between his legs, too forcefully. Soup sloshed over the edge of the bowl and he stared at the spilled broth as dull pain pulsed in his calf. The pangs abated slowly and his appetite returned.

He hated their food. Hated knowing he was dependent on a group he did not trust.

Brat's head moved along with the tray. She sniffed at the soup then turned pleading golden orbs up to him. They gave her the scraps of meat leftover from butchered goats, but still, she pleaded for more. Insatiable. She had grown to the size of a foal and filled much of the tent.

"But the Island woman, Cyrah." Kath dipped the spoon into the soup and fished out a hunk of meat for Brat. "We don't know what they'll do to her."

No one knew, but they were so focused on the Daughter of Scala that they forgot that another had been taken. Kath remembered.

"What about Rain?" Kath found another piece of meat and lifted it for Brat. Her forked tongue slithered out between pointed teeth and slipped the chunk into her mouth. Red watched, and after she swallowed, he responded.

"What about him?"

Kath shrugged. He could not tell Red that he was afraid they would kill the captive. Rain did not matter, but he could not die. As much as he was loath to admit it, Kath had found his fifth life. But he buried the knowledge. Buried it beneath the memory of the silver gun and the fatal bullet.

"Maybe he would know what they'll do to her," Kath said to cover the question and avoid Red's suspicions.

"We are preparing as best we can," Red assured, but it was a distraction from the truth that their plans were not focused on Cyrah.

"Do you hate the Islanders?" Kath asked. If Red was going to remain as long as it took him to eat, they might as well converse. The more information he could get the better.

Red's brow furrowed. "No."

"Really? I do." Kath exchanged the spoon for the flatbread. He dipped it into the soup. As it soaked, he continued, "Scala tried to claim authority and he was cursed. Why do they get blessings from that, what did they do to deserve that?"

"Scala was arrogant." Red's words were carefully measured, eyes narrowed as he gauged the reaction of the Islander and his dragon. "Pride and lust for power brought us here, we cannot make the same mistakes."

"Like the Bu Chak are doing?" Kath stuffed his mouth with the soggy flatbread.

"Exactly."

"So," Kath paused to finish chewing, "why are you doing this?"

"Feeding you?"

"Tattooing yourself, endangering yourself. What does it matter to you?"

"I'm not afraid to die," he said. Kath did not believe him. All Kathka's past was hinged on avoiding death. He quirked an eyebrow and Red added, "Some things are worth dying for."

"Avoiding the past?"

"Creating a better future," Red corrected, though Kath did not see the difference. "I know you are skeptical of him, but Taitos has a great vision."

"Taitos," Kath repeated.

"The Bu Chak will only worsen our situation by bringing more death, but he wants peace. To bring understanding and cooperation."

"Taitos," Kath said a second time because Red had misunderstood. "That is his name."

"Yes."

"Like the Blood King's Chief General?"

"You know our history?" Red questioned, but Kathka did not care what suspicions he raised.

"Like the Chief General?" Kath repeated, demanded, needed to know.

"Yes, like the Chief General," Red confirmed. "Tai is his descendant, and he fell under the Chief General's same folly. Tai was part of the Bu Chak, desiring to overthrow the curse and conquer the world, just like his ancestors. Such arrogance did not end well for either."

"I know," Kathka interrupted, to silence Red. "I know what happened to Taitos."

The clipped words brought heavy silence. Thick and dark. There was no room for further talk, Kathka made sure of that. Red stood stiffly at the tent entrance and watched the foreigner with a narrowed gaze. Brat nudged Kathka's hand, imploring for more meat. He swatted her away.

"I'll get more meat for the dragon." Red excused himself. But he would return.

Kath stared down at his reflection in the discolored

water. The hair grew longer, thickened in coils around foreign features. He slipped his fingers through the hair, but they were not his hands. His hands were not thin and fragile. They were calloused hands dripping with the blood of his General Chief and his wife.

He thought of shattered glass across the floor.

"Traitors," he whispered, to remind himself. But the words felt hollow, and the hurt remained.

Chapter 33

The egg was hidden beneath a deep green blanket and nestled in a cocoon of sky blue wool with teal tassels. Amid such color, it sat in the wooden crate in stark contrast. So simple, so precious. Safe and secure.

Kath looked at it often, to assure himself that it was safe. He cupped his hand around the small object and held it until he felt the pulse of warmth beneath the cold exterior. It was still alive.

He could only hope that Cyrah was as well. Nana had called her a Dragon Priestess. She should have been the one caring for the egg.

The crate housed only the egg. He had scoured it and the trunk on the other side of the tent. That one held bandages, towels, and strong-smelling balms and ointments. A medical trunk for the tent of a patient. The only object that resembled a weapon of any kind was the small blade to cut bandages.

He had no weapon, no provisions. The only advantage he had was the dragon curled against his back. She would not stop growing. She was the size of a young horse and just barely fit into the tent.

"Shouldn't you be resting?"

Kath tugged the green blanket over the egg and closed the lid. He turned to the entrance, leaning against Brat's scales. Tai stood at the entry. Kathka glared at him over the bulk of white. But he could not escape the perceptive gaze of the older man. The guilt cut.

"What do you want?" Kathka asked. Brat growled.

"You complain that we are inattentive, then you complain when I visit." Tai smirked. Kathka could not stand it. The high cheekbones, the straight bridge of his nose, the strong jaw, even the quirk of his lips. Just like his namesake. "It appears you are feeling quite better."

"Appears so." Kathka stood, but he still had to tilt his head upward to maintain eye contact with the man. It angered him.

"Kath." Tai rubbed his fingers over his beard, words slow with great calculation. "I understand your restlessness and distrust. We are preparing as best we can to rescue both Nana and Cyrah."

"I'm sure you are," Kath muttered.

"To help Cyrah we need more information," Tai

continued as if he had not heard Kathka's sardonic interruption.

"I'm not hiding anything."

"Not you," Tai corrected. "Rain."

He dropped his hand from his beard and clutched it with the other behind his back in his most natural posture. A militaristic one. At the ready to relay clipped orders. "We need more information about where she would be kept and what they intend to do. We are attempting to learn more, and we thought you may be useful during the interrogation."

"Useful?"

"He is trained to resist us. But you, the dragon, that may incite him to speak."

Kath smirked, though Tai's face remained set in stony seriousness. He had so little leverage that he took whatever he could.

"Lead the way, old man."

"Follow me, young one." Tai swept the flap of the tent ajar and stepped out. He held back the flap for Kath to follow. It felt like a test, though Kath did not know what result the man desired. It had been days since he had seen the sun, since he had set foot in the sand. He stepped over Brat's tail and followed Tai.

The camp looked untouched, unmoved, since he had first awoken. The tents were still the same, the fire still smoldered, the inhabitants still lounged beneath the shade tents and listened to the metal boxes.

Brat emerged from the tent and stretched her wings, snout pointed toward the sun high overhead. She sparkled in the light, shimmering like a mirage on the desert floor.

All eyes were enraptured by her.

Except for Tai, who looked across his followers, and Kath who looked at Tai.

"Come." Tai led the way through the center of the camp. Their gazes followed their leader and the dragon. Tai set a slow pace, aware of the slight limp of his injured patient.

Red stood in front of a tent on the opposite side of the camp between two spear-wielding guards. He shielded his eyes with his hand and watched their approach. A frown dragged his lips down low.

"The dragon will only draw his anger," Red said when Tai stopped before him.

"We will see." Tai patted Red's shoulder and slipped past him into the tent. Red crossed his arms and glared at Kath as he followed Tai into the stifled heat.

In the center of the tent knelt Rain, hands lashed to a stake driven into the sand. He kept his head tilted down as the footsteps shuffled around him. The three men formed a half circle before the prisoner. Tai resumed his habitual stance with hands crossed behind his back and waited patiently for the dragon.

Kath tugged at the golden heat within him. There was a resistance, a tugging back, as Brat soaked in the sun she had sorely missed. He tugged harder, and the dragon slipped into the tent awkwardly behind the men, curling around herself.

In the muted light of the tent, her shadow fell faintly over Rain. But he saw it, and he lifted his head.

Malice filled his gaze.

"Rain." Tai's voice remained as gentle as it had beneath Kathka's bitter jabs. Kath could not recall ever hearing any fluctuation of frustration. "We have come to ask more questions."

Rain's expression remained fixed. It dripped with the venom of his hatred. Red may have been right — the captive did not seem apt to speak.

"What would the Bu Chak do with him?" Tai motioned to Kath. Rain allowed the shift of his attention. Kath felt like he had returned to the Square as all eyes considered him and determined his fate.

Tai and Red had not yet made their decision.

Rain had.

"We would right the wrongs." He leaned forward until the bindings caught him. "We would end him to scour the cursed from our land. Islander or desert dweller, it does not matter. We will restore the prosperity to—"

"Enough," Red interrupted. "It's only Bu Chak propaganda."

Responses seared into him. Ones he would repeat until his death.

"I am offering you a chance." Tai's voice did not reveal the same vexation as Red's. "We just need your cooperation."

"You cannot stop what has been put in motion," Rain scoffed. "You will kill me as they would kill you. The cycle of death will continue until we sever the curse and finish what Scala could not and kill the last god."

"More death will break that cycle?" Tai asked.

"Yes," he said without hesitation.

Kathka could still hear the gun ringing in his ears, could still see the blood dripping in the jungle. Mell had been innocent, and it had been Rain who had smothered his life. It took all Kathka's concentration to focus on the next twisted words that slipped from Rain's lips.

"It is a momentary necessity. The death will cease, the

shaking earth will become steady, the rain will come, our world will heal. They have seen it."

"Have you?" Red muttered.

"You will see," Rain said, gently, as if he were sorry the man was so blinded. "The Wise One, the cursed, they will be erased from our earth, then you will see."

Kathka did not wait to hear his next words. His hand was about Rain's throat, veins raised as the heat coursed through him. Blinding. His calf pulsed in pain as he crouched before the captive, but his mind was clouded, only aware of Rain's breathless gaping mouth.

"Say that again," he dared. Rain gnashed his teeth, eyes cold, harsh, daring Kathka to kill. Kathka could. So easily. "I will. They won't kill you, but I will."

He would.

But he could not.

Rain, the murderer, was his fifth life.

His heartbeat thrummed loud in his ears and he felt like himself. Like before. He could kill Rain if he just pressed tighter, longer. But hands grabbed him, pulled him back and Rain's lungs filled with air.

"What are you thinking?" Red shoved him against Brat, away from the pole and Rain's heaving body.

"Me?" Kathka shouted back. He was aware of their eyes. Anger, sadness. Any trust shattered. But the rage pulsed in him, and the pain gave clarity just like the snapping bones. "What's wrong with you? Standing there, asking kindly? They will kill Nana and Cyrah. They'd kill you all if they had the chance, and you won't do the same. He won't give any answers, you know that. So, what do you plan to do with him?"

"Kath." Tai rested his hand lightly on Kath's shoulder.

"Don't touch me!" Kathka jerked away.

"Do you want to save them?" Tai lowered his hand back to his side. His voice was smooth, calm, infuriating.

"Do you?" Kathka spat back.

"Do you want to save them?" Tai asked a second time, as evenly as the first.

"Of course!"

"Then control yourself. You are young and brash. You do not realize your actions have consequences."

"So does your inaction."

"Indeed." Tai nodded. "I have calculated that cost. I will save this land from the Bu Chak, and that includes him. You want to save Nana and Cyrah, but for what? While the Bu Chak still exists they have no safety. If you truly wish to save them, perhaps it would be better if you left them to us."

The words were soft, but they were effective weapons. They dulled his fury, welled the guilt.

Kathka left.

He left Tai, Red, and Rain and exited the tent. The camp residents watched him emerge. Only Brat remained at his side, a reminder of a life that was not his. He marched across the expanse as they all watched him. There was silence except for the garbled words of a man issuing from the possessed box. A reminder of a life that was not his.

Everything about him was not his.

He approached the strange box. Tai's followers scrambled to their feet as he intruded upon their shade. His heel landed heavily upon the box, crumbling the metal, silencing the voice.

The pain did not bring the focus he had hoped.

He stood, chest heaving, as around him the whispers began. Ghosts did not lurk within him and haunt him like they did Nana. He was the ghost haunting the living. Tai's words wound in his head, tortured his mind.

The Blood King's kingdom had been constructed on a heap of bodies, on the blood of his unfaithful wife and lying general, and it crumbled under the weight of his arrogance. It was a cruel joke the Wise One played, that Tai was the descendant of the general in whom he had placed so much confidence, who conspired to have him killed. It was a cruel joke that Tai would be one of the lives.

It was an even crueler joke to charge him to save anyone. Tai was right, he did not save people. He was the one people needed to be saved from.

Chapter 34

Kath sat on the sand, knowing that the sun burned him. He did not care. He wanted to think the pain was pleasant, but it just hurt.

Brat sat lower down the dune and tore at the meat the camp had provided for her. Her razor-sharp teeth shred easily through the tough scraps, and they all watched with eyes wide and mouths agape.

She was their hope.

It was her sullen companion they did not trust, the one they wished did not accompany the dragon.

He held no malice against their sentiments. Dangerous

things were to be avoided, and he came with no assurances that the risk would bring a greater advantage.

Staring out over their camp he could almost envision himself as one of them. Apart from the metallic boxes, their camp resembled one he had slept in when he was a boy, before the Wayfinders. A camp his parents had set. His foolish parents who had lived in the desert as if nothing could hurt them.

He had so few memories of that time it was easy to transpose the camp before him onto his memories. The pads of his fingers slipped over his earlobe, and only then did he remember that it was fake. This was not his parents' camp, and he did not belong there.

He did not belong. He had made that abundantly clear when he had crumbled their metal box. But he did not want to belong there. He could not belong there. Not when there were six lives yet to save. Until those six were saved he could belong nowhere.

Save seven lives, retain his second life. He had found five. Mell was dead. Nana was scheduled for sacrifice. Cyrah may have already been killed. Rain, he could kill. Tai was the descendant of Taitos and Zalna and looked at him with sad eyes.

Save seven lives, retain the second life. He had not dwelt on the possibility of failing. He had pushed the consideration to the recesses of his mind, as ignored and overlooked as the fear that plagued him, as the disconnection he felt with his body. But as he sat on the dune, he let the thought occupy his mind.

If he failed, it meant death. Death, and then something worse.

He squeezed his eyes shut and ran a hand down his face. When he opened his eyes, white scales filled his vision. Hot breath swept against his skin as Brat butted her brow against his.

"Hey," Kath growled and tried to shove away her head. She met him with her own growl and butted her head against his a second time. More forcefully. The golden heat in his chest warmed. A gentle heat. A soft calm.

He laid a palm flat against her snout. A rumble reverberated up his arm. She lowered herself back down, heavy head sinking into the sand by his side. His hand remained on her cool scales.

Tai emerged from the tent, Red in his wake. They exchanged a few words. Red nodded, then looked up and found where Kath was seated, overlooking the camp. A few more words were passed, and with one final nod, Red walked to the nearest shade tent. Tai turned and found Kath.

Kathka looked away, but he knew it was not enough to avoid the man.

Brat's nostrils flared and she perked her head up, his hand slipping off her scales. In a fluid twist of her body, she slinked down the dune to meet Tai and the pouch of meat he brought her.

"Deserter," Kath muttered. He tried to impress the spite against the gold, but a cheer pushed back and overwhelmed the petty frustration.

Tai sat with a sigh lower on the dune, Brat at his side. Kath tilted his head to watch the man touch the crest of Brat's brow. Together they looked over the camp, as the people looked on at them. Their leader and their outcast. They whispered, judged, and spread their rumors.

Tai said nothing.

Kath wanted to be angry at him, but the rage had been spent and he was left only with the pain. The pain of Zalna and Taitos' betrayal. He wanted to be bitter, but he just felt exhausted.

"What do you want?" Kath finally asked when the rumors had spread far enough. "Here to admonish me again?"

"Though you did break the radio, no, I am not." Tai's fingers found the grooves of the scales and ran along their edges. Like Kath had done. "I do not wish to fight with you."

"Then why are you here?" Kath asked.

"I have never seen a dragon," Tai said, which did not answer his question. Kath sighed and allowed the man to continue. Tai held to his own schedule. "I have seen sketches from history books and I have occasionally seen their shapes flying by the Islands. I had always imagined that they would be majestic, but I would never have guessed how grand they truly are."

Brat licked her claws of the last residue of meat, then turned her great snout to sniff for hidden food in Tai's pockets. Kath had never thought much about the beasts. There were a great many things he had not cared to learn about in his past life. Regardless of what he thought of the beasts, or what he knew, Brat was bound to him. But now, she only served as a reminder that Cyrah had come, and now she was gone.

"Kath," Tai started, and this time his voice was low and serious. "I do not know you or how you came to be in our land."

Tai slipped his hand from the dragon's scales and slid his fingers across his jawline. He stroked his beard as he sat in contemplation and let his statement rest. There was a gravity in his words that made Kathka uncomfortable. "But I know what the Bu Chak are planning. I was part of them once, and I understand why they must be stopped. They wish for a massacre of the Islands. If we are not cursed enough already, we soon will be."

The weighted words settled heavily between them. Heat licked the sand, and just past the edge of the camp, a shimmering mirage of a great pool flickered into existence.

"To answer your question," Tai continued, "I am here to ask if you will help us enact a foolhardy plan."

Kath watched where the span of water had appeared. It flickered and revealed that the earth remained dry. Dead.

"I will help if Nana and Cyrah are saved."

"That is our deepest hope." Tai grunted as he stood and brushed the sand off his pants. Red stepped out from beneath the shade and watched the two on the dune. "The Bu Chak will not expect a dragon. We will use that to our advantage."

"When will I leave?"

"Soon. Tonight our camp will discuss, we will decide." Tai turned his solemn gaze upon Kathka. "But Kath, remember what I said. We can only save them if you trust us."

Kathka trusted no one. No one was to be trusted, only himself. He had learned that long ago, and the lesson was easy to recall when Tai looked so much like them.

Tai's heavy gaze was insistent and Kath looked away.

"If they are rescued," Kath finally muttered. He clasped

his hands together and squeezed tightly. "I'll do what is necessary."

Tai was at least satisfied with the response. In the corner of his vision, Kath could see him start back toward the camp. Halfway down the dune the man paused and turned back to Kath.

He looked as weary as Kath felt.

"And please," Tai's voice broke. He paused, then tried again. "Protect Red."

The request made little sense. It seemed disconnected, but the man's solemnity pushed away the confusion. There were plans in action, circumstances that could not be stopped, and there was no promise of safety.

Kathka could promise nothing.

Tai inclined his head to accept that reality and turned back toward the camp. When the man had rejoined his people, Kathka chuckled in dark humor.

"He's not on my list."

Chapter 35

That night around the bonfire, they decided. The flames cast twisting shadows across the fabric of Kath's tent. He sat on the cot, Brat filling the rest of the space. He stared at their darkened forms on the canvas and wondered what they said. Their words were too low for him to hear, but they were sharp and tense and charged.

They had not invited him to their camp meeting. They mistook him as an Islander, but he was not. He knew their fires and late nights with the host of heaven stretched above.

He was not one of their ranks, but neither was he a

passive actor.

Kath sat until he grew too impatient to remain. He uncrossed his legs and stood. Brat stirred, but he pressed a firm palm against her snout.

"You stay," he whispered. He willed her to remain and hoped she understood. She growled low in the back of her throat but curled back around herself. "Thank you."

He slipped out of the tent.

The desert chill had descended, but it did not bother the camp gathered around the flames. Some sat close to the heat, though most stood as the discussion grew more impassioned. Red stood and argued some point. At his side, Tai sat with a metal poker and stirred dying embers at the edge of the flames.

No one noticed as Kath edged along the peripheral glow and made his way toward the prisoner's tent.

A guard stood beside the tent, but he stared at the fire and leaned against his spear as he strained to listen. He only noticed Kath when he stopped at his side. With a start the guard straightened, confusion and uncertainty narrowing his eyes.

"I want to speak with Rain," Kath said. The man's eyes flickered between the fire and Kath. "Please."

"Didn't you try to strangle him?" the man asked.

"I just want to speak with him." Kath tried to make his voice mellow and trustworthy. He doubted he would succeed, but the man had paused, so he added. "I simply want to ask about the Islander they took. As an Islander, I have special interest in her."

He worried he relied too heavily on his foreignness, but there was a hesitation and at last the guard resigned.

"I won't take my eyes off you." With the butt of his spear, he swept aside the flap and allowed Kath entrance.

In the partial illumination of the campfire, it was difficult to see inside the tent. Kath sat cross legged at the entrance of the tent, to keep distance between himself and the Bu Chak zealot. The guard kept the flap pulled back to ensure no harm came to the captive.

Rain glared at Kath.

Everything was warped, suspended in bated anticipation. Tai's words circled in his mind. The suggestion to leave Nana and Cyrah to him stung. But maybe he was right, maybe he could not save any of them.

Nana, Cyrah, or Rain.

Tai's words made it difficult to think. They were threaded with the same hope that the older man looked at him with, as if expecting more, though there was nothing.

It was so hard when Rain glared at him, when Mell's blood filled the jungle, when Nana and Cyrah slipped through his grasp. He smothered Acrius' taunting sneer, and instead thought of Tai's words, of Nana's smiles outlined by diamond skies, of the tile game in the Green Quarter.

"What happens to the dead," Kath asked, "when the god of death has abandoned us?"

The warm glow of firelight caught in the hollows of Rain's eyes, in the dip of his cheeks, across the angle of his jaw. His expression remained impassive, though Kath had come to expect only two emotions from the man.

Cold indifference or fevered allegiance.

"Are you here to kill me?" he asked bitterly.

"No," Kath said. He knew his question would go unanswered. Rain, or the Bu Chak he spoke for, would have no answer. No one did. "What do you think became of Mell?"

The slightest twitch of his eyes as they narrowed. As he calculated the ends Kath played toward.

He had no aim.

The guard dropped the tent flap back in place. Sufficiently convinced Kath intended no harm, or otherwise distracted by the voices as they rose around the campfire.

"The servant of Pashka," Kath clarified. Without the watchful eye of the guard, he felt the freedom to be more direct. There was a pricking in the back of his throat. It wasn't anger, but it felt close. "The one you killed."

Rain looked down to the sand. It was difficult to discern his expressions in the muted light. But his shoulders sagged.

"I did not intend for him to die."

Kath laughed. A short harsh sound. "What did you intend then, exactly?"

"I don't want anyone to die," Rain started, but was cut off by another sharp laugh.

"Oh you don't?" Kath leaned forward and rested his elbows against his knees. The dull pain in his calf flared, and he hissed out the next words with the pain. "Then why is Nana waiting to be killed?"

"Sacrifices are necessary." His voice sharpened to the practiced clip of Bu Chak rhetoric. "I do not want anyone to die, but what is necessary, is necessary. To restore our world, some must die, but we will see the blessings again. We will see the rain again."

"So you will kill?"

"As will you," Rain retorted. "You're opportunistic, selfish, and violent."

"And you are different?"

"The Bu Chak is different," Rain corrected. "They provided me with everything."

"Is that so," Kath muttered and straightened, dropping his hands to rest on his kneecaps. He considered Rain. He had come into the tent without purpose. It was better than being alone in his, waiting for the verdict from the bonfire.

If he was supposed to save this fifth life, then he would need to know what to save him from.

"Do you want to be in the Bu Chak?" Kath asked. The question surprised Rain. There was a pause of uncertain hesitation. As if no one had asked him that before, and Kath doubted anyone had.

Rain looked more human in that instant. In the space between his stony exterior, and the hesitation below the surface. Like a child, perhaps a little lost.

"Of course," he said, but it lacked the strength of his previous responses. "They gave me everything."

"Doesn't mean they're good," Kath muttered. The Wayfinders had given him everything and had taught him nothing but rage. "They're asking you to kill mindlessly, they sound horrid."

"It's not mindless," Rain defended.

"Mell was mindless," Kath refuted, and Rain winced at the words.

"They take in orphans who have nowhere else to go," he tried again to raise a justification. "They clothe and shelter them, give them names that mean something and training that will change the world. Does that sound evil to you?"

Rain lifted his venomous glare.

It was a defense woven with history. It was not the words

he had been taught to say, and Kath knew he spoke more than about unknown others.

He spoke of himself.

"They will free our world," Rain continued, mistaking Kath's silence as a break in his defense. "We will rid the world of the Wise One and the cursed, and all will be restored."

"You think you can kill a god?" Kath scoffed.

Rain's gaze remained set upon him. Brow drawn low over determined eyes. Kath understood then that yes, he did. As foolish as the Blood King.

And they were more similar than that.

They were both indebted to groups whose care for them extended only to their usefulness as a weapon. Simple tools used to accomplish dirty tasks. An instrument of destruction. Lied to, used, abused, left to die.

"Try to kill a god," Kath stood swiftly, "and you will be destroyed."

When he stepped out of the tent the desert chill rushed back around to greet him. It filled his lungs with what he knew. Around the campfire the discussion continued, but Kath was too preoccupied to concern himself with their deliberation.

He ignored the guard who had barely acknowledged his exit and moved in the shadows back toward his tent. His heart pounded in his chest, confirming what he feared to be true.

To save Rain, he would have to save him from the same fate the Blood King had suffered. The objective that doomed Rain was the same one Kathka had set out to fulfill in his first, and now his second life.

The destruction of the Wise One.

Chapter 36

Tai stood outlined by the rising sun in the tent entrance. He was silent. Kath turned away from the leader and back to the open crate before him. The egg looked gray in the diluted light.

"We have decided," Tai declared, though Kath already knew. There was a spark in the camp, a general commotion of activity, of preparation, of planning. "You and Red will ride for the Bu Chak fortress. Red will explain where they keep their hostages, you will use Brat to take them by surprise. The rest of the troops will act as a diversion."

Foolhardy.

"And the egg?"

"The most I can offer," Tai said, "is my own protection. It will remain here until you return."

"That's not very comforting." Kath closed the lid.

"It is all that I can offer."

"So be it," he conceded. There was nothing better that he could do for it. He edged along the tent around Brat's scaly haunches to the entrance and the man who blocked it.

In the illumination of the rising sun, Kath could see the slope of Tai's shoulders, the fatigue beneath his eyes, the slight trembling of his arms well hidden by his laced fingers.

"Be careful." It was all Tai could say in the face of such a risky plan. Kath smirked and slipped around the man.

"I'll try." It was all Kath could offer.

Outside the tent, the desert encampment had shrugged off its disguise and transformed into a warrior outpost. Beneath the shade tents rested rows of swords and guns. Men and women outfitted with leather armor sat in the sand sharpening the edges of more weapons. Others tacked horses with protective plates, some metal and some leather. The horses struck the earth with impatient hooves and bobbed their heads. They could feel it, the fire of the rising sun and the knowledge that soon they would ride.

But even the thirty-odd horses were not enough to face the Bu Chak. Not if they were all as well trained as Rain.

Two horses stood separated from the rest of the ranks. Red held the reins of each. Camp members circled between their preparations and wishing their farewells to the warrior. They clapped their hands upon his shoulder and promised their swords, their lives. With each visitor, Red's lips etched deeper in a firm determined line.

As Kath approached, their wary glances caught on him, noted the slight favor of his right leg, then slid to Brat. Their hope. They whispered, pointed, nudged each other to look at the dragon. The beast that could make all their plans possible.

Their hope was thick in the air, and Kath found it difficult to breathe when he did not know if the dragon could accomplish anything. If he could accomplish anything.

"Put that on." Red pointed to a pile of clothes folded on top of a pair of boots at the edge of the shade tent. "Take a weapon."

Kath donned the headscarf, slipped on the leather breastplate, and cinched it tight. It all felt comforting, the boots on his feet, the armor around his chest, the arming sword he took from the stockpile.

He only mourned the loss of his hair. Even garbed in the familiar armor, he felt naked without his braids. Going into battle without the mark of a warrior made him uneasy. He smothered the thought of what he could not change and instead focused on strapping the sword to his side.

His wait had come to an end.

Red watched him with cautious consideration. Kath set his hand on the pommel of the sword then turned to face the scowling man.

"Follow me." Red passed one set of reins to Kath. "We will be there soon enough."

Kath gripped the leather and gritted his teeth. He hated taking orders from Red, but the atmosphere of the camp was heavy and stifled the snide comments forming in his mouth. This was not the time for petty banter. This was a deadly plan. Kath's life was as precariously set as the rest of

Tai's camp.

Dawn shredded the sky, crimson gradually easing into a hazy purple. Beneath the foreboding painted sky, the riders mounted their steeds. Rain hauled himself up, and Kath followed, though his calf ached and spiked pain down his leg.

Tai still stood at the entrance of Kath's tent. Resolute as always with his hands gripped behind his back and face solemn before his army. Kath did not know what would save him.

Red inclined his head, Tai mirrored the action, then Red called out, "To the Bu Chak!"

The men echoed the cry. Their shout rose from the desert, and it burned in the blood. Kath had heard this before, many times. With the Wayfinders, with his own men. But this was different. They gained nothing from this.

Kath looked over the people. They had lingered at the fringe of his attention, unimportant when he had lives to save. Now he looked at them. His eyes swept over their ranks and saw their haggard, determined faces as they prepared to ride into a hopeless battle. Refugees, Tai had called them.

All willing to die to have a chance to save Scala's descendant and stop the Bu Chak.

Kath had never been willing to sacrifice his own life like that.

A single rider nudged his horse forward, calling once again to the gathered forces. The first rider eased his horse into a trot, and they followed.

Red turned his steed away from the rest. Kath tore his eyes from the departing force and followed him. They swung two great loops. Two to the left, the rest to the right. Two paths that both led to the Bu Chak.

Brat roared. She coiled her great muscles and burst off the sand. Her wings beat a heavy rhythm that muffled his hearing. Kath craned his head upward to catch sight of her. He had seen her flap between short distances as a newborn, but this was a sight to behold.

A fearsome beast. A glinting vision of white with sharp teeth and razor claws and the smoke of fire on her breath.

A beast that belonged to his enemies.

His dragon.

Kath ripped his attention back to the horse below and the sand before. He had not forgotten the feel of leather in hand or the roll of hooves beneath. His new body slid easily in sync with the horse. The black mane lashed in a wild dance and his heart beat in rhythm to the pounding hooves.

Above, Brat kept pace with the horses. Her wings tore a jagged black shadow across the desert. As the sun ascended, the shadow shifted across the sand like a dial, reminding Kath that time kept moving, kept marching closer to Nana's death. He pushed his horse faster.

Red fell behind.

"Halt!" The call was a whisper in the wind. Kath wanted to ignore it, but he reined in the horse. Sand flew as hooves clamped into the shifting earth. Pain bloomed in his calf. Brat pinned a slow circle in the sky, rippling shadow and sun over Kath. Red trotted his horse to stand side by side with Kath.

"What?" Kath growled when Red had halted.

"You're running them to exhaustion!" He waved between the steeds. Their heads dipped close to the ground, chests heaving beneath their riders. Kath felt it in his own body. The soreness of his legs, the ache of his back.

"You said we'd be there soon."

"We will."

"Then, they'll make it."

"I set the pace." Red pointed to himself, then turned an accusatory finger to Kath. "You follow."

Red saw it, the resistance in the narrowed eyes.

"Or we risk not saving them at all," Red threatened. Brat's shadow crossed his face, cast it into shadow, then exposed it back to the harsh rays. Red's eyes remained firm. They looked like Tai's.

Red echoed Tai's words, a calculated move Kath was certain. The words haunted him. They tore to his core and left him wounded, knowing that he was not a savior. Red was the leader, and Kath was simply a weapon in his arsenal. Red would be a much better choice of a savior.

"Lead the way." Kath grandly extended his arm in invitation. Red pulled his horse forward and set to slow a pace. Kath prodded his horse to follow.

"How were you cursed?" Red asked. Kath heard the question clearly. Without the swift gait, the wind and the pounding hooves were no longer all-consuming.

"Doesn't matter."

"How did you come to be with the Daughter of Scala?"

"Doesn't matter."

Red dug his heels into the barrel of his steed and spurred the horse ahead. Then he pulled one side of the reins back to his hip and pivoted the horse in a sharp circle and drew it to a halt. Kath jerked his reins tightly back to halt before he collided with Red's steed.

"I don't trust you."

"I don't trust you!" Kath snapped back. Brat crashed onto the sand and roared at the two. The horses stamped nervously.

"What are your plans for Nana?" Red demanded.

"To protect her," Kath replied curtly. Red knew. He knew Kath had other plans for her. She was going back, but not to Red, not to Tai. "And what are your plans for Cyrah?"

"If we can save her," Red said, "we will offer her the same protection as Nana."

"When we save her," Kath corrected. "And me?"

"The same protection."

"And Rain?"

"Rain?" Red shook his head. "I cannot trust you, but for some unfathomable reason Taitos does, and I trust him."

The sound of that name made Kath grimace.

"To save Nana and Cyrah," Red continued, "we need to work together. Can you agree to that?"

Kath nodded sharply and nudged his horse into a trot. Brat growled and launched back into the sky. The riders continued in an uneasy silence.

At the corner of the horizon, a chain of dark mountains sliced through the flat earth. From the opposite side another chain came to meet it. But they never did meet. The middle section of the mountains was gone, flattened to orange earth.

Between the two mountains lay great pits, surrounded by jagged rocky formations jutting from the earth. The pits were not visible yet, but Kath knew they were there. They would remain hidden until the very last moment when they fanned out like great gaping mouths.

Kath had already been to the pits before. It was where he had been leading Cyrah and Nana, the Coran Mountain range. The orange scenery haunted the legends of the past. It was where Scala had been cursed for conspiring against the gods. It was where the Islands had been torn from the earth and the dragons gifted. It was where Kathka had ordered his last charge and where the Wise One had slit his throat.

Kath lifted his eyes to the white clouds looming eternally over the pocked earth. On the occasional days when the clouds thinned the dark undersides of rock were just visible, suspended like dark foreboding stars. The Islands.

He expected to see flashes of white flitting between the floating land, dragons that would descend upon him with their riders.

But Brat remained the only dragon in the sky.

Chapter 37

The Bu Chak had built their fortress down, hewn in the void left from the Islands. Guards dressed in gray patrolled the edge of the abyss with bows strapped to their backs and quivers filled with arrows. They surveyed the protrusions of cracking rock surrounding the underground fortress. The spears of rock provided the perfect hiding places for enemies desiring to creep up to the compound.

Red and Kath crouched behind a large mound riddled with whorls and windswept grooves. They had left the horses at the first large rock protrusion, and, on foot, they darted between one formation to the next. Kath was glad to be rid of the horses. His muscles ached from the ride, and it was good to stretch them.

Brat slinked after them. She was barely able to hide behind the edges of the stone. She was too large, too bright, too noticeable. Red glared at Kath accusingly, but they needed the dragon.

As they crouched immobile behind the rock, an unease unraveled from the knot in his stomach and expanded in his chest. It made his heart pound. This was the same earth that had drunk his shed blood.

He had returned. But he still had so many lives to save.

"How much longer?" Kath asked to keep the unease from suffocating him.

"We wait," Red said unhelpfully. He jabbed a thumb backward, toward the guard they had caught sight of earlier. "Without our distraction, they'll see her and all eyes will be here."

"I hate waiting," Kath muttered. He gripped the pommel of the sword but still, his heart beat a rapid rhythm. A low growl rumbled in the back of Brat's throat.

"Calm her."

"I'm trying," Kath hissed. He willed her to be still. Brat did not still. She did not listen to his silent pleas, but to the pace of his heartbeat.

An arrow buried into the sand beside Red's hand. Fletched with all gray feathers, and a single blood-red one. Red jerked back and rammed against Kath. The two pressed low behind the rock face. There was no shouting, no pounding hooves of oncoming steeds, but there were certainly approaching footsteps and another nocked arrow.

"Great," Red muttered and chewed at his bottom lip as he strategized through the new possibilities. "We have to act now."

"With no diversion?"

"I'll be the diversion." Red unsheathed his sword. It flashed in the sun with the promise of blood. "You fly, attack quickly. They will have Nana in the pit prepared for sacrifice, get her and get out."

"I'm not leaving Cyrah."

"You may not have a choice," Red hissed. Kath wanted to argue, but too much time had slipped past. The guard approached, to retrieve his arrow, to see if his keen eyes had noticed something.

"What will you do?" Kath asked. To create a distraction required the attention of more than one guard, and Red was just one man.

"Focus on your mission." Red's words were rushed, aware that they risked too much by staying so long. He was poised for action. "Get her back to Tai."

Red's face was set for death.

Tai had pleaded for his life.

Kath grabbed the edge of Red's leather breastplate and pushed him against the stone.

"You stay here," Kath hissed. "I will be the distraction. He won't know you're here."

Red pushed away from the wall, objection on his lips. Kath shoved him back a second time.

"Get to Tai," Kath said firmly. He released his hold on the armor and twisted back to where Brat crouched on the sand.

She knew his intentions.

Kath slid his hand along Brat's muscled neck. Her golden gaze followed him. He gripped the ridges of her shoulder bones and hefted himself upon her back. She was broader than a horse with little purchase on her scales. He wrapped his arms around her neck and pressed his sore legs against her chest.

"Don't let me fall, Brat," he whispered.

Great wings unfurled, and with a sweep down, she rose.

The beat of the dragon wings swirled the sand around the stone. The guard had crept to their stone screen. He lifted his arm to shield his face but halted mid-movement with mouth agape as he beheld the crystalline dragon. He would rush to warn the others. But by the time he reached the base it would be too late.

The dragon would have already descended.

Brat trained her head upward as she climbed higher and higher. Kath clung to her and squeezed his eyes shut, focusing all energy on simply not falling. The air thinned and cooled. Forever she climbed until at last she banked, straightened, and all became still.

Cautiously, with cheek pressed against her scales, Kath opened his eyes. He was surrounded by white. All was white. White above, white below. Droplets of water formed against his skin as they passed through the thin mist. The dragon was hidden in a cloud.

It was deeply peaceful there. Still and silent. Serene. Brat rumbled in agreement with his assessment.

The cloud bank broke and revealed the scorched earth far below. The chasm lay below them. In its black depths, a fire burned. Small figures rushed over the earth, toward one side of the fortress. Opposite of Brat's approach. A plume of sand rising from the desert captured their attention. Tai's riders.

"Go down," Kath ordered. It was time. Brat tilted her left wing and dipped into a circle above the pit. A growl reverberated in her chest and through Kath's body. She tucked her wings against her sides and dived.

Down, down to the earth, to the blackness. White exchanged for red, and the rock swallowed them.

With a snap, she spread her wings and swept herself upward before they rammed into the earth. Her talons cracked the rock as she landed. The impact jolted the breath from Kath's lungs.

Kath forced a breath in and ignored the bloom of pain in his calf. He focused instead on the objective at hand.

There were too many men, the first assessment he made. The coming riders had not distracted enough. He had moved too early. Inside the pit, Bu Chak members in their gray uniforms halted along platforms chiseled into the rock walls. There was a bated moment of silence as they simply beheld the white beast that had descended among them. The creature epitomizing all that they hated.

A shout broke the still and bows were nocked and guns raised, all trained at the dragon and her rider.

"Kill the beast!" The cry echoed in the pit. Brat roared and rose on hind legs. Kath lost his purchase on her slick scales and slid onto the rock.

Fire plumed from her outstretched jaws. Wood burned, metal scorched, and the screams of men filled his ears. The heat was against his skin. The terror of her power thick around him. He had heard the myths, but he understood then, as the men fled the destructive force, the power of the dragon. The power he had wielded without even knowing.

He tore himself from the consuming heat and scanned the floor. He searched for Nana, for Cyrah.

Red had said that Nana would be there, in the center, prepared for death.

He found her.

She knelt on a raised pedestal with her hands chained to the ground. Their prize on display for all to see. For all to mock and jeer and loathe. His eyes caught hers. Amid the panic and ruin, Nana smiled.

White scales snaked around him and cut off the sight of her. Arrows glanced off Brat's protective scales. There was thunder, but he could not tell from where or if anything had been hit.

"Nana!" he shouted to Brat and pointed. He hoped she would understand, that their connection would relay the emotions, the fear, that he could not express. He inexplicably knew it would. He ran and Brat followed. She wove around him, jaws gaped and unleashing flames whenever a Bu Chak member ventured too closely.

"Kath." Nana strained against her metal binds as he climbed onto the pedestal. Brat circled the platform, teeth bared and tail swiping back and forth in a snake-like curve. "What are you doing?"

"Saving you."

"Why?"

He had not expected the confusion. He knelt in front of her and tugged at the bindings.

"Because I don't want you to die."

He wondered what expression crossed her face or if she had even heard his response in the chaos that descended around them. It did not matter. He had found her and he would free her. He would save her.

"Prisoner!"

The voice haunted Kath. It was inescapable. He craned his head upward and found the young lord leaning leisurely against the balcony high overhead. A sneer tore across his face. He wore the same hairstyle he had the day he shot Kath.

"Halt!" yelled a gray-robed woman at the young lord's side. "Do not harm the Daughter of Scala!"

Around the pedestal, the Bu Chak halted their advance. They ringed the pedestal, an imposing circle of weapons.

"Is it for sale?" Pashka pointed to the dragon. She bared her teeth.

"She isn't."

Pashka's laugh was easy despite the stench of burnt flesh overwhelming the pit. "Such a shame, I'll just have to take it."

Kath's breaths were shallow. The air burned his lungs. He needed to think.

"Surrender, Islander," the woman shouted down. Her voice was wound tight, her hands clutched at the banister as she leaned over the railing. "You are vastly outnumbered"

"We have yet to see if that is true," Kath shouted back.

"Kath, consider." Pashka clapped his hands together and tapped them against his chin, as if deciding the best course of action to chastise a small child. "You must recognize that this touching show of heroism is doomed."

He separated his hands and swept them wide toward the men who stood on the balconies and those on the floor.

"Surrender." The woman ordered again.

"You underestimated me before," Kath crafted his barb to buy time. He needed a plan. He focused his words to Pashka, the more likely to be lured by the haughty words. "I've escaped you twice."

Pashka's head tilted to the side as he considered the retort. At last, he nodded and shrugged. "We must recognize our failings, learn from them, and not repeat them. It would appear to me the only way to redeem myself would be in your capture, so I suggest you stay right there."

"I'd rather not."

"What would you rather?" Pashka asked. "Your men will be killed soon, then it's just you. Even if you did escape with her, you'd leave the other behind. Imagine, right now there are three cursed in their midst. The Bu Chak have only dreamed of such a day."

Three cursed. The words roiled like poison in Kath's stomach. Pashka had to be lying. A smirk twisted sinisterly upon his lips.

"After you and the girl are dead," Pashka leaned against the balcony, "I'll take the dragon."

Kath had no way to save them both. But he had no time. Pashka had wasted some, but the threats could not protect him forever. He needed to act.

Kath lifted Nana's chains and pulled at the golden warmth in his chest. He urged Brat to swift action before the Bu Chak could respond.

The chain snapped easily in her jaws.

Kath slipped his hands into Nana's and hauled her into the shadow of Brat's outstretched wings. He helped her onto Brat's back as the dragon breathed out another stream of hot flame.

"Cyrah!" Nana exclaimed as Kath climbed on top of Brat behind her. "Pashka didn't lie. She's cursed, they'll kill her!"

Red said to leave her.

But he needed to save her.

"I know." Kath pressed Nana down beneath him and folded his arms around her still manacled ones. He knew, but he was helpless. They were vulnerable and his mind was muddled, and he did not know the next step in his plan. He had no next step. But he had to save Cyrah too.

With the weight of two bodies, Brat struggled to lift from the earth. Slowly she rose. Kath expected arrows and bullets. He could hear their shouts, but there was no retaliation. The men watched their quarry slip through their fingers on the back of the dragon.

He had their prize, the heart of their vision of liberation. They could not risk her.

Kath glanced to the balcony, where Pashka had stood. He caught sight of the lord as he jumped, over the void, arm outstretched.

Pashka's fingers caught the back of Kath's breastplate. He slammed against Brat's side, but his grip remained latched.

Kath clawed onto the juncture of Brat's neck and wing. Her pained cry radiated deep within his chest, but he dared not release his hold. Pashka weighed heavily on his back and threatened to send them both falling to their deaths. Brat kept her course upward, set on the patch of sky high above that sang in tune with her most basic instinct.

Higher the dragon rose, though she labored beneath the weight. She continued upward even after she had escaped from the pit and into the open air. She climbed higher, breaking into a cloud bank and she roared. Roared in agony.

The edge of the breastplate bit into his shoulder. Pashka's ribs dug into the wound in his calf. Pain clouded his vision. Acidic bile burned his throat. He dared not lash out at the lord and risk his hold on Brat.

The dragon punched through the cloud bank and back into the clear blue sky. Pashka cursed and kicked his legs, seeking purchase on the slick scales. Nana cried out as his knee dug into her calf. She twisted backward and elbowed him firmly in the ribs.

His fingers slipped.

Pashka fell into the open space.

Brat abruptly evened her body and Nana and Kath crashed against her scales. Nana's breath stopped within her. The stillness filled him. Sunk everything within him.

They stared at the falling body, arms still outstretched to the beast above until the clouds swallowed him and he was gone. Only then did Nana's lungs fill and empty in a rapid pace. He could feel her shaking.

"I killed him," she whispered.

He wanted to calm her, to whisper sweet promises, that she was safe, that he had saved her. But those were lies. No comfort could come from the Blood King. He could not count the number of lives he had ended. Blood was thick on his hands. She mourned for the one. He had forgotten how to mourn such loss.

He set his hand upon her back, a subtle pressure. She continued to shiver.

Brat veered to the right and rammed her riders against her body. She swept along the edge of a cloud bank, narrowly avoiding a collision with a great crystalline beast that rose from the field of white.

A dragon.

It shimmered in the sunlight and blinded Kath.

Brat banked a second time as another rose. She swept in a circle as more white dragons appeared from the thick clouds and hemmed her in. They dwarfed her young form.

Upon their sparkling scales sat riders. They wore black wooden masks with thin slits for eyes and blue feathers flowing down their backs. They held spears, all leveled against the unknown dragon.

Six dragons surrounded Brat. Below a dragon circled, and when Kath craned his neck upward, he found another circling above. He gritted his teeth as Brat roared in defiance.

A single dragon banked closer. The rider clutched a spear in one hand and splayed the other across Pashka's back as the desert lord clutched the leather saddle.

The rider's voice boomed over the whooshing of wings.

"You are under arrest."

Chapter 38

The riders kept a tight circle around the smaller dragon as they directed her upward through the sky and closer to the Islands. Nana could not stop shivering beneath him. He kept his attention on her, a good distraction from the approaching land.

"I'm scared," she whispered.

The eyes of the masks watched them. Void, lifeless, hostile.

"Me too."

They passed outcrops of rock that hung suspended in the air, small fragments of land that had crumbled from the larger islands. As the floating earth grew larger, thin brittle grass sprouted on its surface. Life so far above the earth below.

They approached a great suspended rock with sheep grazing in a fenced pasture, ignorant to the fact that the next bit of solid ground was far beneath their hooves. From their island, a rope ladder looped precariously up to the next island inhabited by a small village with rock houses situated along the slope of the land. There was not a single wood house, only stone. Strands of rope looped from roof to roof, fluttering squares of blue strung along their length. Upon the paths walked people.

People so far above the earth below.

Little children pressed against the stone fence wrapped around the island, waving at the dragons as they passed. A few of the bravest ran up the slope of the bridge that connected their island to the next one hovering above. Over the beat of dragon wings, their cheers were not audible.

With the periphery islands behind them, the larger loomed overhead. Trumpets blew from watchtowers as the dragons flew past the first of the greater islands. There were houses and gardens, pastures, and roads. An entire infrastructure perched on all available space.

The riders kept their path trained upward, toward the jagged black underbelly of the greatest of the islands. Bridges looped to the floating rock, tethering it to all the closest settlements, the hub of Island life. The dragons crested its craggy edge and shifted their course. They directed Brat over the crammed city.

There was no green on this island, just houses with blue-tiled roofs, and the fluttering blue flags. People crowded the streets, faces craned upward as the riders passed overhead.

The dragons followed the rise of the land to the peak of the mountain. At the summit, the rock had been hewn into a castle. The shadows of the great beasts rippled over turrets and open gardens, barracks and the peaks of grand halls. The riders directed their course downward to a green lawn at the very edge of the castle wall. It was the most green Kath had ever seen. A sea of grass hemmed between the castle walls and a protrusion of black rock jutting out over the steep city incline to meet the blue sky and nothingness.

The riders forced Brat to bank and circle over the green expanse. Lower they forced her, and lower until Brat's claws scraped gauges spitefully into the lawn and she landed. The dragons landed around her, their riders dismounting before their claws touched the earth. They approached the young dragon with raised spears.

A low snarl rumbled in Brat's throat, echoing the disquiet Kath felt. A spearhead tucked against Brat's jaw and forced her snout upward to the sky.

"Contain her," a rider commanded. Kath did not know how. A rider grabbed his arm, another Nana's, and dragged them down to the ground so high above their world below. It dizzied Kath to think about.

The riders uncinched the sword from his waist and removed the breastplate before searching over the rest of his body for hidden weapons. Brat roared. The other dragons growled with stretched jaws, fire kindled in the recesses of their throats.

"Contain her!" The rider's hand about his forearm tightened. "We mean her no harm."

But the spear remained against her jaw, his sword was in

their hands, and his arm firmly in their grasp.

"Brat," Kath hissed. She twisted her neck to escape the spearhead, but the rider turned with her movements and kept the tip pressed against her scales. Another rider brought a great metal cuff and skirted close to the beast.

"Can you not control her?" The question lacked judgment and held only confusion.

"Where are you taking her?"

"To a holding stall," the rider clutching his arm replied. "The dragons are all put in the caves, she will be cared for while we discern who you are."

Kath gritted his teeth as the metal cuff clanked around Brat's neck. They led her across the lawn to the dark mountain peak with its gaping black caves. Kath focused all his willpower on keeping her docile, but she responded to the undercurrent of his distrust.

Surrounded by the other dragons, Brat did not seem quite so large as she had on the desert floor. The darkness of the cave swallowed her frame. He felt her growl deep in his bones.

Kath did not trust the dragon riders or the land to which they brought him. They seemed as uncertain about him as he was of them.

"Kath!" Nana cried.

His focus on Brat broke and he wheeled toward Nana. The grip around his forearm jolted him to a halt. Two riders gripped Nana's arms and led her, along with Pashka, into the shadow of the towering castle. Brat's scream ricocheted through the cave.

"Stop!" Kath jerked his arm, but the rigid hold remained. "Where are you taking her?"

"We simply want to speak with her." The words were meant to assure, but, muffled by the looming wooden mask, they sounded hollow and threatening.

"Why separate us, if you just want to speak?"

"We do not trust you together." The response was forthright and dangerous. There was nothing in the flat words and the blank eye sockets that reassured Kath. The Islands were as hospitable as the world below. "Come."

The rider led Kath across the lawn, two riders in their wake. The fluttering feathers added to the rider's height and, surrounded by so many, he felt small. Powerless.

The rider took him through an arched doorway and into the fortress. The dark was icy cold. Down the hall they walked, then up a curving flight of stairs.

With each step, Kath's lungs burned. His pace lagged, though the riders behind pressed him forward.

"The heat of their air affects even a rider?" the rider behind him muttered. Kath wanted to be angry, but it was hard when his lungs labored for breath.

"Come, it is only a little further." The rider in front prodded Kath onward.

Kath was glad when the stairs ended.

The rider led him a short distance down the hall and into a small room. The two trailing riders remained in the hall on either side of the entrance. One shut the door and Kath was alone with the dragon rider.

The man released his hold on Kath's forearm and strode across the room toward a shelf built into the wall. Kath rubbed his hand over his injured calf and took a steadying breath of the thin air.

He waited for danger.

The rider laid his spear against the wall and began to light the candles lining the shelf. There was no false light here, only raw fire like Kath had known. He glanced upward but found no round bulbs.

As the light filled the room, Kath scanned the rest of the narrow chamber. The room was empty except for the golden candelabras set on the shelves on either side of the room. The wall across from the door had a large arched window. From the window came a sound, like an incessant wind.

Kath stepped to the banister. He slid his hand over the damp rock and peered over the edge and down at a cascade of falling water. It tumbled from a river that ran beneath the room and splashed over moss-covered rocks and into a pool far below. The mist wet his skin and coated his lips. Life-giving water.

It was mesmerizing.

"I am to interrogate you." Behind him, Kath could hear the rider approach. "Custom guides us, the customs set forth by our ancestors, but custom cannot guide me now. You are quite outside of it."

Kath tore his eyes from the lull of the water and peered at the rider. The soft glow of the candles warmed the black of the mask to an earthy brown. The pits of the eyes were still cast in utter darkness.

"Who are you?" The first question was even and calm. The sun lowered beneath the island, an early sunset. The flames flickered peacefully. The waterfall sang its rumbling lullaby. Everything seemed gentle.

It all trapped Kath in the moment and coaxed his lips to form the words, his tongue to reveal its secrets. He firmed his lips and refused. He thought of the chocolate room, of

Pashka's tactics. These riders were no different.

They would do whatever necessary for information.

The mask tilted to the side, and the rider accepted that Kath would not divulge the truth.

"Why were you in the land below?" The rider posed his next question then let the pause sooth his captive. Kath resisted. Beneath the mask was a stranger, behind the door was a hallway leading to the unknown, and somewhere Nana was being asked the same string of probing questions. "How did you obtain the dragon?"

The rider took deliberate steps closer.

"Who are your companions?" The string of questions continued, each spaced with calculated intervals. "Why were you at the ascension ground?"

Kath's breaths were even, and he counted in sync with the rider and waited for the next question. It did not come. The mask was close, the feathers stirring in the breeze from the crashing water. A calloused hand splayed across the black wood and removed the headdress, revealing cropped hair and a chiseled face with deep-set black eyes.

Knowing eyes.

"You are far from a brother member." The voice sounded different without the mask to distort it. Lighter, fatigued. "But I will give you the respect of one."

Insults crowded upon Kath's tongue, scathing and taunting. They would revolt against the answers the rider's questions had attempted to elicit, but Kath did not allow them to pass the gates of his lips. He understood that the man offered mercy.

"You have broken all the customs of the Ja Nrai," the man said. Kath frowned at the title. "You were not approved by the Dragon Priestess, nor confirmed by the brothers. You are a stranger to us. A danger. You have brought those from the world below into our sacred midst and have threatened our very fabric of existence with such blatant disrespect to the order the gods established."

"Then why haven't you killed me already?"

It was the rider's turn to remain silent, carefully formulating a response. "Though you may dishonor all of our customs, we still abide by them. You will be treated kindly if you simply explain. If you do, I can offer you some protection."

The rider searched once more, for any break, any tell. All he found was the stubborn frown and resolution hardened by experiences far beyond the young countenance. There would be no further words. The rider slid the mask back over his face. The slitted black gaps were not kind.

"I will report your response to the king."

The rider left, blue feathers waving behind him, wishing Kath goodbye as the door shut and he was left alone in the room with the roar of the river behind.

Kath breathed out heavily. He wished he could give the man something, to appease his sense of decorum and earn leverage in the unknown. But the truth would only endanger Nana and himself more.

The Ja Nrai had been searching for Cyrah.

He did not trust them.

Chapter 39

T he sun had set when the door opened and a rider entered. Beneath the mask it was impossible for Kath to tell if it was the same one who had interrogated him. They looked identical with the wood and blue feathers.

But then, it did not matter who this rider was. Silently, the man grabbed Kath's arm and forced him away from the waterfall and out of the room.

Kath was his enemy.

The two riders guarding the door fell in behind Kath as the rider led him down the twisting hallways of the palace.

Their footsteps echoed in the vacant corridors. Flames lit in the wall sconces twisted shadows across the gray stones. The flickering light obscured the doorways and corners of the complex network of halls. Kath quickly lost track of how to return to the green lawn.

Down a spiral flight of stairs the rider led him. At the bottom, the stairwell opened into a high domed passageway with twin pools of water flowing on either side of the stone path.

A red fish startled as the four walked down the path. It darted away from the movement and disappeared beneath the walk. A moment later, it reappeared on the other side and bumped against a smaller fish before careening back beneath the stones.

The pools stretched alongside the path until the hall ended in an archway and the water slipped beneath the wall and flowed into a vast pool that stretched outward on the other side.

Round columns supported a domed ceiling above the pool. Striped between the stone pillars the velvet starry sky stretched endlessly.

The riders allowed Kath no time to consider the marvel. They led him steadily down the walkway that maintained its course straight over the pool until it terminated before a set of massive stone doors.

Delicate images were carved into the doors, dragons with their dragon riders. Around the edge of the doors looped the marks of the curse. Kath nearly collided with the carved Ja Nrai before the doors swung inward.

Riders with their black masks lined both sides of the purple carpet that rolled out from the doors to the dais and its throne. Upon the throne sat the king of the Islands, a golden circlet upon short black curls. His young face was set in a solemn transfixed gaze as the riders brought forth the captive.

The rider halted Kath a few feet from the shallow stairs of the dais. He tilted his head upward to maintain eye contact with the Island king.

"This is the stray brother," the king stated and the rider at Kath's side inclined his head. The king silently assessed him then said, "Let him stand."

The rider released his hold and took a step to the side. The two riders remained set behind him. Kath stood resolutely still.

"Why did you stray?"

Kath did not give his story and the king nodded.

"They said you were closed-lipped, quite unlike your friend. He is verbose, though speaking nothing useful."

"He is not my friend."

The corner of the king's thin lips perked in the slightest smile.

"You may not be part of the Ja Nrai but certainly you understand that court etiquette insists you wait for the king's permission to speak?" he said with a soft tone, but he paused for the weight of the words to settle before he continued.

"He did share one piece of information," the king continued as if Kath had never interrupted. "I believe you will find it as fascinating as I did."

He rose from the throne, and as he spoke, he moved across the dais, closer to Kath. "He claimed there were two Islanders in the desert."

With an even pace, the king stepped down the stairs and

allowed his comments to remain unclear. The king's eyes were a weak gray as vacant as the open sky. He watched Kath, consuming any tells he revealed, and he had revealed too much. Kath's breath was shallow in his lungs, and the king knew.

"Is his story true?" The king was barely taller than Kath, but he tilted his chin up and gazed down at him over his nose.

Kath clenched his teeth together.

"Perhaps my question is vague, let me rephrase. Was Cyrah with you in the desert?"

Kath refused to answer. His teeth ached. The pain distracted. It made him think of the throne he had once sat in. One that he had bloodied.

"As it is customary to wait until the king speaks, so it is customary to answer when the king asks you a question." The king turned aside his devouring gaze.

Kath released his hold upon his teeth and breathed. Slow steady breaths.

The king motioned to the rider at Kath's side, then returned his gaze to Kath, a smile formed upon his lips.

"I realize you may be unaccustomed to our ways. You may not even know who I am. I have been discourteous, forgive me. My name is Altan, I am the king of these islands. I am heir of Caizin, the first blessed by the gods, and I bear his blessing."

Altan's gaze flicked to the rider, and the man tugged Kath's shirt down to reveal the edges of the tattoos on his skin. Kath jerked away, but the black had been seen.

"As you are also blessed," the king murmured. "Tell me, Kath, that is your name correct? Tell me, why are you blessed?"

"Blessed?" Kath scoffed. "I am cursed."

Finally, an emotion passed across the king's face. His eyebrows twitched low, confused.

"Cursed?" Altan repeated. Kath snapped his mouth shut and the king saw the clench of his jaw, the refusal to speak further. A light sigh passed his lips and he turned to the rider still at his side. "Bring Cyrene."

"Let the lady enter!" the rider shouted down the hall. The doors groaned open and down the carpet footsteps padded softly, nearly silent.

"My lady, I would like you to speak with our fallen brother."

A woman skirted Kath to stand beside the king. A woman clothed in deep purple, hair twisted in an intricate braid. Cyrah. The same dark hair, same narrow chin, same high brow.

"It would appear—" Altan extended his hand and the woman rested her fingertips lightly against his palm. "That Cyrah is alive."

This was not Cyrah, only a mirror of her.

A mirror that tugged at his soul the same way Cyrah had.

Altan's features remained impassive, but the lady's, Cyrene's, sparked with irritation. Her lips were taut, and her eyebrows bunched over her eyes as she considered Kath with a venomous glare.

"You say he has a dragon, is it he who spirited her away?" she asked, and even her voice was Cyrah's.

"His dragon is too young, it was born below," Altan replied and her frown deepened.

"You're looking for the eggs?" Kath asked to break their

private counsel. They both scowled at him. "Then why was Cyrah trying to keep them from the Ja Nrai?"

"Insolent," Cyrene snapped and turned to Altan. "You say he is blessed?"

"Indeed." Altan considered Kath's smirk then turned his focus to Cyrene. "Not of royal lineage."

"Nor of the dragons." Cyrene eyed Kath's disheveled shirt, where a bit of black marking could still be seen on his chest. A replica of the ones peeking from the edges of her gown.

Pashka had not lied, as Nana had attested. If Cyrene was cursed, Kath could be sure her mirror below bore the marks as well.

"We cannot afford such unknown." Altan rested his hand momentarily on top of her fingertips still resting in his palm, then dropped her hand and faced his captive. Kath squared his shoulders and straightened to match his stature.

"You will tell me the truth," Altan declared. "Perhaps not today, or even tomorrow, but you will comply. The desert lord says you were in league with Cyrah and that you know where the eggs are. I am very much interested in knowing the truth of these matters. You will enlighten me, won't you?"

Both knew that Kath's defiant stance was a farce. He stood powerless in the room of dragon riders. The Island king had all the leverage, and Kath had none.

"Prepare your account, I will call you to my presence again." The king waved him away.

Two riders pinned his arms against his side and forced him back down the hall and toward the shimmering pool of water. Cyrene's malicious gaze followed him, haunted him.

Cyrene, his sixth soul.

Chapter 40

The riders took Kath from the throne room, the king, and his sixth soul.

They took him back across the pool through the archway and down the hall. There they altered their path. Instead of the small room with the waterfall, they led him through the twisting halls to a steeply descending staircase.

Kath understood then the reality of his situation. He was far from a brother rider. Far from an Island citizen. He was their prisoner, nothing more. Altan was incorrect to interpret his insolence as ignorance. He knew of courtly etiquette, not on the Islands but he had been a king and he knew how to interpret the stately game they set. He knew the danger that lurked, the price of placing the wrong piece. The world above was not so unlike the world below, and the king had just revealed his pieces.

This was a warning, danger was to come.

The stairs paused in a landing before plunging further into the deep heart of the mountain. Upon the landing stood a woman with hands on her hips. She smirked as she watched the riders descend toward her.

The escort halted on the landing.

"Your Highness." The lead rider's voice crumbled with wear as if he already knew his words were insubstantial before the young woman. "We have our orders."

"From the king?" Her bared shoulders rolled in a nonchalant shrug. The motion slipped through her arms, and she dropped her unyielding pose and stepped forward. Her silk garbs flowed smoothly around her. "Do you think he's in the throne room, counting every second to ensure you don't pause?"

"Where is Nakota?" The rider refused to bend, though they had not advanced past her.

"Mikael," the woman cooed, "you worry too much. The king can't be angry about things he doesn't know took place. Nakota can't be punished for things the king doesn't know took place."

The lead rider remained rigid, mask blank and fixed before her sly words. But the lack of rebuttal was a concession and her smile softened. For a moment, she rested her hand on his shoulder, then she slipped past him and planted herself before Kath.

A well set piece or a stray one Kath had not yet decided.

The woman waved aside the riders behind him, and they released their grip on his arm and stepped backward.

"So, traitor." She tilted her head to the side and set a hand upon her hip. Her eyes meandered over his body. "Your name is Kath?"

"Yes."

"You speak!" Thick eyebrows rose over gray eyes. She looked like the king. They shared fine bones, thick hair, and vacant eyes. "They said you didn't. Since you gave me your name, I'll give you mine. You may call me Jayla."

He knew the name.

It was the same name Cyrah had spoken when she had accused him of being sent after her. The name breathed out after Ja Nrai. Why this powerful woman's name had been uttered alongside the king's guard, Kath did not know. But she seemed pleased by the way he cautiously considered her and allowed him a moment of confusion.

"I'm interested in you, Kath," she continued. "Nana says you're not what you appear."

"You spoke with Nana?"

She was taller than the king and looked down at Kath as the pause stretched and she contemplated her response.

"She's sweet." She settled on those words with their vague meaning. Jayla watched the frown deepen upon his face then added, "Though she is the Daughter of Scala."

He did not think there was a threat in her voice, but it was hard to tell. He could not tell with any of the Islanders, with their strange phrases and ridiculous protocol.

"What will he do to her?" he asked. If Jayla knew Nana's identity, the king certainly did as well. Though he had not mentioned that in the throne room. As if he did not even care.

She heaved a sigh and crossed her arms over her chest. Her smile was strained. "Am I my brother?"

"So, you're powerless?" Kath matched her bite with his own unamused words. Her smile twisted into a cutting grin, and she leaned close, nose inches from his.

"Don't be so arrogant." Her eyes bored into his. "Worry about you, not her."

"Should I worry about you?"

The princess blinked twice in quick succession and straightened, smirk intact.

"You are interesting," she said. "But perhaps he is counting."

Her arms brushed against his sleeve as she passed. The pungent fragrance of her cinnamon perfume engulfed him.

"Be careful."

He said it before the scent had left. Before his mind had cleared. Before he could think reasonably and remember that she was one of them, and that Cyrah had asked if she had sent him. But it did not matter. The pull on his soul was so strong.

Jayla, the princess of the Islands, was the seventh life.

His final life.

With their obstacle removed, the riders continued their descent. Kath tore his mind from the princess and focused instead on the uneven stairway. The stairs eroded from clean-cut rock to rough-hewn shallow steps pooled with the water dripping from the damp ceiling. At the bottom of the staircase, a narrow path stretched into the darkness. The fire of the sconces flickered unevenly over the chiseled surfaces and only dimly revealed the dungeon.

"Hail, Riders." Guards without masks inclined their heads respectfully as the masked men passed. In their servile stance, they snuck furtive glances at the prisoner hemmed in by the Ja Nrai.

The riders led Kath to the far end of the hall, to a cell tucked deep beneath the castle. In the very bowels of the mountain itself. The iron gate whined as it swung outward and stirred the stale air.

Inside the cell, chains jangled. The flickering firelight highlighted the curve of Pashka's smile as it grew into a sinister hyena grin.

The riders brought Kath into the cell with the desert lord. They clapped cuffs around his wrists and retreated from the dank space. Leaving the false brother behind.

The guards eyed the two prisoners. Once the riders had disappeared up the stairway, one gave a harsh chuckle. He muttered something to his comrade, and they laughed. Two other guards moved closer to join the conversation and in their closed knot they formed the sensational bits of gossip that would spread across the whole of the islands when the guard shift changed.

Kath lowered his gaze to the cuffs and did his best to ignore the hiss of their whispers.

"I would never put my prisoners in such a place as this." Pashka's voice was raised for the guards, casting alluring tidbits to twine into their tall tales. The lord's presence was wearisome.

"Of course," Pashka said, and this time his voice was low. He spoke for Kath alone. "I would never share quarters with my prisoners anyway."

It took great effort for Kath to remain silent. He

experimentally tugged at the cuffs. The cool metal pressed into his flesh and promised raw gashes if he persisted in trying their strength.

"Where's Nana?" Pashka asked. "Perhaps she gets special treatment, being the descendant of their greatest enemy. Or do you think they've already killed her?"

"Why did you tell them?" Kath conceded to his prattling. He dropped his hands and looked across the cell to Pashka. In the weak light from the hall, it was hard to distinguish the expression twisting his features, but he saw the slight shrug of his shoulders.

"I told them many things, you'll have to be specific."

"About Nana."

"I'm not trying to protect her," he scoffed. "It's in my best interest to be helpful. Of course, I would tell them."

"Then why didn't you tell them where Cyrah is?"

He laughed and shook his head. "Why would I help them? Your people are my enemy, Kath. I'll play their game, give them enough information to keep me alive, retain enough information to keep me alive. I'm quite good at it."

"They'll still kill you."

"Probably!" He laughed again. "But I will die with the peace of knowing that you will soon follow. Perhaps they'll use a dagger with a golden handle, that would be nice. Inlaid with sapphires. No, rubies. Gold and rubies. I wouldn't even mind if they gave me a long death with that blade. Do you think they have rubies?"

"Be quiet."

"Sliced throat, I'll lay there in a pool of my own blood. Not bad. Not like I imagined, but it will do."

"I said, be quiet."

"It's kind of romantic," Pashka continued, Kath's opposition only strengthened his rambling speech. He was too loud, the guards too keen to listen. "A song will be made of my death. Not that anyone would know. Which is better. I'll be immortalized, carried away on the back of a dragon, never to be seen alive. I'll rival even the myths of the Blood King and Scala!"

"Will you be quiet!" Kath shouted though he hated that the guards heard. He glared at Pashka, but the lord had lost interest in him. Trembling fingers traced up his neck, over his cheeks, and into his loose curls. "What are you doing?"

"Headache." His voice was subdued. He tugged at his hair, then tugged harder. "Gram said the leaves could be crushed and brewed and it'd ease even the worst headaches. I don't remember the plant though."

Pashka jumped to his feet and kicked the bars of the cell. The bang snapped the guards to attention. He strained against the cuffs and kicked the door a second time.

"Not that it'll do much good here!" he shouted at the guards as if they personally kept the herb from him. They watched with amused bewilderment.

"You're addicted," Kath said, and Pashka's attention focused back to him. He glowered at Kath. Standing closer to the light of the hallway sconces, Kath could just make out purpling bruises lining his cheekbones.

"I'm lord of the Square." Pashka drew closer until the chains snapped taut and lurched him to a halt a few feet from Kath. "Of course I am!"

"Of course you are!" Kath could not help but laugh. The situation kept worsening.

"Quiet!" Pashka groaned and collapsed onto the damp

floor. Kath obliged. Another groan escaped Pashka's lips, and he threw his arm across his eyes to block even the faint light. With Pashka silenced, the guards resumed their talk, spinning new rumors with all the details Pashka had divulged.

Kath lowered himself to the floor and sat cross-legged in front of the lord. He wondered how much of his condition was from the lack of a pipe or from the high elevation. With narrowed eyes, he watched the quick rise and fall of Pashka's chest and tried to discern how sick he was. His condition could be from the air. It could be too thin, and his body too used to the ground below. Or he could be suffering the effects of his pipe being gone for too long. Or both coupled together.

Pashka remained still, face half-covered, no longer in control, no longer powerful, but broken. But then, he had never been powerful. He was a man hollowed by greed into a mere shell, possessing nothing truly and ravenous for everything. Kath could recall the immense hatred he had felt for Pashka at one time, but it felt pointless now. Pashka deserved pity more than hatred.

Kath tried to remember the faces of the merchants who had first found him in the desert. He had sworn to kill them, but he could no longer recall them. Only Pashka remained. He tried to pinpoint when he had forgotten Calster's features.

The Blood King would not have forgotten.

Kath closed his eyes and breathed out evenly through his nose. A dull pain throbbed in his calf. It roused memories of guns and blood. In the calm, there was too much time for the past and present to haunt him.

He had expected swift, abrupt actions with constant questions and forceful anger. Not this void. Not the spaces for the fear and the pain to creep back and settle in the cavity of his chest.

They were trapped in the floating world. Six lives would pass through his fingers. This truth was no longer a possibility but a horrible reality. He had been arrogant before, to believe that he could save even one of the seven. They were each a heavy weight and his soul was collapsing beneath them all.

He had forgotten how much it hurt to care.

The darkness settled thickly around him, but Kath kept his eyes firmly shut. It reminded him of when he had died. When the Wise One had killed him. His purpose then had been to kill the Wise One and accomplish Scala's Revenge. A revenge he had begun when he executed his unfaithful wife and her lover, a revenge he would complete by killing a god he had not even believed existed. It had not mattered what he believed when he had set out to the pits, he simply had to prove to himself that he was powerful. The most powerful. So powerful that he needed no one.

His purpose had been foolish. Had been impossible. He recognized that now. That motivation had ended his first life and had been prepared to end his second one.

But that was no longer his purpose.

He had not been aware of the shift. When the faces of the merchants had slipped from his mind, a new goal had settled in their place. It had been subtle at first, and he had ignored it. But the longer he left it unattended, the stronger it grew, until now it filled his soul and it hurt.

He wanted to save them. Nana, Cyrah, and Tai.

In the darkness he imagined the moment when the Wise One had turned, when he had asked if Kath would accept his deal, if Kath would save seven lives. He must have known that he asked an impossible task.

Perhaps the Wise Man knew he would not succeed. Perhaps he had planned it that way all along.

Chapter 41

"Hail, Riders."

The greeting cut through the aimless conversation of the guards. A warning that passed quickly down the hall. They scrambled to their feet and resumed their positions as if they had never yielded. The greeting repeated down the hall until Kath could see the black masks emerge from the shadows.

He glared as they approached. At his side, Pashka still lay with an arm across his face. Kath assumed he was asleep and wondered if he was dead. A small part of him wished the desert lord was awake, he would certainly have no qualms hurling witty insults at the masked soldiers.

Kath restrained himself. A multitude of petty comments circled through his mind, but he stayed his tongue. It would gain him nothing.

He expected the riders to take him, but they halted before an empty cell. One stepped forward and unlocked the door, and then they parted, and between the blue feathers of the headdresses, Kath saw her.

Nana.

He rushed to his feet. At the sound of the jangling shackles, her eyes flitted to him. Just briefly. Then the riders ushered her into the cell and clamped manacles around her wrists.

They did not even glance at the other two prisoners before they left without a word. The guards, however, exchanged a great many words as soon as the riders had departed. Cruel words, lewd jokes, and grating laughter. Nana looked around the cell with a curled smile, as if she did not even hear the words they spoke about her.

Her dark eyes fell upon him, and his heart lurched.

"Nana," he said.

Her smile widened.

"Are you okay?" His eyes scanned her body for any signs of misuse. He had feared her dead.

"I'm fine," she whispered back. Her soft smile assured him that she told the truth.

"Hey." A guard whacked the butt of his spear against the bars of Kath's cell. He glared at the guard who simply scowled back. "No talking."

"Careful," another guard called out. "They say he's feral."

A dry chuckle scraped from the guard, and he jabbed the

butt of the spear between the bars. Kath leapt back, narrowly avoiding the blow.

"Next time," he growled, "I'll use the other end."

The guards laughed, and one clapped the spear-wielding guard on the shoulder as he returned to their tight knot. They exchanged jokes on Kath's behalf, but otherwise seemed distracted once again from the prisoners.

Kath eased back toward the bars, as far as his restraints would allow. He shifted his attention to Nana and opened his mouth to speak, but she held up a hand. Her eyes passed swiftly to the guards and back to him. He glanced back at the Islanders and found one guard still watching.

He clenched his jaw shut. If Nana was equally perturbed by their attention, he would not have known. She shuffled about her cell, kicking aside clumps of dirt and peering into every puddle. Finally, she settled, cross-legged upon the damp floor and adjusted her skirt over her legs. There was an ease in her disposition, in stark contrast to Kath's wound energy.

She had been a prisoner many times before.

Her eyes lifted and caught his.

"They don't know what to do with you," she whispered. Kath spared one more glance to the guards, who had started a game, then focused entirely upon Nana.

"Did they hurt you?" He brushed aside her comment. He didn't care what they thought about him. He cared about her.

She shook her head.

"Did they threaten you?"

Her shoulders shook in withheld laughter.

"Of course they did," she said, and he could hear the

amusement in her voice. "I'm Scala's Daughter after all."

"They shouldn't know that," Kath growled, all too aware that the desert lord was only a foot from him, oblivious.

"Don't blame him," Nana chided. "He's just afraid."

Kath scoffed. The noise earned a glance from a guard. The two fell silent. The man stared for a moment, until another guard nudged him to play his turn.

"Did they take you to the king?" Kath asked a moment later.

"They did," she said slowly. She wrung her hands together and frowned. "He is not a kind king. Cyrah was there. Well, her lookalike was. She never mentioned having a twin."

"I think there's a lot of things she didn't mention," Kath huffed.

"They are alike. They are both…" She searched for the right description. "Desperate."

"They are not the same," Kath muttered. "Whatever her ends, Cyrene is to be as trusted as their king."

"Perhaps," Nana murmured. A smile had returned to her lips. It was difficult to argue with her resolute certainty, so Kath conceded to Nana's beliefs about Cyrah's twin.

"Nana," he whispered and she straightened. "We need to get to Brat. If we can get to her, we can get out of here."

"How are we to do that?"

That question he had no answer to. The golden warmth in his chest felt hot. Too hot. It burned with Brat's anger. Her fear. Somewhere on the island she was caged, as he was. She pulled at him, but he could not offer her comfort. The same anger and fear coursed through him.

"I will find a way." He attempted to sound certain, but

Nana's lips quirked.

"It's okay." Her whisper was low. "I'm willing to die to protect the egg."

"Absolutely not."

He said it too loud. A guard stood, spear in hand.

"Hey! What did I say about talking?" In quick steps, he reached the cage and thrust the spear in. Tip first. Kath jerked to the side to avoid the jab. "Careful, imposter. There's only so much space for you to go."

Kath glared at the guard. Rage boiled in his blood, intensified by Brat's own emotions that echoed his own. But across from him, Nana sat perfectly still.

Her dark eyes found his.

Buried beneath the anger was the helplessness. He wanted to protect her, he wanted to save her, but he was trapped. He was trapped and down below Cyrah was still held by the Bu Chak.

Brat's warmth burned, but it was the six other attachments tearing him apart. Each life was a heavy weight upon his soul. Six lives, and he was utterly aware of each individual one. Their pull was incessant.

But he was helpless to save them.

Chapter 42

Kath slept fitfully.

He had not intended to sleep. The anger and the fear had coursed hot in his blood, but slowly the adrenaline filtered away and left him exhausted. He could not resist the rest his weary body craved.

The blackness was haunted by their faces, the seven lives he was tasked to save.

A bang jolted him awake.

A guard rattled the bars with the butt of his spear and chuckled at the reaction. The noise worsened his pounding headache. The guard shoved bowls filled with pasty white gruel beneath the bars. It was cold and tasteless. Pashka refused to eat, Kath was not so arrogant. Nana was given nothing.

In the dungeon far below the castle, everything was twisted into an eternal night. There was no understanding of time down there, only the changing shift of the guard kept any semblance that the hours marched onward.

Nana refused to speak with him. Every time he tried, she would glance at the spears and shake her head. It was unnerving not to hear her speak.

To fill the vacant time, Kath eavesdropped on the discussion of the guards. He could only catch words and phrases intermittently, but it was a good distraction. It kept him from thinking too much. That was the king's plan, just as it had been Pashka's. Use time against him, to show that they had the power and slowly break his resolution.

He refused to let the king triumph.

When the four masked riders returned, he had not yet caved to the king's desires. He had not caved, but he also had no further plan of action.

The guards' talk ceased at the appearance of the riders. They pressed flat against the damp walls at sharp attention. Kath stood as they approached, resigned to be taken. It was futile to fight the inevitable. The king had promised that he would call upon Kath again.

One rider opened his cell, another Nana's. They unshackled both and led them out, Nana before and Kath following behind.

"Goodbye," Pashka called after them. "I hope to see you both again!"

They led the prisoners back up the steep stairs, but this

time there was no interruption on the landing.

Nana labored to breathe, lungs not finding sufficient oxygen. But they pressed her onward. Kath's Islander body had already adjusted to the new atmosphere, but he slowed his pace to match hers.

As they mounted the stairs, a hazy natural light replaced the torchlight. The more they climbed the more it solidified into something real. The light pierced the darkness, probing rays growing more confident and pressing back the clawing black.

At the top of the stairs, Kath squinted in the morning sunlight. It filtered through the windows and illuminated the hall. It stung, but it was beautiful. It was the same sun that shone down upon the desert so far below.

In the castle halls they crossed no other Islander. Everything was still and empty. Empty except for the lurking disquiet. Something was wrong, but Kath could not pin it down long enough to discern what.

Down a staircase the riders guided them, then through an arched doorway that lead to the grassy expanse where Brat had first been forced to land.

The sun rose in the brilliant azure sky. It shaded everything in a hazy pink glow. It was almost possible to imagine that the islands were surrounded by a deep blue sea and not the formless expanse of air.

Altan stood in front of the stone precipice that jutted from the castle, Cyrene at his side. In his hand was a sword in its scabbard. The Ja Nrai stood in rank facing their king, forming a walkway that the four riders led Kath and Nana down.

They halted Kath before the king and in front of the

ranks of Ja Nrai. Nana, however, they stood at Altan's left.

Nana kept her head bent and stared at her bare feet. Hot anger beat in his chest. He did not know Altan's game, but the pieces were dangerously set.

"Kath." Altan's voice echoed off the castle and resounded in the space. The riders listened attentively to their king. At the name, Nana's eyes flickered up, though her chin remained tucked against her chest. "I have been patient with you, but unfortunately, I cannot shield you from our customs forever. Though you may not be a rider, you will be judged as such. You shall be sentenced before the Ja Nrai, with the Dragon Priestess Cyrene as judge in accordance with Ja Nrai tradition. Do you understand?"

Kath did not. Altan did not wait for his response but turned to Cyrene and, with a gentle touch on her shoulder , said, "My lady."

She inhaled a shallow breath and stepped forward. The long white skirts of her robe caught in the wind and fluttered around her like wispy clouds.

"Ja Nrai." Her voice was weak compared to the kings. There was a tremor she could not contain. "I present to you a traitor."

Cyrene paused and took another shallow breath before she continued.

"The eggs were stolen from you." She continued, words careful in their precision, "From us. Our sacred duty was to protect the eggs, to keep them safe until the binding ceremony. And this man."

She untwined her laced fingers to lift an accusing one at Kath.

"This unworthy man with no blessing of mine possesses

our greatest gift and treasure, breaking everyone tradition we hold dearly. He mocks us and he has brought our greatest enemy to us."

Her accusing finger swung to Nana.

Nana looked at her not with the anger that Kath felt, but with soft eyes. Gentle. Kath knew how undoing that gaze was. Cyrene faltered. Her hand balled into a fist and dropped to her side.

"We have asked for explanation." Cyrene tore her eyes from Nana's as she continued. The tremor had returned. "You have demanded, the king has demanded, you all know he refuses to answer. He is a danger to the Ja Nrai, to our king, to the Islands. I, Dragon Priestess of the Islands, blessed of the gods, reject his claim to the Ja Nrai. Are you in agreement?"

Her eyes swung over their blank masks. There was no objection. She let her gaze pass over the ranks a second time.

"With no objection," she said and turned her gaze to Kath. The unease that had settled in his chest swelled and pressed against the back of his throat to suffocate him. He swallowed hard. He knew her next words would be a crushing blow. "This traitor will receive just reward for his crimes. Though blessed, he will be stripped of our blessing, and he will speak."

The masked soldiers remained silent. They were passive actors in the play unfolding before them. Puppets in the hands of their lady. Cyrene allowed the silence as response and turned to the king, who inclined his head in the most solemn resignation.

A puppet in the hands of her king.

"Bring her forward."

At the king's command, two riders broke rank and crossed the grass toward the caves. Cyrene turned away to look out at the sunrise, focused on a point on the far horizon. She did not watch them disappear into the darkness, but flinched when the high-pitched scream rent the air.

The black masks emerged from the recesses of the cave. Each step they planted firmly one after the other as they forced the dragon from the cave with great iron chains. At the first glimpse of sunlight, Brat stretched her head up high and screamed again. She could not roar, her jaws were lashed shut.

Kath's heart beat in a rapid rhythm, a rhythm she felt. He could not calm her. He could not calm himself.

"What is her name?" Cyrene asked.

"Brat." At his voice, the dragon lowered her head and swung her great gaze to him. Her golden orbs latched onto him, and her struggles eased. She rumbled a greeting in the back of her throat. A cold washed over Kath though her warmth pulsed within him.

"An unworthy name." Altan's voice twisted with disgust. Kath paid him no heed, his gaze was transfixed on the dragon. His dragon.

The Ja Nrai strained to lead her onto the rock precipice. There they linked her chains to bolts in the stone. She was pinned, immobile.

Metal flashed in the sunlight as Altan drew the sword from its scabbard.

"No!" Nana grabbed Altan's arm and pulled it back before he could set the sword in Cyrene's open palm. "You can't!"

"Nana!" Kath lurched forward but two riders caught his

arms and dragged him back. Pinned like his dragon.

"How dare you!" Altan tried to jerk away, but she wrapped her arms tighter around his. A rider descended upon her and wrested her from the king. Still, she struggled against him.

"You can't!" she cried again.

Altan handed the sword to Cyrene. Her fingers curled around the hilt.

"No," Kath whispered.

Uncontrolled, uncontrollable. That was what Cyrah had said. A beast so untrained was a threat. Kill the beast, they would be free to kill the unknown brother.

"Stop!" Kath fought against the riders as Brat strained against the chains. Cyrene stepped closer to the dragon. The riders forced Kath to his knees and pinned his arms behind him, but still he struggled. "Don't you dare!"

Cyrene ran her fingers up the crystal white scales of Brat's neck and knelt beside the dragon. Brat's straining eased as she considered the woman at her side. The Dragon Priestess's touch was gentle, palm pressed flat against her scales, just below her jaw. They simply looked at each other.

"Traitors do not deserve such fine beasts." Altan's words were low and harsh, and Cyrene lowered her gaze.

One straight plunge, just beneath the jaw, in a gap between the scales. In, then out, and deep scarlet ran down white scales and pooled across the rock. There was no struggle, just a final working of the jaw, then Brat's head fell limp.

Dead.

Bright white pain seared his soul. It was sharp and deadly and sliced her life from him. Her golden warmth ripped away. Pain pricked in the back of his throat, in the back of his eyes.

The blood ran in rivulets along the cracks in the stone to the edge of the precipice. In fat drops of sticky red it fell. A rain of blood on the world below.

Cyrene stood as two riders approached the carcass. They unfastened the chains and, with great effort, shoved the body over the edge. Brat's wings unfurled in silky sheets and fluttered aimlessly.

Brat returned to the desert where she was born.

The Dragon Priestess did not watch the dragon fall. She bowed her head and considered the sword still in her hand, stained deep scarlet.

"Cyrene," the king said and she lifted her head. He beckoned her and she returned from the precipice, her footsteps red. "Justice is accomplished."

He took the sword from her as she passed. In the grass, the bloodied footprints disappeared, wiped away by the green. But the stains on her hand and the hem of her gown proclaimed what she had done. She stopped in front of Kath.

"Is the desert lord telling the truth?" she asked. Her hands balled in tight fists at her side. "Did he have her?"

"He did, and if she has the same marks as you—" Kath answered through the pain in his chest. He met her direct gaze. Their features were the same. Same square jaw, same rounded nose. But so different. Cyrah was desperate, Cyrene was despairing. "She will be killed."

Her blank expression did not change, as if she had not understood the words he had spoken. Or decided not to believe them. The next words that slipped from his mouth were not angry, maybe defeated, but they were harsh. Because he wanted to save her, but not this one, not this imposter.

"She may already be dead. But what do you care?"

"Insolent," she hissed low under her breath. "How dare you, she is my sister!"

"Then why was she all alone in the desert!"

She raised a bloodied hand, but Altan caught her wrists. Slowly, gently, he lowered her arm. His other hand rested on her shoulder. His lips brushed her hair and he spoke low words in her ear. Tears shimmered in her hazel eyes. Her fingers clutched the folds of her dress, and she was silent. Still. Altan's grip slipped from her wrist, and he stepped aside. His hand remained on her shoulder.

"Traitor." His voice boomed across the expanse and focused the attention of the black masks away from the cracks that formed in the wake of Kath's question, and Cyrene's outburst. Distracted from the answer the question demanded.

"You have received just punishment for your treason. Are you now prepared to give your true account?"

"No," Kath growled. He felt hollow without the golden warmth. He had not realized how comfortable he had become with it. With her.

Her loss strengthened his resolve.

"I see," the king sighed. "When you are called forth again, you will answer our questions. Or more extreme measures will be necessary."

He glanced back to the rock precipice where the rider held Nana. Tears wet her cheeks. So close. Yet unreachable, unsavable. He wished he could touch her, comfort her, but she was so far away, and the king's threat rooted him.

If he did not comply, Nana would be the next sent with a dripping necklace of red back to the land of her birth.

Chapter 43

The dice rattled across the wooden table. The guards, huddled beneath their cloaks for warmth, all leaned forward in anticipation as the dice bounced against the wood. Black dots announced the winner of the round. A guard barked a harsh laugh and accepted the begrudging coins from the others. Kath had learned all the games to play on long watches, but he did not recognize their game.

The previous winner initiated the betting and with wagers placed, the dice hit the table. The dots declared another round of losers and one winner.

Kath tried to focus on learning the game, but his mind

returned to blood slipping across stone, into the undergrowth of a jungle. His chest still ached where her warmth should have been. The absence made the pull of the other six lives more noticeable.

He almost wished that Pashka was not passed out in the corner. At least then, there would be inane comments to distract him. But the lord slept, only offering the occasional mumbling comments about the color of napkin rings and the number of fish missing from his pond.

He did wish that Nana was awake, but she slept curled about herself in the corner of her cell. It was rare that she slept, so he was glad she did. She would jerk in her sleep, and he wondered if Scala haunted even her dreams. She felt distant. He wondered if, so far away, his soul was any help in staving off the specters.

The dice tumbled. The clattering snapped his attention back to the guards. But it was an insufficient distraction from the hollowness in his chest. The living and the dead. Blood and pain. He thought of the boy. The first life he had tried to save. It hurt to think that Mell had trusted him, that the spark of hope was so viciously snuffed.

Nana would face the same fate if he had nothing to offer the king.

Another round of dice, and Kath noticed that when the sixes and ones were rolled the player on the thrower's right smirked. He stored the piece of information as the coin was collected and snide remarks exchanged.

He should sleep. But the dark haunted him, it felt too close now when death pressed around him. He should plan his response to the king, but his mind was muddled with the past and the present. It was difficult to think when Nana was across from him but all he could see was a knife to her throat.

As the executioner placed one to Zalna's.

The Blood King and King Altan were more similar than he cared to acknowledge.

All sixes were rolled and laughter exploded from the table. The guards all thumped the back of the poor soul who was the biggest loser. Another two rounds, and Kath had mapped out the game in his mind.

A guard glanced up, eyes staying too long on Nana before flicking briefly to the other cell. He found Kath glaring at him.

"Hey," he leered. "You done gawking? Or do you want to play?" The other guards chuckled, the overconfident one persisted at his joke. "Well? What do you wager?"

It was a game of luck. There was no way to guess what numbers would fall. Each call was based on statistics and how bold the player felt that evening.

"My freedom," Kath said, feeling very bold, "on all threes."

The guard paused, stunned he had received a response. But the others waited for him to continue his jest, so he laughed off the uncertainty and snatched the dice from the table.

"A worthy wager."

The four dice fell upon the table. Bounced. One fell, two fell, then the other two. All threes. The guards stared, frozen. Then the overconfident one laughed and shook his head, gathering the dice back up.

"I'll let the king know you're a free man."

"I'd appreciate it."

The prisoner's win dampened their interest in the game. They exchanged dice for cards. It was a small deck, with only ten cards. A guard deftly shuffled and dealt two to each. It was another game Kath did not recognize.

Kath did not bother to learn it this time.

He should not be focused on dice or cards. The king and his ultimatum needed to be at the forefront of his attention. Altan wanted something. His focus was singularly upon Cyrah and the eggs, so much so that even the Daughter of Scala was unimportant in his regard.

Cyrene needed something, but Kath did not think he could help her. Not if it meant that Altan would welcome Cyrah back into his realm.

Kath drew in a steadying breath and closed his eyes to the cards. It seemed a simple game, much simpler to master than the game Altan had set.

The pieces were placed, the next move was up to Kath.

The princess had a plan, perhaps one he could use to his advantage. But she had not been on the grassy field, nor in the throne room. Jayla may be a princess, but the title seemed to possess little true power. She slunk behind the king's orders, so Kath dismissed the possibility of help from her.

The Ja Nrai were hostile, controlled by the king. The Dragon Priestess was equally controlled. Trapped, crushed beneath his will. Her sole support had likely been her sister, who was now trapped in the world below.

It was a dizzying board.

Politics was like Crowns, Zalna had assured soon before he killed Acrius. Assured him that he would be as adept as a ruler as he was at the game. She had been wrong. It had taken him much too long to realize she traitorously plotted with Taitos.

In the desert there were no games. It was simple, survive or die. He tried to imagine the rolling dunes, but a guard barked a harsh laugh and he flinched. He opened his eyes and peered across the dungeon to where Nana slept.

It was easy to keep her safe down below. But not here.

If he brought the king to Cyrah, she would be doomed. But if he refused the king, then Cyrene would be doomed, and Nana killed.

It was an impossible game he played.

Chapter 44

Two riders entered the dungeon with no words and swift actions. They unchained Kath and Nana and dragged them from the cells.

Altan had lost patience.

Yet Kath had no answers to offer the king. He had hoped for more time. All he had determined was that he could not bring him to Cyrah, but the king would not accept that response.

He was keenly aware of Nana's footsteps behind him.

In the palace, the rosy light of the morning washed the stone in a cool hue. Despite the light, a cold void filled the castle. Kath had yet to see anyone walking the halls apart from the riders who led him.

The castle was lifeless.

The riders led them up the spiral staircase of a turret. Nana labored to breathe, and Kath almost asked for them to pause when the staircase ended in a room filled with color.

Stained-glass windows lined the walls. Triangles and rectangles of color elongated across the stone floor, shading the circular room in a rainbow.

"Your Highness," the rider on his right announced their presence.

One square of sky remained unshaded where a window stood open. A breeze found its way through the opening and, as the princess turned, it caught the coils of her hair and brushed them against her face. She smiled at the prisoners.

"You're both alive!" Jayla shut the window with a clink and severed the wind from its source. Her hair fell lifeless around her face. "It's wonderful to see you."

Kath stared at the princess. She was a ghost in the space, pale dress absorbing the hues around her. He was sure if he reached out to touch her, she would be no more tangible than the swaths of color. She laughed at him.

"I am used to astonishment, but this is flattering."

"What are you doing?" he demanded. The riders remained stalwart pillars at his side and kept him firmly planted between them. He wondered what power she possessed over the Ja Nrai, over the guard, over the crown. He had underestimated her.

"Do you know?" she toyed, as if she was enjoying it all.

"You want your brother's crown."

"I already have one." She waved aside the guess. "Why would I want another?"

"Because his comes with power," Nana said. Kath could not see her around the headdress of the Ja Nrai.

Color rippled over Jayla as she stepped closer. Blue and green and purple, a great kaleidoscope that settled when she stopped before them. So close that amidst all the color he could see the reflection of his own face in her eyes.

"Do you know why you're here?" she asked.

"Because you need to be saved from Altan."

She raised an eyebrow. "That's a strange way of phrasing it, but perhaps you're not wrong. You're here because he wants the eggs, but I don't want him to have them. I hid Cyrah so he wouldn't get them. Do you see why you complicate that?"

"You sent Cyrah to her death," he stated bluntly in a spark of anger on Cyrah's behalf. In the foreign world below Jayla's name had slipped across Cyrah's lips in a desperate hope, but she had been left to die.

Light rearranged over the princess as she shifted backward with a sigh. She looked at him with her head tilted.

"You truly don't understand."

"Jayla," the rider to his right said, voice low in caution. She held up her hand and he said nothing more.

"She knew that risk, but if Altan found those eggs many more would die. He has this dream." She turned her lifted hand and let the colors drift across her skin. "A dream of leading the Ja Nrai on a glorious white dragon to exact revenge upon the lower realm through fire and ash."

In her empty palm rested a red square.

"All he lacks is a dragon of his own."

"Aren't you an Islander?" Kath tore his eyes up from the red to meet her gaze. "Don't you want revenge?"

"Revenge?" Her fingers closed over the red, but it remained painted on her skin. She dropped her fist and shook her head. "It's not about revenge, Kath. It's about how to keep us from dying. We don't have enough. Not enough land, not enough wood, not enough food. We are dying. That's what concerns me, but Altan uses our plight to convince our people that we need to take from the world below. That doing so is our right. Do you know why Scala was cursed?"

"He killed Caizin," Nana murmured.

"Then why would Altan be praised for killing all of the world below? He is insane, but they follow him because he is blessed. They all follow him."

"Except you," Nana interjected and the princess smiled. A forlorn sort of smile detached from the rest of her face.

"Except me," she agreed. "I know my brother's cruelty, as does Cyrah. I refuse to commit the same mistake my brother will, the same mistake Scala did."

The same mistake the Blood King had.

"How will you avoid that?" Kath asked.

"By returning you to the ground," she said with great certainty in her words. "Altan cannot find those eggs. You will not lead him to them."

"And the other dragons?"

"I will worry myself with my realm, you with theirs. Agreed?"

In the swell of color, his vision warped. Everything was a distortion in the realm of the air. Death permeated his lungs and Jayla offered an escape. To save the other four lives, he would have to abandon the two above.

He did not reply. The princess' smile faded.

"I don't think you understand, this isn't an offer. If you stay here, you will die. It doesn't matter what you say, he will kill Scala's Daughter and eventually, he will kill you."

Kath did not know how to save the princess.

"We're wasting time." Jayla's voice shifted, amusement transforming to heavy seriousness. "You will be taken to the land below."

She turned her attention to the riders. "Mather, distract the Ja Nrai. Nakota, take them away."

The rider on the left, Mather, bowed and retreated down the staircase. The rider on the right, Nakota, stepped forward. His black gloved hand took the princess' bare one.

"Be careful," he murmured. There was no smile to be found upon her face. The rider turned and ushered both prisoners back down the stairwell of the turret.

Leaving the princess with a multitude of colors and glistening tears in her eyes.

"Do not speak," Nakota instructed as the three descended. His fingers pressed firmly around Kath's arm. Nana trailed behind. "Just follow me."

At the bottom of the stairs, Nakota released his hold and flicked his wrist to motion down the hall. His booted heels clicked an even pattern across the stones as he led the way with confident strides. Kath followed the swaying blue feathers.

Nana was at his side. He glanced over at her and found that she was already looking at him. Her dark eyes so deep whole galaxies were certainly lost within them.

Kath slipped his hand into Nana's. Her fingers twined

with his as they followed Nakota. He held her tightly, perhaps too tightly. It was unnecessary, but he did not let go of her hand.

They rounded a corner and two women stood in their path. The first Islanders he had seen who were not guards or royalty. They both wore gowns threaded with beads in intricate patterns.

Nakota's pace did not falter, even when both women turned toward them. Their conversation halted, and they pressed against the wall to allow clear passage for both the rider and the couple who followed him. Their eyes followed the three as they passed.

Grime layered Kath and Nana's bodies. The stench of the dungeon followed them, the damp and stale sweat tinged with the putrid scent of the chamber pots the guards seemed loath to change.

They passed without contention.

Down the hall, Kath could feel their eyes follow. He expected a reaction, it was impossible they were so oblivious to the state of the two. Yet they demurely remained silent.

When the three rounded the corner, Kath heard the spark of renewed conversation.

"They don't question." Nakota veered into a stairwell. "They would never question those who have received a blessing."

"Would they question me?" Kath asked. It was strange to consider the tattoo the mark of a blessing. The blue feathers shivered as Nakota nodded his head.

"You bring uncertainty to his reign. That is why you are so dangerous to him."

The king required unyielding support to his cause, and

the people had no reason to withhold their loyalty. He was blessed. They would follow their mad king on his quest for revenge. They would follow him until the desert ran red with blood, all on the promise that the destruction of their enemy would mean their own survival. The same promises that the Bu Chak had proclaimed down below.

At the top of the staircase, a bridge spanned from one tower to the next. They crossed over and into the dark hallway. It intersected with another, one that Kath recognized. It was the same one he had been led down when they had first landed on the island, and again the day prior. Straight ahead was the green lawn where Brat's blood stained the rock.

The tang of bile rose in the back of his throat as he stepped from the stone hall to the green lawn. The sun was still low on the horizon, but it was bright and it burned.

Nakota halted.

The lawn was empty, except for the woman who stood beside the bloodstained precipice. She looked like Cyrah. But this was not Cyrah, this was Cyrene.

She stood with her arms wrapped tightly around her body, staring out over the horizon. Nakota held up a hand and all three stilled. He pointed to the caves, but then Cyrene stiffened and turned.

She looked at them with tight lips.

"Cyrene," Nakota whispered. Her eyes flickered to the Ja Nrai rider, then back to Kath. The stranger of her own kind, the rider she did not bless.

"I should have known that Jayla would be plotting." Her voice was thin, her fingers gripping her forearms.

"Her Highness seeks to protect the Islands," Nakota

began, but Cyrene shook her head and he fell silent.

"She does what she thinks is right. But if you escape …" she spoke to Kath alone, and with each word the resolve in her pale eyes hardened. "I will never see my sister again."

"Cyrene, please," Kath said, though it hurt to speak the words when he could still see Brat's blood dripping from the sword. But there was pain in her eyes, and he needed to save her. "Let us go. If I can get to her, I can protect her."

The words fell brittle from his mouth, hard to believe. He had spoken honestly, but there was no reason for her to trust him, a stranger and foreigner. She did not know his desire for Cyrah's safety.

Tears slipped down her cheek.

"I want her back with me."

She called for the Ja Nrai, for the king. Kath lurched forward to grab her, but Nakota caught his forearm and tugged him back.

"We need to go." Nakota pushed him toward the cave. They ran across the lawn and into its dark recesses.

Kath tripped on the rocky path and caught himself on the ragged wall. Stone bit flesh, and there was blood, sticky on his hand. He forced himself forward, though he knew it was futile. He gripped Nana's hand tighter.

A dull light filled the cave. They entered a cavern with one wall chiseled away to reveal the blue sky and white clouds. A fully tacked dragon sat perched on the edge of the drop-off. It chittered and flapped its wings as Nakota approached.

"Get on!" Nakota ordered, but as his hand came to rest on the white scales, another dragon burst through the opening. Its wings snapped open and blocked the sunlight.

With its back claws, it landed on the rock edge, with its front it clamped Nakota's dragon against the rock. Nakota lurched backward, narrowly avoiding the razor-sharp talons.

"Kasain!" he called to the rider atop the beast. "Stop y—"

A spear thudded into the wooden mask and knocked Nakota to the ground. Kath dragged Nana behind him and pressed her against the cavern wall. Her fingers remained tightly laced with his.

Nakota groaned and clawed at the mask. He tore it from his face and flung it to the ground. It tumbled across the rock and disappeared over the edge.

Another dragon rose into the shallow cleft, jaws wide as it roared and forced Nakota to scuttle backward on his elbows until he hit the wall. Down the hall more riders appeared, spears raised against the prisoners, against their fellow brother.

A rider grabbed Kath's shoulder, another Nana's arm. Their fingers tore apart. The riders hauled Nakota to his feet and led them all back up the cave path and onto the lawn.

Cyrene stood in the middle of the expanse with her arms still wrapped around her body. The Ja Nrai spilled into the lawn and shouted amongst each other in the confusion. There were orders to search for the king.

Fire and ash, Jayla had said. The embers had been stirred.

The Ja Nrai knocked their brother member to his knees. He remained stoic, face set forward to gaze at nothing. He was young, though his broad shoulders bowed like they carried a weight far beyond his years, and his forehead was indented with the eternal knitting of his brow.

Nana and Kath were forced down beside Nakota. The

riders kept a firm hand settled upon the shoulder of each of their captives.

The blue feathers swirled in the commotion, but amidst the blue and the green she stood in stark contrast in her white dress. The one still stained with blood.

"Cyrene." She flinched at his voice. "Do you think this will save her?"

A rider whacked the butt of his spear against Kath's ribs, and he hissed in pain. Cyrene refused to look at him and wrapped her arms tighter around herself. He wished she would break from the structure of tradition, of her blessing, and defend herself.

But the Ja Nrai parted, and Cyrene looked up at her king.

"Well." Altan stood before the three prisoners, face set in a stony scowl. Murderous. "It appears we found another traitor amidst the brothers."

Nakota refused to look up at him.

"I am disappointed with you. I trusted you to guard my own sister, and you have betrayed her. You have betrayed your king."

"I am fulfilling my duty," Nakota interrupted the tirade, "to protect both her and this land."

Altan's hands curled into fists, then uncurled, and he breathed evenly through his nose. His jaw worked as he contemplated the brazen disrespect.

"You are well aware that the penalty for treason is capital punishment. It is a shame." He turned to Cyrene, "That another dragon should die."

Her eyes widened, but her mouth remained pressed shut. "Wait."

The king looked at Kath, lips contorted in obvious

disgust.

"Nana and Nakota." Kath spoke before the king could chastise him. It was the beginning of a concession, and Altan allowed the interruption.

Kath set a dangerous game. There were too many people to save, too many lives, all twisted together. He had been a fool to think that he could save any of them, but he could protect some. He could at least try.

"If you spare them, I will take you to Cyrah."

Chapter 45

The Ja Nrai rallied. They grabbed their spears and swords and fitted their dragons in leather saddles. The haste of the upheaval seared the air and danger flashed in its current.

Each member of Jayla's escort was held back. The four riders stood separate from the activity, not to be trusted. Apart from them, Kath counted fourteen riders. Fourteen dragons. He started recounting when Nana pressed her elbow against his arm.

"Kath," she whispered. In the movement swirling around them, she was an oasis. Voice calm and soothing. "What are you planning?"

Her eyes trained upon him. When he glanced at her she had already found that deep part of him, the tangled part he did not understand. The part that was broken, the part that was tired, that was hurt. The true part.

"Trust me." The words fizzled between them and left nothing tangible to grasp and cling to. He would not have accepted the two simple words; he had given her no reason to.

She knew. She knew his secrets. She knew that the blood of the Wayfinders, his wife, his best friend, and hundreds of others stained his hands. She knew the pain that cracked his heart, his hatred of the Wise Man, his confusion. She knew of the unjust world and how he had fractured it further. She knew that he was incapable of saving Mell or Cyrah or Rain or Tai or Cyrene or Jayla.

Or her.

"I trust you." The gift was the most precious thing he had ever received. Beneath its weight, his soul snapped.

Then she was torn from him, hauled back by the riders. Gloved hands hefted him to his feet and forced him toward a saddled dragon. Kath craned his neck backward to watch as they wrestled Nana back into the castle.

She vanished from his view.

He swept his gaze over the lawn, noted every dragon, every rider, and where Altan mounted a dragon behind its rider.

"Up," the rider ordered. Kath grabbed the saddle and climbed up behind the dragon's rider. He clutched the smooth back of the saddle for balance as the dragon rose to its hind legs.

"For the Islands!" Altan called, and the riders roared the phrase in unison. A thrum of zeal that promised the demise of the world below. The dragons speared into the sky and left Cyrene on the green grass.

All alone.

The wind crashed cold against him. The dragons pinned in the open air then one by one each tucked their wings against their body and plummeted toward the earth. They kept in a tight formation. The islands streaked past them, then the thick bank of clouds, and only when the desert unfolded before them did the dragons snap out their wings and veer their course.

The dark craters of the Bu Chak fortress were small and insignificant as they passed below them. Shadows were not important to the physical world. For the moment, Kath allowed the cult to remain unimportant to the riders. It was the Bu Chak who had Cyrah, but it was to Tai's encampment that Kath led them.

The dragons covered the distance swiftly. Their black shadows rippled like water over the dunes. Soon the tan slopes of the campsite rose between the rolling red sand.

"There!" Kath shouted over the wind. The rider motioned sharply down with his spear, and the dragon dipped toward the sand. Three dragons descended as the others circled above. Carrion vultures waiting for their meal to die.

Kath brought destruction upon the camp.

Panicked cries reached his ears as the dragons swept lower. The wind stirred by the leathery wings whipped up the flaps of tents, tumbled the shade stands, and covered the campfires with sand.

The camp rushed to protect themselves as the first dragon landed upon the desert. Children were ushered into the periphery tents while the adults armed themselves with swords, spears, bows, and a few glittering guns, whatever had been salvaged after the attack on the Bu Chak camp. There were few horses, fewer people, even fewer to fight.

Tai's people leveled their weapons against the beasts crowding the center of their camp, but they held them loosely. As if they had already submitted themselves to their fate. The fear plain on their faces.

Upon the desert floor, Kath's plan looked desperately inadequate. His fingers tightened around the saddle and he racked his brain to cobble together something that would not end in all their deaths.

Kath needed Rain.

Altan's boots hit the sand.

The Ja Nrai pressed their dragons and spears close behind their king, prepared to intercept any who dared approach.

The rider in front of Kath reached back and tugged him off the beast and onto the ground. He hit the sand hard, calf pulsing in pain, air shoved from his lungs. He spit sand as he pushed himself up and knelt on the ground.

He glared up at Altan.

"Where is she?" Altan demanded and ignored the stares of the desert dwellers.

"Who are you?"

The three simple words caught the king's attention. The question calm amidst the fury of the forces that crashed into his encampment. The words possessed authority. They were a threat. Altan faced Tai.

Before his people, the old man stood with his back straightened in steely resolve, weaponless in the face of legends. The shadows of the dragons above danced over him.

"I will excuse your directness," Altan said. "I assume you do not know to whom you speak. I am Altan, king of the gods blessed. I have come to reclaim what is ours."

"Please continue to excuse my directness." Tai approached and the spears tilted toward him. He stopped between his people and the dragons and lifted an empty palm toward Kath. "I must ask for clarification, I only see that you have returned someone to us."

"Get Rain." Kath stood. Altan snapped his fingers and a rider descended from his dragon and grabbed Kath's forearms.

"You are in no position to give orders."

"They're not orders," Kath snapped back and glared at Altan. "If you want Cyrah, you want Rain. He'll lead you to her."

Altan's scowl was cold in its derision. Though he had no choice but to cave to Kath's words. He was an outsider of the world below, Kath was not. The king turned to Tai and snapped, "Retrieve Rain."

Tai pressed his palm against his chest and inclined his head. "Of course."

He raised a hand, and Red joined him in the space between the camp and the Islanders. His brow knit in confusion. He looked from his leader to the dragons, the king, Kath, then back to his leader. Tai gave short orders, too low to be heard from where Altan and Kath stood. Altan frowned.

Red left Tai's side and slipped into the crowd. Tai remained with back ramrod straight and smile upon his lips. There was an uncomfortable moment of restless still. Before the king could become impatient the camp began to stir. Slowly, person by person, the group parted, and Red returned with Rain at his side.

Rain looked murderous.

Faced with his enemy, his eyes were stormy with years of trained hatred. These were the Islanders from on high, descended to mock his captivity. The full brunt of the curse come to taunt him.

"Rain," Tai said when the two had halted beside him. Rain focused unwaveringly on Altan. "They have questions."

Rain spit into the sand. Altan crinkled his nose.

"I refused yours," he growled. "I will refuse theirs all the more."

"They are all so impertinent," Altan muttered.

"May I speak with him?" Kath requested, an appeal to Altan's sense of structure. Though it pained Kath, the request seemed to sate the king and he nodded.

"Order him to direct us to Cyrah."

The riders released their hold and Kath approached the bound man. Kath could not find the right words, the ones that would convince the man who hated him to side with him. But he did know what drove the man, a twisted belief that he could help his people.

"He can't have the egg," Kath whispered as he untied the rope binding Rain's wrists.

"I would not help him," Rain hissed.

"Good." Kath dropped the rope to the sand. Rain rubbed his raw wrists. "Help me, or he will destroy you all."

A rider grabbed Kath's shoulder and pulled him back as another grabbed Rain and shoved him toward the dragons. Rain did not look at Kath.

Red did, and he dipped his head in a very slight nod.

"What did you say?" Altan demanded as the rider led Kath back to the circle of dragons. Kath remained tight-lipped. "I grow tired of this disrespect."

The king turned to Rain. "Answer me simply, where is Cyrah?"

Rain glared down at Altan. The pause lengthened and Altan's eyes narrowed. But before the king could demand again, there were words. Each slow and forced through clenched teeth.

But they came.

"The Bu Chak has her."

"And where is this Bu Chak?" Altan pronounced the name with pursed lips, derision on his tongue and it was not a pleasant taste.

"I can show you the way." Rain looked away, proud stance breaking into a defeated slump.

"Show it," Altan ordered and motioned to the riders. They grabbed Rain and Kath and dragged them off the sun-soaked sand.

Kath remounted the dragon behind the rider as ordered. Rain resisted the rider, until he threatened to throw the desert dweller across the saddle and Red grudgingly complied. Tai and his people remained with weapons raised, ignored by the Ja Nrai.

"Which way?" Altan asked.

Rain glared at him. Gaze venomous. But the words did come. "In the pits, below your islands."

"We ride!" Altan commanded. The dragons roared and stretched their necks to the sun with a flash of their needle-sharp teeth. The camp dwellers lifted their arms and pulled their loose clothes over their noses and eyes to protect themselves from the sand stirred by the flapping wings. Tai remained staunch in the windstorm, and after the dragons had risen from the ground, Tai's eyes opened, and he craned his head upward to find Kath still gazing down at his shrinking form.

Tai gave him a single nod.

Trust was a delicate thing.

Chapter 46

White flooded the scar on the desert floor.

The sound was deafening. The screech of beasts, the shouts of men, the thunder that rumbled and reverberated and promised death.

Kath ducked close behind the rider, fingers curled around the saddle as his heart thudded in his chest. He wished that the thunder would cease. The dragon landed upon the rock and fanned its wings wide, a great sheet of white that blocked Kath's view of the men running along the walkways far above. The dragon roared.

Kath shoved the heels of his palms against his ears. The

rider slid down the dragon and dragged Kath down with him. Crouched in the relative shelter of the beast's great body, the rider ripped the black mask from his head. A young face lay beneath. A young face contorted in pain and gulping air in jagged breaths.

He gripped his side, blood pooling over his fingers.

"Stop it," the rider gasped. Kath wiped his sweaty palms against his pants and stuttered through a reassurance, but the rider halted him. "Make it stop."

Kath met his dark eyes and saw fear.

"Keep your hand on the wound," Kath instructed as another volley of thunder echoed over them.

"Stop!" Above the cacophony, Rain's voice was barely audible, but still, he persisted. "Halt! They—"

A rider grabbed Rain and shoved him backward. He rammed against Kath's back and collapsed beside him and the injured rider.

A shrill whistle rent the air. A signal.

A sea of flames poured through the stone fortress.

Brat had injured their ranks with her flame. But this fire was different. It was insatiable and devoured everything. Beside the dragon, Kath could feel its burning fury. Despite the heat, he felt cold.

"What have you brought upon us?" Rain whispered.

Another whistle and the dragon jaws snapped shut and the fire ceased. But the burning continued. Wooden structures snapped and cracked, railings and platforms crashed in charred heaps to the rocky floor. The scent of burnt flesh, left unmasked by the raw heat of the flames, was stifling. After such intensity, the lull was reverent.

The dragons kept a tight, protective circle around their

riders, some wounded from a blow without a source. The rider beside Kath had gone dreadfully still. Kath could not bring himself to look down at the young face. Instead, he watched as the Island ruler surveyed the carnage he had inflicted. A glimpse of what was to come.

"You have one of our own," he called into the void. "You will return her."

A wooden walkway splintered and collapsed in response. The Bu Chak remained recessed in the darkened entries of the passageways they had bored into the earth. They faced the impossible and their hatred alone could not defeat the foe.

A woman emerged onto a section of walkway that remained, flanked by guards with singed armor. It was the same woman who had stood at Pashka's side when Kath had freed Nana. In the hesitation, the Bu Chak all looked to her.

"Are you their leader?" the woman asked.

"I am their king," Altan gently corrected, with enough emphasis on his proper title that the woman would not again be mistaken.

"I see," she muttered.

"We have come for one of our own, is it true that you have her?"

The woman said nothing.

"Mirati," Rain hissed, and the woman's eyes darted to where he crouched amidst the dragons. "Get her, save the rest."

"Silence," the woman growled. Rain stiffened. "I will not bend to the will of the heathens, as you seem so capable of doing. You say you saw visions of rain, it seems you saw nothing more than this."

She motioned wide to the ash falling gently down upon the rocky basin.

"She is cursed, she will be sacrificed. The curses will be satisfied and the Islands will crumble—"

"She's in the cells," Rain interrupted the tirade. "They would have moved her after Scala's Daughter was taken. In the upper cells, straight up the stairway."

Mirati's jaw slackened with each of Rain's succinct words.

"You," she whispered in shocked outrage.

"It appears that he speaks the truth." Altan nodded to the riders. "Rain, escort the riders."

A rider shoved Rain forward, out from the circle of dragons. He stumbled before he caught himself and stood in the precarious space between the Ja Nrai and the Bu Chak.

Mirati glowered at him, but the dragons remained a constant threat and kept her pinned in place. They could easily destroy all the Bu Chak had labored to create, and she knew.

"We will give you the girl." Mirati caved. "If you give us the Daughter of Scala in return."

"Why would you think we have her?" Altan asked. His features schooled to impassivity.

"He took her." Mirati pointed to Kath. "You have him, so you must have her. You seek one of your own, we seek her. You return her to us, and we will return yours."

Altan tilted his head to consider the fortress. The ash fell gently around him, his vision of destruction come to life, and it pleased him.

"I will consent to that. The Daughter of Scala will be yours, but only after you return the Islander."

"Agreed." Mirati snapped and a Bu Chak member

disappeared into the dark hall behind her.

Rain remained in the in-between. Vulnerable, alone, forgotten. His head remained tilted up to Mirati, but she kept her eyes bored into the king.

"To think that we were once part of this wretched world," Altan muttered, words icy with resentment toward the earth and those who had sided with Scala. Around them the wood continued to smolder and another walkway crashed to the earth. "The Daughter of Scala will be destroyed alongside them all."

Crazed and murderous.

Kath poised himself for action. His plan was coming to an end, and he did not have a next step. He knew he had to protect Cyrah and Rain. He could not allow Nana to be given to the Bu Chak.

It was difficult to think when death filled his nostrils.

A guard emerged from an entryway in front of Rain, Cyrah towed behind him. At the smell of the burning, her nose wrinkled and she lifted a hand to block the stench. Her eyes swept over the charred wood, past Rain, and halted at the sight of the dragons.

"Cyrah," Altan murmured in his low, melodic voice. It should have been soothing, but her eyes widened in terror. She was trapped before the man she had fled. Kath had brought him to her. She stopped a few feet in front of Rain. The two lives, caught between the two worlds prepared to destroy them both.

Altan waved his hand and two riders slipped past the protective circle and into the empty expanse. They advanced toward Cyrah. She was unable to move, unable to flee. They grabbed her forearms and forced her closer to the dragons.

Altan stepped to the edge of the protective barrier and slipped his fingers around her wrist. He lowered her hand from her face and smiled.

"I missed you." His lips brushed hers briefly, and as he pulled away, he asked, "Where are the eggs?"

Confusion knit her brow. Altan's soft smile turned sour.

"Cyrah." His voice struggled to maintain the calm facade. "What have you done with them?"

Her lips parted to speak, but she had no response because she did not know. Her eyes darted to Kath and Altan noticed.

"You." He released Cyrah's wrist and marched to Kath. "How dare you mock me."

Two riders grabbed Kath's arms and forced him to stand before the king.

"I have brought you to Cyrah," Kath answered. "Just as I said I would."

"Answer me simply, where are the eggs?" Altan's jaw clenched tight as he seethed.

Kath still had no plan past Cyrah's rescue. She was freed from the Bu Chak, though delivered into Altan's hands. Rain was freed from Tai's camp but turned to an even more hostile force. Three below, three above, and he did not know what more he could do.

"You cannot defeat the inevitable," Altan snarled. "Smell, listen. Soon this whole world will be cleansed and the gods will return to bless me."

"Bless you?" Kath scoffed. "You are more cursed than we are!"

The statement made the king pause. The words incongruous with the reality he had constructed around himself. A narrative he had twisted from the fragments of tales handed down through one-sided myths of what had happened so long ago. Kath had received the other side of the tale, of harbored resentment against those who had been raised, a resentment that grew into the Bu Chak. It had all made sense until he had died.

Until he had met the only god who had not abandoned them. Until Kath had seen his weariness.

"Impertinent," Altan muttered and pushed aside the surprise Kath's words caused.

"I can take you to the Wise One." The words rushed from Kath's mouth. He could not save the six lives, but the Wise One could. "He will tell you all."

"Do not take me for a fool!" Altan snapped and grabbed a spear from a rider. He flipped its tip against Kath's neck. The razor edge brushed against his skin. "You are a liar and a pretender. You will tell me where the eggs are."

"No."

Frustration twisted Altan's face. The impertinence tested his patience, but as he opened his mouth to speak, a shout silenced him.

"Altan!" Cyrah cried, then covered her mouth. The king turned as Rain unsheathed a Ja Nrai sword from the rider's scabbard.

This was not an end that Kath could allow.

Before Rain could enact his foolhardy plan, Kath acted first. He dropped to the ground, swept up the spear from the dead rider, and thrust it forward.

Red. All blood was red. Islander or desert dweller.

The spear dropped from Altan's hand and clattered upon the rock. Altan opened his mouth, but no words passed from his lips before he collapsed on the ground before Kath.

His blood spilled across the stone.

Rain and Kath stood on either side of the fallen king and stared at each other in the poised moment of shock. The Ja Nrai spears flashed to level against them both.

Mirati's laughter was sharp from overhead. It mocked the king, but it felt like it mocked Kath. Kath who had killed again. He released the end of the spear and raised his hands over his head.

"Stop!"

The riders halted at Cyrah's voice. Black masks swung to her. She stood firm beneath their heavy gazes. There were cuts on her hands, bruises on her jaw, dirt and sand soiling her dress, but she commanded their attention. She was their Dragon Priestess, blessed by the gods.

"Retrieve the egg," she ordered. "And bring these two to the Islands, the queen will decide their fate."

Chapter 47

In his corner of the cell, Pashka would not stop laughing. It began as a chuckle but continued until he wiped away tears and shook his head. Rain watched him for a while. If the altitude had affected him, he hid it well. Hid it until the laughter grew too loud and he winced. Finally, he asked the question Pashka waited for. "Why are you laughing?"

Kath sighed and lifted his forehead from against his knees. "He's in withdrawal."

"You killed him?" Pashka blurted, accompanied by another round of laughter.

The rumors spread quickly. They began when the riders

had brought Rain and Kath to the dungeon. The guards whispered between themselves and cast furtive glances to the two prisoners. They were on edge, gripping their spears, stances firmed as the unease and uncertainty tainted the air. The king's absence left a gaping hole that was deep and dangerous. The glances at Kath were murderous.

He did not care what the Islanders thought. He cared that they had taken Nana, that she had not returned to the dungeon since the two prisoners had been brought down.

Kath's lack of response only gave Pashka the freedom to continue.

"You killed your king?"

In the flickering torchlight, he could see the grin spreading across Pashka's face. Both Pashka and Rain watched him, the prisoner they had once exchanged. Now they all sat chained in the same cell. Kath shook his head.

"He was never my king," he said.

"You're an Islander." Pashka waved his hand in the air to dismiss the firm words. "Of course he was your king."

"And your king," Rain added with forceful words, "was prepared to destroy us."

Kath was tired. In the aftermath of the day's bloody events there was only exhaustion.

"Why did you kill him?" Rain asked.

"You were going to kill him," Kath muttered, too tired to skirt the truth with coy phrases. Rain looked away to escape Kath's direct gaze.

"Did you think that he could live?" Rain questioned darkly. "He would have destroyed everything."

"The Bu Chak is no different," Kath retorted. "If they had their way the Islands would be destroyed."

"Good," Pashka muttered.

Rain clasped and unclasped his hands multiple times before he asked, "Then why didn't you kill me?"

"Because," Kath began. Rain looked at his hands, at the shackles around his wrists. "You chose a different path."

Pashka laughed at that, but Kath ignored him. Rain said nothing more. Kath rested his head back against his knees and waited for the Ja Nrai to come. He knew they would return, that the crime would be punished.

The blood on his hands deserved justice.

Acrius had told a tale one evening, as he sat on watch with Kath and Zalna while the other Wayfinders slept. He told a tale of a conquering king who let nothing stand in his way. The story had settled deeply in his soul, resonating with his own desire for control and it resulted in his sweeping conquests. He wondered if Altan had been told such a tale in his childhood, if Rain had.

As Kath waited for his judgment, the story wound through his mind, twining between the visions of red blood slowly sinking into sand and slipping across stone.

He wanted no more blood on his hands. He wanted nothing more to do with the Wayfinders and their twisted lore. He wanted nothing more to do with the Bloody King and his vicious rule.

He only wanted to save the six lives. He didn't even care if he had accomplished his side of the Wise One's deal. He just wanted to see the six safe.

A rider came for him.

Chapter 48

—

"It's their wood," she explained. In the room, a large hearth filled the far wall. Warmth rolled against him as he stepped across the threshold and sent a shiver up his spine. Flames licked at the wood and slowly, slowly gnawed it to blackened embers. A log snapped and he flinched.

He thought of collapsing walkways. Of burnt flesh.

Before the fire, a woman stood with her back turned toward him. Her hair was tightly braided, and she deserved that right.

She wore a soft dress with a large wool shawl draped over

her shoulders. She also flinched when the fire cracked and sent a spray of embers into the air.

Behind him, the rider shut the door. Kath wondered if he would find Nakota or Mather behind the black mask. The rider, however, remained silent and still beside the door.

"We don't have enough resources," the woman continued. "So we take it from them."

"Cyrah." At his voice she turned. A small, tired smile graced her lips. "Are you okay?"

"I am." Her shoulders rose a fraction. "No more harmed than I'm sure we harmed Nana."

She sat on a low bench that stretched before the hearth and patted the stone. Kath moved closer to the heat. The flames wavered in their mesmerizing dance and lulled him into a displaced serenity. He should be unnerved, but the cracking of the wood eased from threatening to comforting.

He thought of warmth on cold desert nights.

"Her Highness let me bring you here," Cyrah began when he had taken his seat beside her. "To explain what is going to happen."

She faced him. Half of her face glowed in the firelight the other was thrown into deep shadow. Her smile was gone.

He already knew what she would say.

"Tomorrow Jayla will be crowned queen," she said. "Then they will ask her to kill you."

Kath chuckled. He knew.

"She will have no choice but to comply," she continued, and turned her face away from the fire as if there was something else to consider. Something other than the heat and the stolen wood and the promise of death. "You did kill our king."

"I understand." Kath knew he should have felt rage. He should have felt anything other than the calm. Maybe it was the exhaustion, or the warmth, but he felt only the calm. The resignation to his fate.

There was blood on his hand. From the past, from the present, he could no longer run from the sins. There was only one thing pricking at the back of his mind. Only one thing causing unease.

Cyrah had turned back to face him, carefully searching for any emotion his expression would betray.

"What will happen to the others?"

"They will be free to go," Cyrah assured. "I will make sure of that. They committed no crimes. I won't let them do anything, not to Nana."

"Good." Kath whispered. He meant it. So he repeated, "Good."

"I'm so sorry, Kath." There was pain in her voice. Kath concentrated on the fire. He did not want to see the pity in her eyes. "I should have been the one to intervene."

The fire snapped. The wood burned. It was comforting, it reminded him of the caves. When there was nothing between them but a begrudging trust. The moment would not last forever.

"Thank you." Her voice was thick with emotion. "I owe you my life, my sister's. Truly, I owe you my home. And I am sorry."

She paused. The moment was coming to an end. Time moved onward and what Kath had put into play would draw to its conclusion.

"I am sorry I cannot save you."

Kath chuckled at her wording, then shrugged. "It is just."

At the gesture, Cyrah closed her eyes and took a measured breath in.

"No, it is not." When her eyes flicked open, there were shimmering tears. Always so quick to reveal her emotions. Kath smirked.

"Don't waste water," he murmured to maintain the casual detachment.

With the tips of her fingers, she pressed away the tears at the corners of her eyes. The smallest of smiles perked her lips.

"I do have one request," he said slowly.

"Ask it."

"I would like to see Nana."

Her smile broadened. "I knew you would."

She nodded to the rider at the door. The door clicked open. Kath stood and turned as Nana stepped into the room. They had given her a new dress, a simple blue one. But she looked clean and unharmed.

He smiled.

She frowned.

"Mather will be at the door, let him know when you are ready." Cyrah stood and pulled the shawl tight around her shoulders. "Unfortunately you will have to be escorted back to your respective cells to be held until …"

She took a shaky breath and Kath allowed his gaze to break with Nana's long enough to set a hand on Cyrah's shoulder. His touch felt stiff and heavy, but she did not shrink from the attempt of comfort. Instead, she brushed her fingers lightly against his own.

"Thank you," she whispered, then she left. Nana took the Dragon Priestess's hand in hers briefly as she passed. The rider dipped his head then stepped out of the room and closed the door. When the latch clicked shut, Nana's attention snapped to Kath.

"Did you kill him?"

"I did."

She inhaled a long, slow breath and nodded. Her gaze turned toward the windows and considered the stars. For a long moment she was silent, and Kath let her be. Because she needed it, because he did not know how to break it.

After a time he did not count, she stepped past him and took a seat upon the bench. The gentle glow of the fire made her skin warm and rich. Kath lowered himself onto the edge of the bench, poised, but for what he did not know. He felt ill at ease and thoughts crowded his mind until he could no longer piece them intelligibly together. Nana said nothing.

"Do you still want to go to the Wise One?" Kath asked. It was the easy way out, the simple way to make her speak. But it was not what he wanted to ask.

When she did not respond he tried again.

"After I killed them, I went to kill the Wise One." He had been waiting for her to say the first words. His were timid, hers were always strong. Confident in what she needed to say, even if it was difficult. She was the one who began the conversations, he felt awkward as he made his bold start. "I executed Zalna and Taitos in rage, and that rage brought me to him. I think he was waiting for me. He knew that I would come."

"Why did you want to kill him?" she asked when his voice had faded to nothing, and he needed direction.

"Because I thought if I killed him it would prove I

needed no one. But then he killed me. He offered me a deal. If I saved seven lives, I would be given a second life."

It was strange to hear the tale forming upon his lips when he had guarded it for so long. It sounded more like a myth than a reality they inhabited.

"I accepted the deal. I thought when I obtained my second life, I could have a second chance to kill him. A second chance to …" His words failed. He did not know how to properly express the pain that his two closest confidants had caused. The only two he had trusted. Killing the Wise One would make him feel invincible, powerful, and calloused. "To be all powerful. I don't want that now. I don't think it's possible anyway."

His second life had always felt a fragile thing. The body was tangible, but the soul within was only loosely connected. Nana knew. She could feel the disconnect, the truth that lay beneath his skin.

When his words had died and he had nothing left to say, Nana offered no further prompting. She did not look at him, which only made him feel more unstable.

"Nana?"

"I don't think it's possible to understand," she whispered.

"No, I don't think so." Though he wished she did. "Do you think I saved them?"

"The seven lives? Does it matter?" she asked. "You will die anyway."

"It matters," he murmured. Though he could not say why. She tilted her head to the side in thought. "Though, I already know the answer. I couldn't save Mell, I messed up the whole thing from the start."

"You saved him," she said with such assurance he felt

wrong doubting her. He did though.

"He died."

"You saved him from a life that had him trapped," she insisted. "His death is not on your hands."

"Even so," he conceded because he did not have the energy to contest her claim. "I had to save seven."

"Who are the seven?"

"Mell, Rain, Tai, Cyrah, Cyrene, Jayla." It was difficult to say each name, to admit each soul that he had been charged to save. There was a long pause before he turned to look at her, to admit the one that laid the heaviest. "You."

She looked at him with her dark, perceptive eyes. In the silk dress, with her coils of hair, she looked far from the prisoner he had first met.

"I don't know how to save you." The words were a painful confession, a hoarse whisper he wished she did not hear. But she did, and she already knew. "I want to."

"I don't know if anyone can," She whispered. "I think he tricked you."

"I guess he did," Kath chuckled, but she did not join his humor. "I'm so sorry."

She smirked finally. A beautiful sight. "What for? I will go free, you're the one who is going to die."

"That doesn't matter." He shrugged. "It is just, I deserve it."

Her lips were still quirked. She raised an eyebrow.

"It doesn't matter," he repeated, to assure her of the truth of his words. To assure himself.

"I don't believe you."

He had cried once. His arm had been broken, and Acrius had set it. The tears were hot on his cheeks. Acrius had laughed at him and told him that no strong man ever shed tears.

He had not cried since.

Now, the pain built in the back of his throat. In the wake of her words, everything came crashing down, and he did not know what to do with all the shards. They cut, and they hurt, and he did not know how to respond to her.

The guilt of blood clawed at his heart. The yearning to live constricted his chest. His first life had been constructed around survival and conquest. He had crushed everything in his path. His second life had begun with the rage to destroy what he could not in his first.

It was all worthless.

He wanted no more breaking bones, no more blood, no more death.

He wanted to live.

Tears slid down his cheeks and he angrily tried to wipe them away. A waste of water. Nana caught his fingers and gently lowered his hand. Her dark eyes were cool and calm. He let her arms wrap around his body.

He cried, and she cried with him.

Chapter 49

Altan's crown sat upon the Jayla's long, loose curls.

It was hers now. The crown passed through the royal lineage, from the first king of the Islands until now. She sat upon the dais comfortably, as if she had always occupied the throne.

On Jayla's right stood Cyrah, and on her left, Cyrene. Both were garbed in the same white dress, hair styled in the same braid. Kath could only tell them apart by the faint bruises speckling Cyrah's face. She smiled at him, a tight, pained smile.

The Ja Nrai lined the room just as they had during Kath's

first visit, but now behind their ranks stood nobles in their regal garb. They whispered between themselves in a dry, scraping sound that swirled in the throne room like locusts. The noise buzzed in Kath's ears as he, Rain, Pashka, and Nana were led to the queen.

The four prisoners were halted before the throne. A silence descended amongst the nobles, and in the silence, his apprehension grew. Nana's fingers found Kath's and twined with his.

"Well." Jayla's simple word riveted the focus of the gathered nobles. Altan's voice had been smooth and soothing, Jayla's burst with energy. "What a strange assemblage you are."

She smirked as some grand joke had been told. The four prisoners before her were not so enthused, even Pashka had the sense to remain silent before the sovereign. The queen's eyes scanned each prisoner then settled on Kath.

"Kath," she said. "You appear in the desert with no family, no place in our society, no past at all. You are blessed, bound with a dragon without the blessing of a priestess, and you killed our king. Still, we do not know who you are. So, who are you?"

"I'm no one," Kath said. Jayla's expression remained impassive.

"Cyrah told me an interesting tale." She motioned to the woman on her right. "She said that you saved her."

"The last egg is safe because of him," Cyrah added and the queen allowed the interjection. Cyrene lowered her gaze, hands wringing around each other. "He saved the last dragon, for that we are indebted to him. I am indebted to him."

A restless murmur passed through the court. There was confusion. Questions raised by the younger royal who presented a reality so starkly different from their previous monarch.

"However." Jayla's voice cut sharply through their noise. "You have murdered our king, an act of treason that cannot be overlooked. An act of treason that deserves death."

Behind the line of impassive masks rose a low whisper of agreement. Nana's fingers tightened around his.

"He saved her," Rain muttered.

"Do you wish to say something?" Jayla asked Rain. He glared up at her. "You may speak."

"He saved her," Rain repeated, voice snapping in the throne room. Indignation boiled in him, and he looked upon the queen with disgust. "Truly, he saved you all. Your king was crazed. You're going to kill him for that?"

Hisses of outrage filled the throne room. Rain stood staunchly amidst the flurry of their anger. Jayla tilted her head to the side and considered it all. When their fury showed no sign of cresting back into silence, she lifted a hand.

"Tell me." She lowered her raised palm when the uneasy silence returned. "What is your name?"

Rain glared up at her, hands balled into fists.

"Dailin," he said. Kath glanced at the man. Dressed all in gray, he cut an imposing figure in the colorful hall. But that was not the name he had come to associate with the man. The man who saw visions of rain.

"Well, Dailin," Jayla said, "I hope you understand that because of this man you will go free."

Rain, Dailin, opened his mouth again but Jayla shook her

head.

"You will be released to your own land." He tried to speak again, but she snapped her fingers and a rider stepped forward and lay a heavy hand upon his shoulder. A subtle threat. "You do not belong in ours, and you will not be tolerated here." She waved a dismissive hand at them all. There was a shout from the crowd. A call for the Daughter of Scala. The ripple of unease passed through the crowds and the queen heard.

"Even the Daughter of Scala," she proclaimed. Still there were whispers. They wanted her dead. Kath squeezed her hand.

"The gods have already decided her fate." It was not the queen who answered the unrest. It was Cyrene. "It is not ours to meddle with."

Cyrah looked over at her twin with widened eyes. Jayla's expression remained unchanged, as if she had not even heard the Dragon Priestess's words.

Three lives for one.

"Kath." Jayla rose from the throne. She looked like a queen, power and prestige swathed her so naturally. "You will be executed for high treason, the murder of King Altan."

Judgment proclaimed, the nobles erupted, clamoring to be heard. Calling for justice, for a swift execution.

Kath looked over at Nana. Her dark gaze was already upon him. She would be safe. She would be returned to the world below, and not to the Bu Chak. Tears glistened like stars in her eyes.

He smiled.

She smiled back.

Chapter 50

They took him to the precipice where they had killed Brat.

A rider led him across the green lawn to where the grass grew sparse and yielded to the rock. He lifted his gaze from the gray rock to the sky stretching endlessly before him.

The rider halted him, and just over the edge of the rock, Kath could see where far below the sky gave way to the desert. Orange, red, and brown all mixed in a tapestry of colors that was familiar. It was home.

The rider kicked the back of his legs and his knees hit

hard on the rock. Pain laced up his injured calf. Beneath him, the stone was still stained with the black dragon blood.

From the lawn, fabric rustled as the nobles positioned themselves to watch the spectacle. Their whispers were barely constrained. He caught snippets of their hissed remarks, frustration at the queen, bewilderment of her decisions, anger at his crimes.

Jayla heard it all.

She was there as witness, as were the Dragon Priestesses. The prisoners were not brought to watch the execution, and he was glad for that.

He did not want Nana to watch.

Footsteps approached. A light tread. Kath's breath was sticky in his lungs. Inhale, then exhale, and every moment stretched to eternity and yet happened all too quickly.

A Dragon Priestess stood at his side. Cyrene, not Cyrah. Kath looked up at her, and she lifted the sword in her hand. The same sword she had used to kill Brat.

"The eldest proceeds over executions of riders." Cyrene's fingers gripped the scabbard tightly. The pommel was inlaid with rubies. "I asked the queen to allow me to instead."

In the face like Cyrah's, Kath could see the same expressions he had grown accustomed to. The same remorse. The same pain.

"It's better that way." Kath looked away from the woman who looked too familiar. He dropped his gaze back to the desert and ignored the blood on the stone.

"I'm sorry," she whispered. "Cyrah explained it all, and … I am so sorry. For doubting you. And I am so grateful that you brought her back to me."

A smile perked his lips. It no longer mattered if he saved

any of the seven, not when he would die, but there was some small solace that perhaps, just perhaps, he had saved one.

The blade rang shrilly in his ears.

Fear strangled his heart. Fear and sadness. He had not planned to lose his life this way a second time. Throat slit, blood across the ground. But three others would be released unharmed.

That was, after all, a worthwhile sacrifice.

His blood spilled onto the rock.

Chapter 51

Kath was dead.

The silver edge had sliced his throat, and his blood had pooled in the cracks and crevices of the stone. There he died, while the other three went free.

In his first death, the Wise One had been his constant. Tethered to the god, there had been a semblance of reality to cling to.

Now there was nothing. An oblivion abandoned by the god of death. He had dared hope that he would feel the pull of Nana's soul. But it did not work that way she had said. He knew, but he had hoped.

This is how he would truly die.

Alone, severed from the six lives and all their demands. He had grown accustomed to their pull on him. It had become a calming assurance, that they were there, that he was alive. The pain he had felt when Brat's life was severed still scarred his heart, but this new pain was worse.

He felt empty.

In the pitch darkness, he was left only with the memories. The unpleasant ones of his first, and the pleasant ones of his second. He tried to cling to the most precious ones. The nights spent walking across sand, playing Crowns with Mell, Nana's arms around him. But already he felt them slipping away, crumbling to time.

He was truly alone.

Until the gentle tug at his soul. A pull toward something he could not place. It felt familiar.

It felt like the dry desert, like the cool spray of water on the Islands. It felt like old books and dried plants. It felt like the Wise One.

Around him the blackness warmed. Black to blue to red to orange. The life-giving colors of a fire faded the darkness into the stony outline of a cave. A cave chiseled into a study, illuminated by the firelight flickering off the chipped edges.

His soul returned to the cave where the Wise One sat scribbling and did not acknowledge the newcomer. His soul returned to where it had in his first death.

A long time passed, or no time.

"Kath." The Wise One swiveled on his stool to lock the soul in his gaze. There was the slightest of smiles upon his lips. "It is good to see you once again."

Confusion.

And pain.

The two emotions twined through his soul. The rage had left. The anger, the fury. Those had left and had uncovered the pain.

The Wise One nodded.

"Why did you kill him?" the Wise One asked. Guilt speared through Kath. Though he could not speak, the scene played vividly through his mind. The Wise One saw it all. The spear in his hand, Altan's widened eyes, the blow, the blood. Rain standing with the sword in his hand, face contorted in shock and horror.

Dailin hated violence. Rain needed to be saved from it.

If he had not, the world below would have been destroyed. The lives he was tasked to save would have been destroyed.

"Is death ever justified?" the Wise One sighed. The guilt pressed afresh at his soul. He had thought so, at one point. The Blood King had killed so many. Even his own chief general, even his own wife. His hands were covered in blood, another life should be insignificant.

But it meant everything.

The weight of all the lives he had tried to save. The weight of the single life he had taken. He understood now why Nana had cried.

"Tell me." The Wise One leaned against his desk and considered Kath with his gray gaze. It was a heavy gaze, but not the repressive one Kath had first imagined. It was an old gaze that understood, that perceived, that held the weight of wisdom, and the weight of the world the other gods had abandoned. It was a kind gaze. It was a pained gaze. "Did you save seven lives?"

No.

It was the only honest answer. Kath had no assurance that any of the six lives had been protected, and though Nana thought otherwise, he knew he had failed the first life.

"You are right. It may be a difficult question to answer." The Wise One nodded. "Though, you undeniably did avert a great tragedy."

Questions rolled through him, but he did not know which one to ask first. If he could ask any. The Wise One chuckled and stood. He shuffled closer to the fire and stood before it, considering the tendrils flickering in the hearth.

"They are safe," the Wise One responded to one of the many burning questions within Kath. "They will be safe. The Islanders returned them wherever they asked to go."

His response only spurred more questions in Kath's soul.

"So many questions," the Wise One chuckled. "We could easily spend a whole lifetime addressing your many concerns. Shall we focus on the most pressing?"

His voice was jovial, but Kath's need for answers burned. It consumed him. They crowded in his consciousness. The Wise One turned his attention back toward the soul and considered a moment.

Nana. She was the most pressing.

"I cannot intervene," he answered. "Nana's curse is one made by multiple gods. The power of it is beyond me."

The injustice tore him apart. The Wise One nodded and turned back to the flame.

"Indeed," he murmured. "But their power is waning. The more time that passes since their desertion of this world the more their power weakens. Someday, perhaps, I will be able to break even that curse."

Kath did not fully understand the answer.

"I understand, it is hard to understand." The Wise One pushed back his sleeves and stretched out his hands toward the flames. "When the gods left, they abandoned you to the destruction begun by Scala and Caizin. The islands and the desert squabble and the earth groans to be reunited. The seven I chose are only a few of many trapped in the cycle of chaos. You may not have saved them, but you did protect them. Perhaps that's the same thing, perhaps it is different?"

Kath remained confused. The god of wisdom was incomprehensible, his words riddles that Kath could not decipher. Though he tried. So desperately. Because he wanted so desperately to understand.

"The gods' powers are waning, Kath. I will bring down the islands to rejoin your world. And perhaps your actions will pave the way to mend the chasm created by Scala and Caizin."

Each life carefully chosen. Each drawing their world closer to the Wise One's vision. A reunited world. Kath could not picture that world in his mind.

"In due time, all the curses will be removed." The Wise One turned to face where Kath's soul filled space. "But first, Kath, I have a deal to make with you."

The words did not feel dangerous as they had the last time, though they still felt precarious, and Kath did not know how to handle them. "I will give you a third life, if you seek an eighth life to save. Do you agree?"

A trick, a trap. Seek what he could never accomplish.

But while death had marked his first life, life had marked his second.

It would mark his third as well.

"Then Kath, we have a deal."

Chapter 52

He awoke in the desert.

His lungs filled with chilled air, and his eyes snapped open upon a sky filled with sparkling diamond stars. They stretched in an endless array.

A breath in. A breath out.

He felt whole.

Kath splayed his fingers against the midnight sky. His hand, the same dusty complexion, same callouses. He dropped the hand to his ear and slipped his fingers over the round sphere of his mother's earring.

His own body. His soul returned home.

Kath sat. He dropped his hands to the sand and pushed them into the cool granules.

The desert stretched flat around him. In the distance, the mountains cut shadows on the horizon, framing the patch of starlight between the two separated chains. The Bu Chak fortress below, the islands above that blocked out great swaths of stars.

The Wise One had placed him so near where his second life had ended.

He tried to imagine a world without the floating islands, one with a complete mountain range. The Wise One had promised, but it was hard to envision when he still saw the islands so far above the world below.

Kath wrapped the coat tight around his body, and stood. He spun a slow circle, and calculated. By his estimates, the sun had only recently set, which gave him plenty of time to reach the edge of the mountains. There were no large cities near the pits, at least there had not been, and with the Bu Chak occupying the land, he doubted that had changed. But there was a small village about two days' walk from the pits. He was sure she would have gone there, and if not there, to the nearest city, or to Lyria.

He would find her.

The day would dawn, and Kath would be alive. The morning would grow quickly hot, and he would have to seek out shelter and provisions. The day would dawn, and he would be one morning closer to the fall of the Islands, to the start of a new era. Free from the past, and free to seek out Nana and an eighth life.

Kath was alive.

About the Author

Lydia MacClaren has been writing stories since her earliest memories. *Seven Lives Saved* is her debut novel. She lives in rural Pennsylvania with her loving husband and sweet daughter. When she is not chasing around her baby, she writes. When she is not writing, she dreams about her fictional worlds.

For more information about her future novels, including *The Bound*, visit www.lydiamacclaren.com.

If you enjoyed this story, consider leaving a review!